Claudia McCants

Broken Angel

Guiding Light Press
Jacksonville Florida

Broken Angel

Published by
Guiding Light Press
Jacksonville, Florida

Cover Art: Christopher McCants Design

ISBN: 978-0-615-78610-0

Printed in the United States of America

Dedication

For Jan

Preface

The people and events described herein are fictional. Any resemblance to any living person or situation is purely coincidental. Sabal Palm Island and Sea Turtle Beach exist only in my mind, and are loosely based on the barrier islands of Northeast, Florida.

The golden moments in the stream of life rush past us and we see nothing but sand; the angels come to visit us, and we only know them when they are gone.

George Eliot (1819-1880)

Prologue

Lenore walked into the warehouse and locked the door behind her. Inside, the building was dark and gloomy like a cold empty cavern. It felt different at night when nobody else was working. Even her footsteps echoed as she walked.

She turned on the overhead lights but they did little to alleviate the knots in her stomach. She dreaded what she had to do next, but it had to be done. She felt nauseous.

She fished her cell phone from her purse. "Marlene," she said out loud, and the phone automatically dialed the correct number. After four rings, an answering machine picked up.

This is Marlene. Sorry to miss you. Leave a message and I'll call back.

"Hey, Sis, it's me. If you're screening calls, please pick up. I'm in a jam and I need to talk to you tonight."

She listened a few seconds only to hear continued silence.

"I guess you're really not there."

She thought a few more moments, considering her options.

"Call me back. I'm not sure where I'll be, so try my cell when you get home."

She switched on a gooseneck lamp at her station and began to set up her tools beside the marvering pad—tweezers, rods, rod cutter, holding fingers, glass shears, flameworking pliers, and a scoring knife. It was hard to concentrate. Her temples throbbed with an awful headache that had been tormenting her for hours.

She reached back into her purse, took out a plastic zip-lock bag and tossed two dry white tablets into her mouth.

How had she been wrangled into this predicament?

Just before she fired the torch, she saw headlights flash through the window beside Marlene's workbench. She took several deep breaths and tried to calm her racing heart as she walked across the room.

She unlocked the latch and opened the door to greet her visitor.

"Oh!" she said, feeling a bit startled. I wasn't expecting you."

1

Thursday, March 16, 2000

8:00 p.m.

Lenore's long blonde hair draped gracefully over her evening gown like liquid gold. The last time I had seen her in that black crepe dress was just a few months before, at a company function—a cocktail party to celebrate the 50th anniversary of Crest Glass. She was an effervescent young woman that evening as she worked the room, graciously visiting with each of our valued by-invitation-only guests.

In death her face was expressionless. As she rested in the expensive rose-draped casket, I felt the need to touch her. She was stone cold. A statue. But she was still my sister.

I leaned forward and whispered, "What a stupid way to die."

"She looks serene, doesn't she?" my matronly great aunt said almost as sweetly as the lilac perfume she wore. I barely knew Aunt Geertie, yet she was telling me that my sister was at peace.

"Yes, she does." What else could I say?

She dabbed her eyes with a pink embroidered hanky, squeezed my arm, and hobbled away toward my mother.

I scanned the room. Many of the same people who had

been at Crest's celebratory bash were at the wake: my family, assorted relatives, employees, clients, friends and a few people who were strangers to me. This time their faces were somber. There were even some dignitaries in attendance. The mayors of Sea Turtle Beach, Fernandina, and nearby Jacksonville were cloistered in a corner, and Florida's favorite native son, Senator Winston Wythe, was holding court in the foyer. I recognized him from a recent photo in the local newspaper that showed him at the *Concours d'Elegance* at Amelia Island, a stylish auto exhibition that features classic and vintage automobiles. The show had ended on Sunday, but I figured he stayed over to do some campaigning for the impending November election. Our banker, Thomas French, stood so close to the senator that I thought they would both topple over.

If it had been me lying in that coffin, Lenore would have been performing her normal hostess duties and consoling each guest. But I'm not Lenore, and to tell you the truth, I didn't care how they handled their grief. I didn't even know how I felt. Mostly I was numb, but on some level I was mad at Lenore for dying and at myself for not being home when she'd called.

Suddenly my mother was at my side. "She looks good, doesn't she?"

"She's dead, Mama. Or haven't you noticed?" I regretted the words as soon as they tumbled out of my mouth, but I couldn't help myself. Nothing would make Lenore come back, and small talk at the casket wasn't my strong point. Mama's pain reflected back to me from her glistening eyes and I was sickened by my indiscretion. In truth, Lenore did look peaceful. Then I realized why my mother and aunt had made their comments about Lenore's appearance. It was a safety mechanism. All they had to do was imagine Lenore sleeping so they didn't have to confront reality. I could do that too. Or could I?

I studied her expressionless face.

Nope. What remained of my sister was a lifeless corpse. She wasn't going to wake up and make some miraculous recovery. But I decided my mother and my aunt were right. Lenore looked exceptional that evening. No contusions or lacerations were visible. If her complexion was discolored, the mortician had disguised it with cosmetics. That struck me as funny because Lenore rarely wore makeup, and even then only a little lipstick to dress her up for a special event, like a cocktail party…or a funeral. I stroked her silky smooth hair and told her, "You're beautiful, Sis."

My mother eased closer. "You need a break. Get some fresh air, Marlene." She touched my shoulder and added, "In fact, go home."

I didn't argue. Mama was right. I needed to get away and I couldn't escape from the funeral home fast enough. I said a silent goodbye to Lenore as I whisked out of the parking lot in my Jeep.

It was a perfect evening to ride with the Wrangler's top off. The night air was pleasantly brisk and the winter sky was clear and studded with a blanket of sparkling stars. There were better ways to pay tribute to my sister than to stand by her dead body and weep. I decided then that I wouldn't attend her funeral. I popped in a CD by Lenore's favorite Jacksonville band, *Lynard Skynard*, lit a cigarette, and whisked through the night singing the lyrics to Freebird until my throat hurt.

❧

I woke up around noon the next day. Somebody was pounding on my front door. I knew who it was. I slipped on my robe and walked, zombie-like, to the living room. Daddy was bound to be upset with me for missing the memorial service.

He marched into my house, demanding, "Where were you? And why didn't you answer the phone?" He knew where I'd been because I was still in my pajamas. He also knows I turn the ringer off when I'm dead tired. It was his typical way of inviting me into an argument. I was expected to explain or make excuses so that he could rage on about how I had embarrassed the family yet again. Under the circumstances, I decided to let him vent and walked back into my bedroom without uttering a word of apology.

I hid my head under the covers. Eventually, he realized I wasn't listening. He sat on my bed and touched my hand. "Are you okay?"

"I've been better," I grumbled. "Are you angry with me?"

"Frustrated is more like it."

"Mama?"

"You know your mother can never stay mad at you."

"So she is upset with me."

He patted my hand. "Not angry, Marlene. She's worried. Have you been drinking?"

I shook my head. I knew he didn't believe me. "You always ask me that, Daddy. It would be nice to think you're pulling for me instead of waiting for me to screw up."

He stared at me blankly.

I am the first of three children. My brother, Matthew,

came in between Lenore and me. He's the kind of son a father can be proud of, and my father has always been proudest of Matt. Lenore was my mother's prize. As the oldest, I'm the kid they expected the most of, and I'm also their biggest failure. I have been sober for a long time but my father still waits for me to relapse. I'm sorry that he still stays on edge when I'm around him, but I do understand. At least I try to understand, which is what I wished he would do for me. I felt the urge to shake him to get a response, but I knew we had reached an impasse.

He removed his suit jacket, loosened his tie, and walked into the kitchen where I joined him. He prepared a pot of steaming hot coffee, making it strong, the way he always served it to me when I was recovering from a hangover. We sipped cup after cup of the strong brew in silence. "Shouldn't you be home with Mama?" I knew he was missing the buffet that her Women's Guild was catering at the church hall following the service.

He winked. "I go where I'm needed."

I hugged him. "Thanks, Daddy." I was pleased that my father had come to keep me company, probably at Mama's request. That he stayed, despite my foul mood, was a tribute to his fortitude and his love for me.

We sat together on the living room sofa and leafed through my collection of photo albums. The more I looked at snapshots of my sister, the angrier I got. I resented that she had been snatched away from us. I studied my father as he admired a photo of Lenore. At 62, he was still handsome even though he was no longer the strapping young man shown wrestling with three young kids in our family pictures. He was dressed in a proper church suit—black trousers and charcoal wool jacket with a fashionable silk jacquard tie, but his weary face betrayed his age. I felt sorry for him and I felt sorry for me. "I love you, Daddy," I soothed, brushing a lock of gray hair away from his glassy eyes.

I didn't anticipate his tears. His body began to shake against mine and I listened to his sobs as he wailed in protest of the death of his youngest child.

"I should have attended the service," I apologized as I fought the urge to explain that I'd sat up most of the night, crying until I had no more tears. The black dress I had selected to wear was still hanging in the closet.

I felt guilty for expecting too much from him. Realizing that, I gave into my frustration and held my crying father nestled within my comforting arms.

❧

The Terhunes are glass artisans. Glassblowing has been our family's hallmark for six generations, since before my ancestors migrated from Europe to North America. Like my brother and me, Lenore was a professional glassblower. Our father passed the trade to us, just as he had inherited the craft from Papa Henry. We apprenticed in Daddy's studio before going away to various schools to perfect our skills, and all of us continued to work in the family business after graduation.

Crest Glass Studios is located in a large nondescript warehouse complex on Sabal Palm Island. It's where our family spends most days. Mama manages a small but elite gallery in Old Towne, the trendy part of Sea Turtle Beach. My father oversees the rest of us—a total of 56 employees. Although we are a small company, our creations are shipped to exclusive stores and our glass is exhibited worldwide. Crest Glassware is also a permanent feature of the White House collection. My father is somewhat pompous about that accomplishment.

There are two kinds of glassblowing at our establishment. Larger glass manufacturers often specialize in one form, but Crest Glass is renowned for both.

One form of glassblowing is called lampworking. It involves working with glass rods and a torch. That was Lenore's specialty. Matt is the chief gaffer in the larger workroom located in our second warehouse. He labors in front of a fiery furnace, blowing hot blobs of liquid into vases, pitchers, art pieces and enormous chandeliers that hang from ceilings in renowned hotels, museums and even cathedrals. I'm trained in both techniques. Sometimes I helped Matt's team, but most days I was stationed with a torch at the bench beside my sister. The two of us were the Custom Glass Department. Everything we blew was made to order.

We were closed for business on the day of Lenore's funeral, yet I went to work that afternoon. It was the first time our factory had been shut down in its fifty-plus-year history. I guess Daddy figured nobody would feel like working. Lenore had a lot of friends.

Glasswork isn't just a job. It is part of who we are. I always tell people that liquid glass flows through Terhune veins. For me, glass working can be a way to meditate and escape from the rest of the world.

I sat on my stool and surveyed the cavernous building. Its emptiness only depressed me more. I could almost feel my sister prodding me. *You know you'll feel better behind the torch.* I slid a safety shield over my eyes and lit the burner, which usually fires me up. That day, I wasn't inspired. I glanced over at Lenore's workbench. It was as dismally empty as I felt inside, but I still sensed her presence lingering. I kept hearing her say. *Do it!* I shut off the fire and screamed at the top of my lungs, "Leave me alone!" My words echoed off the walls. I rested my head on the cold marving table and moaned, "Please don't leave me alone. How will I ever work again without you beside me?"

A few minutes later, Tony shouted from the outside yard. "Marlene, unlock this place and let me in!" Tony is a good friend of mine. He works as a bit gatherer on Matt's team. He's also the unfortunate guy who discovered Lenore's body early Monday morning when he'd gone into work to fire up the furnace.

I unlatched the door. "What are you doing here?"

He sat on Lenore's stool. "Same as you." Tony rubbed the metal bench surface reverently and closed his eyes for a moment. "Did yelling help?"

I was a little embarrassed. "Not much."

He shook his head. "I can't believe she's gone."

Tony Gilman is a large man, but that day he seemed to shrink as he slouched against the countertop. I felt the depth of his sorrow. Grief weighed so heavily on me that my heart ached. I stared at the floor and emptied my mind. I didn't want to think.

That's when I saw something sparkling. Tiny pieces of glass were scattered like snowflakes beneath Lenore's bench. I gazed at the shiny flecks on the cement floor and Tony stooped down to pick up a fractured angel's wing, still intact. Suddenly a vision of Lenore holding the crystalline figurine entered my mind.

Tony fetched a broom and swept the residual glass dust from beneath our feet, gathering the larger pieces of broken glass. I emptied my lunch into a trash can, placed the fragments into the brown paper sack, and stashed it away into my canvas tote bag.

Tony picked up a scrap of paper.

"What's that?"

He crumbled it up. "Just trash."

"Let me see." I held out my hand.

He handed me the paper and I spread it out before me. It was a prep list from the floor beneath Lenore's bench. While he continued to sweep, I tallied it up and arrived at a total of 525 sea shells, crystal flowers, bees, ladybugs, doves, hearts and 250 assorted swizzle sticks—some clear glass, some hand-painted. At the bottom of the list it said, 'lots and lots of butterflies.'

"It's an order."

"Who's it for?"

I shrugged. There wasn't a name or address on the form. Instead, there was just the alphanumeric number the front office encodes a purchase order with when a customer asks to remain anonymous. I was astounded that Lenore hadn't told me about the enormous project. We always tackled large tasks together. I searched our department, including all of the shelves and boxes where we store our creations until a job is complete. There wasn't a flower, bee or ladybug in sight. Apparently she had started the angel first, which puzzled me since we save the larger pieces until last to avoid the possibility of breakage.

I combed through Lenore's file folders, hoping to find

artwork for the project. I required detailed drawings to show me what the client had in mind, knowing that I would finish the order by myself. Finding nothing, I was discouraged. I didn't even know the deadline. "I can't believe this," I groaned. "I won't be able to get started until Monday."

Tony shook his head in disbelief. "What are you talking about? You're in mourning. Cut yourself a break."

I pivoted to face him. "I need something to keep my mind busy."

He took my arm and guided me to the door. "Let's get out of here."

The remainder of the evening, Tony chauffeured me around in his vintage Karman Ghia. We enjoyed two chocolate double-dips from the Twisted Treat, a cute little frozen custard stand that is housed in a building that looks like an ice cream cone. Afterward, we threaded our way through the streets of the historic district, admiring quaint antique shops along Middle Avenue, and the bed and breakfast inns hidden in quiet neighborhoods nearby. Tourists sat on porch verandas of grand antebellum homes, rocking lazily in wooden chairs.

As we rounded a corner, McGregor's Pub was overflowing with St. Patrick's Day patrons. It was the first time in years that I wasn't sitting in there on a barstool with a mug of frothy beer pressed to my lips. I wondered how anybody could celebrate on the day when Lenore was put to final rest.

A few minutes later we parked and the two of us quietly strolled along the shores of Sea Turtle Beach. I took off my shoes and waded in the gentle evening surf. Ten brown pelicans skimmed the top of the water.

It was a calming moment, but my heart still ached.

Tony was right. No amount of work—not even a sunset stroll—could take away the pain or make me feel better.

2

Saturday, March 18
3:30 a.m.

Saturday morning started with a thunderstorm and a blinding migraine. A few years earlier, it would have been from drinking too much alcohol, but my Lenore headache was due to lack of sleep. I kept analyzing scenarios, trying to get a fix on why she'd died.

I checked my clock. It was only 3:37.

Before I went to the living room, I stopped in the kitchen and washed down a couple of extra-strength aspirin with a swig of cold milk. Then I sat in my favorite leather recliner with a wet cloth plastered against my forehead. Except for the sound of rain splattering against the windows and an occasional rumble of thunder, the house was silent.

What was it Tony had said? I concentrated until his words came back to me. "Lenore's head was resting on her arms like she was asleep...but she was dead."

No wonder my temples throbbed. Tony had found my sister slumped against her workbench, overcome by noxious fumes spewing from the lamp burner near her head. My beloved sister had taken a nap and slipped away into another world. Why didn't she go home if she was sick or tired? She should have known better.

The first rule of glassblowing is caution. Blowing glass can be dangerous, so glass factories, like ours, always have safety rules, procedures and equipment. Every glassblower takes extra precautions to protect self from harm, but accidents can still happen.

That's what Daddy called Lenore's death—an accident.

I wasn't buying it.

I was certain Lenore would never do something as stupid as falling asleep at her bench, and I knew she would have turned on the fans to ensure proper ventilation while she worked. The more I thought about it, the more my head pounded, and the more I contemplated the possibility that Lenore had committed suicide.

What had she wanted to tell me?

Eventually, I drifted into a fitful sleep that lasted less than an hour. When I woke up, I showered, dressed and hit the road.

I was in line for the St. John's Ferry before 5:30. There were only three cars in front of me, one behind me, each of us parked in the dark with our motors running and our headlights on, waiting for the first crossing of the day. The rain had slowed to a drizzle and the morning fog was disappearing. The gentle rhythm of my windshield wipers lulled me into a tranquility I hadn't experienced during the night.

I scrunched down in my seat and managed to claim another twenty minutes of rest before a scruffy little man in a yellow slicker banged on my window. "Wake up, Missy! It's time to leave!" My heart raced and pounded in my chest, an unsettling reminder of all those mornings when my mother had yelled for me to get ready for school.

I followed the other cars up the ramp as the boat's diesel engine roared to life for the 6:10 crossing from Ft. George Island to Mayport Village. The trip takes just eight minutes but I still got out of my car and stood by the railing, admiring a river that has been traversed through the centuries by everything from dugout canoes to aircraft carriers. The mist cooled my face and I finally felt awake, even though I had only slept a total of three hours.

I was starved. I stopped at a little food mart in Mayport and purchased a six-pack of sodas—the kind with lots of sugar and caffeine—and a few items to make breakfast at Lenore's place. I was sure there weren't any groceries in the pantry. Lenore's car knew the way to every fast food restaurant between St. Augustine and Brunswick, Georgia. That always irritated me because she was the perpetually thin sister. I gain five pounds every time I smell grease.

The neighborhood was quiet except for a mockingbird's pleasant daybreak song coming from a nearby date palm. I used my own key and slipped into Lenore's townhouse unnoticed. Mayport Naval Air Station's weekend employees were already at their posts. The rest of the world was either sleeping in late or watching cartoons.

I had lived there when I was married to Steve, but after our divorce, my sister had taken over the lease. I purchased a house that was located just a few minutes away from work. She had welcomed the chance to live on the other side of the river, away from my parents' watchful gaze, especially since living close to a naval base provided her with plenty of dates.

That made me sad for many reasons. Missed opportunities. Dying young.

The apartment was sparsely furnished. The focal point of

the living room was a framed Patrick Nagel serigraph of an exotic woman with a hibiscus in her hair. Beneath the artwork, a small television sat on a pine tray table with a few bright red throw pillows tossed on the floor in front of it. There was very little furniture except for a faded denim futon chair left over from Lenore's dorm days at the University of Florida in Gainesville, and four bright red plastic crates stacked beside the patio door, each brimming with tattered paperback books. Lenore was an avid reader. She also loved plants. The walls were lined with an abundance of split-leaf philodendron, lush tropical ferns, baskets of Christmas cactus still in bloom, and a corn plant that was taller than me. There wasn't even a lamp.

I stumbled into the kitchen to unload my sack of groceries. When I flipped the light switch up, a fluorescent ceiling fixture flickered and hummed before it illuminated both rooms so brightly that I had to squint. As expected, her refrigerator was almost empty. I found an unopened pack of cheddar cheese, a plastic container of mustard, a jar of baby dills, and a frozen candy bar in the freezer that I immediately claimed. Typical Lenore cuisine.

I had planned to pack up her belongings to save my parents from the ordeal, but there wasn't much to do. I ran the vacuum through every room, spritzed and cleaned the sinks and tub, and thought about Lenore. That was the real reason I was there—to be closer to the essence of my best friend. I needed to be surrounded by her possessions—things she had left behind. I watered her indoor garden, tending to the plants as if they were my kin.

The towels in her linen closet were stacked neatly and undisturbed. I selected a fresh pillowcase to fill with a few items from her bedroom, including her Bible, an inlaid shell jewelry box, a tattered address book, and a self-help book she had been reading before her death. On the bottom of the closet floor was a large cardboard container cluttered with rolls of toilet tissue, combs, brushes, sprays, lotions and a box of feminine napkins. I picked out a few items and put them beside the entry door to take with me.

I crawled into her bed around nine o'clock, wrapped myself in our grandmother's hand-stitched quilt, and napped with the spirit of my beloved sister watching over me.

⁂

People often said Lenore and I looked like twins: same hazel eyes, same honey blonde hair, same fair complexion and freckled nose. Sometimes we even sounded alike. The only difference was our age and the extra thirty or so pounds I sometimes pack around my hips. When I'm sober I tend to chunk up, but friends still remarked about our similarities and that sometimes caused confusion. Like that morning.

I awoke about two hours later when the mattress moved and I felt a strong, warm hand grabbing my shoulder. A deep voice announced, "Time to get out of the rack!" I rose up and hit the intruder in the stomach with my elbow, following with a punch in the face and a robust shove off the mattress. I recognized my assailant when I had him pinned to the floor. It was Steve, and even though my former husband had trained me in self-defense, I'd managed to catch him off guard...the same way he had just caught me off guard. Seeing his face rendered me temporarily speechless.

Frozen in amazement, he stared up at me. "Marlene!

What are you doing here?"

I stumbled off his body. "Me? You're lucky I didn't kill you!" As if I could really hurt a 6 foot 2 inch, 225 pound Navy guy who works out at the gym every day.

He rubbed his left eye. "You pack a powerful wallop, woman!"

There was a time when I would have been ecstatic to see Steve come home after six months at sea.

"What are you doing in my sister's apartment?"

He rolled over on his stomach and groaned. "If you'd paid attention to the news, you would know Big John is back."

That didn't answer my question. "Why are you here?"

"Lenore invited me to stay with her."

"How'd you get in? Do you still have a key?"

He ignored me and glanced around. "Where is she anyway?"

"She's dead. Now get out of here!"

I would have stormed out of the room, but I realized I was standing in front of him in my bra and panties. I slipped on my jeans and blouse and tried to seem impervious to his presence.

He sprung to his feet. "Did you just say dead?"

"She killed herself." I left him in the bedroom to brew over that dose of reality while I tried to figure out if my ex-husband had been sleeping with my sister.

Steve stayed in the bedroom. I could hear his sobs and began to feel guilty for acting vicious yet again.

Three years after our separation, I still tried to keep him at a distance to shield me from his penetrating gray-blue eyes. My parents adore him. So did Lenore. And although I would never admit it out loud, I still cared deeply for him. A lump lodged in my throat and I fought an anxiety attack as my heart rate sped up. I hated that I had sabotaged our relationship, and I still took out my frustrations on him. All I knew that day was that I didn't want him there. I wanted to be by myself, even if Lenore had invited him back into my life.

I busied myself in the kitchen by throwing together an omelet with the eggs, cheese and salsa I had purchased at dawn. "Come have breakfast!" I shouted when the toast popped up. I figured I might as well feed him before I kicked him out the door. I heard the water running in the bathroom and a few minutes later he appeared recovered, apparently refreshed by a cold splash in the sink. For the first time, I realized he was dressed in his whites.

Breakfast was good but the silence was awful. "How long have you been here?"

"I just got back this morning. Lenore was supposed to greet me when I got off the ship. When she didn't show up, I hitched a ride with a buddy who lives down the street."

"You know I'm not talking about when you got back in port. How long have you been living with my sister?"

"Since you and I divorced, off and on. Six months at sea got me out of her way, but when I was in town, I'd crash here until I shipped out again. I helped her pay the rent and a few bills." He said it without a bit of discomfort or shame.

I was amazed. As a kid, Lenore could never keep a secret, yet she had managed to hide Steve's presence from me for almost two years. I could have been angry with her, but remembering how many times she'd told me, "Steve's a good guy, Marlene." I figured she had fostered the connection with my ex-husband just in case I ever realized my mistake. Unless they were sleeping together, which presented a whole different scenario I didn't want to consider, and that possibility increased my anxiety level.

"She killed herself?"

I just stared at him.

He pleaded, "Tell me you're lying."

When I didn't respond, Steve grabbed his sea bags, slapped a key on the table in front of me and walked out without saying another word.

I felt a ton of emotions weighing me down. I was sad about my sister, glad to see Steve, mad that he was in Lenore's apartment, and on top of it all, so much guilt about ruining his day that tears welled in my eyes and spilled down my cheeks.

I'm sure it wasn't the kind of homecoming that he had expected.

I live in a region called Florida's First Coast. At least that's what the politicians and newscasters tell us when they hype the area in the media. No matter what you call it Northeast Florida is a great place to live. The biggest town in our area is Jacksonville with a population of more than 800,000 inhabitants. It covers 840 square miles, which makes it one of the largest cities in the nation.

The St. John's River flows northward through the center of town and empties into the Atlantic Ocean. The Timucua Indians already lived here when the French landed at the mouth of the river in the mid 1500's, close to where the ferry crosses. Pirates, bandits, and runaway slaves roamed its shores. Some parts of the area are still as unspoiled as they were hundreds of years ago.

That's why I adore Sabal Palm Island. You won't find a major hotel chain, high rise condominium, or golf course on Sea Turtle Beach. Our small secluded barrier island—with the Atlantic Ocean on the eastern shoreline and marshland to the west—is still undiscovered except for a few people who on occasion stray off the main thoroughfare and amble into our picturesque community. Those lucky families often revisit, year after year, enjoying our uncrowded beaches and acres of thick coastal forests. It is hallowed ground—pristine untouched wilderness.

My parents' house is a sturdy 90-year-old waterfront dwelling that would look just as perfect on a sprawling farm with its white clapboard siding, tin roof, and wrap-around porches. The lush azalea bushes surrounding it were in full bloom with abundant pink and purple blossoms.

I found my father in the backyard resting in the shade, his hammock stretched between two ancient Live Oak trees. Their twisted branches were draped in Spanish moss. Daddy's face was hidden beneath a fishing magazine. I checked for fire ants, kicked away a few acorns, and sat on the leaf-covered ground beside him. He snored softly as I watched him sleep.

The Intracoastal Waterway kept me company. It was a chilly March afternoon. A beautiful white Egret flew out of a rookery in a cedar by the marsh and swooped into the sawgrass where it easily plucked a brim from the brackish water. A flock of Canada geese squawked overhead. I felt like I was in a Norman Rockwell painting, Florida style.

My father stretched and moaned. "How long have you been here?"

"About ten minutes."

"That long?" He rubbed his eyes and chuckled. "Guess I needed my beauty rest. Have you seen your mother?"

"Not yet."

"She went inside to make me lunch just before I dozed off." He raised himself on his elbow and looked back at the house. "Ah, there's my gorgeous bride!" On cue, my mother came down the wood chip path with two bagged lunches and a small red cooler that she placed by my feet.

Mama looks like my late grandmother. She still pin curls her hair every night to create what she calls finger waves, a style reminiscent of the 1950's. Except for a strand of silvered hair on the left side of her forehead, she's still a stunning brunette. That day, she wore slacks and a rust-colored cardigan sweater that matched her lipstick perfectly. My father sat up and smiled, admiring her as if she was still the 16-year-old cheerleader he had courted and married.

"I saw you from the kitchen window." She gave me a kiss on the cheek. "I imagine you're here to go fishing." Now that I'm sober, I cast a line when I'm down in the dumps.

"And I imagine you'll soon be at a shopping mall," I teased back. When my mother is depressed, she shops.

She looked at my father. "Are you going fishing, Mason?"

He glanced at the skiff and back at her. It took him an instant to decide. "No, Darlin'," he drawled like a true southern gentleman. "I promised to spend the afternoon with you." He winked at me and slid out of the hammock. "You don't mind, do you?"

The prospect of spending time alone with my favorite rod

was appealing. "Not at all. Go have fun with Mama."

As he walked toward the house, hand-in-hand with my mother, he called over his shoulder. "Will you still be here when we get back?"

"Do you want me to be?"

He waved as they went through the back door. "Catch us some fish!"

❧

By the time my parents departed I had already consumed my bologna sandwich, my father's shaved ham sandwich, and both cream sodas.

It was still early in the afternoon. I studied the wetlands and wondered how many fish I could bring in but I didn't move. Instead, I stayed in the hammock with my leg lazily draped over the side, rocking myself, and considering still another nap. I stared at the sky. It was magnificent—Robin's egg blue with white puffy clouds stacked all the way to heaven.

Where are the angels? I heard Lenore's voice as clearly as the day she asked me that question on a flight to Baltimore for a visit with our Aunt Sarah. It was the first flight for my little sister. I can still see her nose smudge on the window. *If we can't see angels, how do we know they exist?*

When I was just thirteen, I, too, was mystified by the question she posed but I responded easily. "There are just some things you know in here." I'd patted my chest just above my heart and she had beamed, obviously delighted with my explanation.

On that beautiful Saturday afternoon, as I reclined

beneath a glorious Florida sky thinking about my sister, I realized I had been right. My eyes misted. I knew what I had to do, and it wasn't fishing for anything the river had to offer. I turned on my stomach and considered my parents' empty house. They would be gone for at least three hours.

I raced inside and dashed upstairs, giving my old room a cursory glance. My mother had remodeled it into a den, and Matt's former habitat had been converted into a sewing room. But a few doors down the hall my sister's room remained untouched. It had been a shrine since the day she'd left for college.

I trembled as I walked inside. There was a shelf of knick-knacks, including the first piece of glass Lenore had made—a paperweight. A curio cabinet in the corner showcased her porcelain doll collection. Photos covered the wall: a few of me, one of Matt, and twenty-or-so snapshots of Mama, Daddy and assorted friends were thumb-tacked to a bulletin board. There were pictures of Lenore the cheerleader, Lenore proudly holding up her diploma, and Lenore with Jonathan Lucas, her high school boyfriend, at the prom. I hadn't thought about him for years, but now he was in the headlines

A search of her closet and dresser didn't reveal anything that might hint at why she had been depressed. Granted, she hadn't lived in the house for several years, but I sensed there was a clue in her room. I found a few tattered letters and greeting cards that I stashed away in my purse.

A car door slammed outside and I sprinted down the steps, arriving in the foyer just as Matt opened the front door.

He looked up the tall staircase. "Find anything?"

"Excuse me?"

He smiled. "Just joking. Where's Dad?"

"Shopping with Mama."

"Figures."

I followed him into the rustic farmhouse kitchen at the end of the hallway. The *Home Sweet Home* plaque over the deep soapstone sink had been hand-painted by my mother in an arts and crafts class, but that's not what made me feel cozy in the recently remodeled room. That mood came from the imaginative mind of my sister. Lenore had dedicated immeasurable hours, literally months, working with our mother, an architect, and a contractor to create a laid-back atmosphere.

They had asked me to contribute my ideas to the project, but I had rejected the invitation, as usual, preferring to isolate myself from family affairs. I saw the room for the first time that afternoon. My arms tingled and my face flushed as Lenore's passion, wisdom and ingenuity were displayed before my eyes. I wished I could tell her how much I admired her design.

The vaulted ceiling was constructed from knotty pine planks. Above my head, a stunning brass chandelier with six daffodil lights was suspended from a thick hand-hewn beam. My brother was busy searching the pantry for a snack and barely noticed the elaborate light, even though he and his team had produced it.

I walked across vintage dark wood floors to examine pewter hardware on the distressed black cabinetry. A white stone countertop and a restored 1890's stove added to the old-fashioned motif. Tangerine colored walls made the room feel warm and inviting. The only hint of a more modern era was the refrigerator my father had insisted upon, a stainless steel commercial-sized monstrosity.

Matt opened both doors and stared inside. "Why do they always have boring food? Boiled eggs, raw carrots, celery, pickles. Salad stuff. No leftovers."

"You hate Mama's leftovers."

"I was hoping Dad cooked last night."

We both laughed.

I peeked through the window at the dock and the empty boat.

"What are you doing here?" He reached into the pantry and took out a can of sardines. "Fish calling your name?"

"Yeah, but I'm ignoring them. Why are you here?"

"I came over to discuss business. The folks have been loading up the Prevost and they're heading out. I'll be in charge for awhile."

My parents have visited 49 states in their enormous motor home, so that didn't surprise me. Under duress, my father takes to the road in his elaborate house on wheels. "When are they coming back?"

He placed the tiny oil-soaked fish between two pieces of bread, covered them with mustard, and took two giant bites of his sandwich. He mumbled, "In a week, maybe two."

"Probably a month, knowing them."

He shoved the last bite into his mouth before preparing a second one. "Dad wants you to go with them."

"No, thanks."

He stuffed three more huge bites in his mouth, "You should go, Marlene."

I poured a glass of milk and slid it to him across the counter. "That's out of the question. I'd be crazy to put them or me through that."

He swallowed hard. "He's giving you time off from work, with pay."

What could I say to get out of a trip to who-knows-where with Mason and Trudy Terhune? I had to think of an excuse fast. "When do they plan to leave?"

Matt gave me one of those 'I know what you're thinking' looks.

"Tomorrow morning." He chuckled.

My parents are the champions of avoiding uncomfortable situations. They stick together, stay busy, steer clear of conversations that make them feel uneasy, and shed their tears privately. I was sure my father was already fretting over crying in front of me. My mother, on the other hand, controls her emotions with a prescription.

The prospect of being confined in close quarters with them sounded exhausting, especially when I knew that talking about Lenore would be taboo. And since I don't drink anymore, I figured I had to get out of Sea Turtle Beach as fast as possible. I grabbed my purse and headed for the front door. "Tell them I said to have a good time and I'm sorry about dinner. I'm out of here. I'll see you at work on Monday."

Matt laughed so hard I thought he'd choke on the carrots he'd pilfered from the refrigerator. "We'll see about that. You know Dad has ways to track you down."

I trotted to my car and sat in the driveway, motor purring, as I deliberated my destination. I needed to hide for just one day in order to avoid an uncomfortable situation with my father. The only reason he could want me to accompany them was to keep tabs on me. He was afraid I would drink to forget about my sister's death.

I didn't need a babysitter, I didn't want liquor, and I would never forget Lenore. I turned right and headed northbound, feeling confident my father would never find me in Georgia.

❦

Amy is one of my favorite people in the world. She may be Steve's older sister, but she's the closest thing to a sister that I have left. When I divorced Steve, I didn't divorce Amy. I called her from my mobile phone and she said, "Sure, come right up!" Twenty minutes later, I pulled to her curb and she ran outside to give me a welcoming hug.

Behind her, Steve stood in the doorway.

I felt like a doe standing in the headlights with a car speeding toward me. I wanted to sprint but I was glued to the pavement. I glanced at Amy, then Steve, and then back at Amy again. Why hadn't I figured he would be at her house? He turned away and his sister snared my arm to guide me inside. "He'll be fine," she assured me. But when we went into the living room, Steve was gone...again. Chasing him away was getting to be a habit.

She disappeared into the kitchen and reappeared a few moments later with a cold glass of southern sweet tea—the kind that sets your teeth on edge. Yummy! We settled in the living room, comfortably talking like we had for so many years. They'd been discussing Lenore before I arrived, and she picked up the conversation where they'd left off. "I can't believe your sister committed suicide."

"Actually, that hasn't been proven yet."

Steve reappeared. He had a real shiner, thanks to me.

"What? You said—"

"I know what I said, but I misspoke."

"You lied."

"No. I just said what I think may have happened."

Steve dropped onto the couch and slammed his head against the back cushion. "What did happen, Marlene?" The emphasis he placed on my name made it apparent he was very annoyed.

"They found her at her workstation. She fell asleep with the burner on and was asphyxiated from oxygen deprivation."

"No way! She wasn't that stupid!" Steve jumped up and paced the room. "What about the exhaust fans?"

"They were off."

"Was she sick?"

"I'm not sure."

"And you buried her?"

I nodded.

He leaned forward. "Without an autopsy?"

"They performed one."

"What were the results?"

Steve watched me intently and I suddenly felt stupid. I took a sip of my drink and stared at the television. Amy noticed and switched on the evening news. Her brother stood up and turned it back off, standing in front of the screen to get my attention.

"What were the results?" he repeated. His head cocked and his arms folded over his chest.

I looked at him and announced clearly, "I don't know."

Amy sat on the edge of the sofa beside me and took my hand protectively in hers. "Leave her alone. Can't you see she's grieving?"

He threw his hands up in the air and marched down the hall to the guest bedroom. "That's right, Amy! Be like the rest of her family. Poor, poor Marlene. We have to shield her from everything because she's so fragile. All I can say is you'd better hide the booze."

"Steve!" Amy stood up to defend me but he slammed the door behind him, leaving both of us reeling from his angry outburst.

I gathered my purse to leave. "I should go."

Amy pressed me back into my seat. "Stay. He's just upset, like the rest of us."

❧

Most of my time at Amy's house was spent on the sofa where I considered Steve's words.

He was right but not about the liquor. I had promised Lenore I would never touch another drop and I meant that, but he was absolutely on target about my family's penchant for protecting me. He had also introduced me to another line of thought that I hadn't previously considered. What did my parents know that they weren't telling me, and what were the results of the autopsy?

I was profoundly depressed, consumed with guilt for missing her telephone call, and becoming more agitated every minute. I had run to Georgia to avoid my parents, but my mind was so full of uncertainty about the circumstances of Lenore's death that I was losing sleep.

Amy came out of her bedroom Sunday morning, looking adorable in a swingy matte jersey dress. "I'm going to catch the first sermon. Would you like to go to church with me?"

"Nah," I said through a yawn. "Maybe another time."

I figured she needed an excuse to escape from Steve and me for a few hours of peace. Not that we had been fighting. He had managed to avoid me by sneaking in and out of the house while I catnapped. I felt sorry for Amy. She'd been tiptoeing around both of us like she was walking barefoot on crushed coquina. Living with both of us for two days was more than any person could be expected to cope with, even imperturbable Amy. It was an awkward situation for her, but for me it was better than a land cruise to nowhere with my parents.

"Are you sure you won't change your mind?" She stood there studying me, waiting for an answer I wasn't ready to give. "Well, then I'll see you in a few hours."

Balanced precariously on stiletto heels, Amy descended the steps to the sidewalk cautiously. I stood in the doorway, watching her shoulder-length auburn hair bounce as she walked away from the house. Too quickly, she disappeared around the corner and out of sight.

It had been years since I'd attended my own church on Sabal Palm Island. Steve and I had married there, and I wondered if he had found another church—perhaps the one Amy attended. Church had been my mainstay in life, the place you'd always find me bright and early every Sunday since I was just a babe in my mother's arms. But I had forsaken my church prior to our divorce, and that thought disturbed me. I pushed it down into the place where I store hurtful memories.

It was just 10:35. If Steve hadn't snuck out earlier in the morning, he was still locked behind closed doors.

I felt abandoned with the whole day looming ahead of me. More time to think. More time to fret.

I settled into a comfy wicker chair on the front porch with a fresh copy of the Florida Times-Union. It had been two weeks since I had picked up a newspaper. Nothing in particular caught my eye. The world was conducting business as usual without Lenore. How sad.

I flipped through page by page, barely reading a word until I came to the obituaries. As I skimmed through the names—all people who would be sorely missed by their families and friends—I realized I was not alone in my grief but I imagined they all knew why their loved-ones had died. Was I being selfish in my grief? Did I have the right to pepper my family with questions, or should I just shut up and accept the undeniable truth without delving into the ifs and whys?

That's when I heard the rhythmic beat of a basketball approaching. I turned to see Freddie walking toward the house. "I'm happy to see you today." I was pleased to see the tall, lean pre-teen climb the stairs effortlessly, still bouncing the ball with every step. I needed a dose of his smile and energy that day.

"My mother is visiting some lady she knows from her job." Freddie's house was located several miles away, near King's Bay Submarine Base, but I'd met his family a few years before when they were neighbors of one of my Jacksonville friends. Kids sure do grow up fast, and at 11-years-old, he already towered above me. "Amy called Mom last night and told her about your sister." His charming smile faded and he looked pensive as he drew closer to me. "I'm really sorry, Marlene."

"So you came here just to see me?" I already knew the answer.

"Yes, ma'am."

"You're a good friend, Freddie. I'm happy to see you."

He blushed.

I pointed to his basketball. "Are you any good?"

"Of course!" He bounced it three times. "I'm getting better every day. You wanna play a game with me?"

I laughed. "Oh, no…I prefer the comfort of this chair."

He bounced the ball a few more times, looking introspective. "Amy said you've been depressed."

"I'm okay." I tried to sound convincing.

He spun the ball between his fingers. "I would be devastated if I lost my parents or my sister."

Looking at my fingers, I admitted, "I am sad, but oddly enough, I haven't cried yet. I can't figure that out. It's natural to cry. Why can't I?"

Freddie crouched beside me, his basketball held between his knees. "Maybe you're afraid that if you cry, you'll have to admit to yourself that she's gone."

I looked down at his hands holding mine. "I don't want to let her go."

He stood up. "You can't lose her. Lenore is in here." He placed his hand just above his heart. "And she's in here." He pointed to his head. "And she's with God, and God can see and hear anything…so maybe she can too. Maybe she is watching us talk about her."

I felt better just hearing him say those words. "Maybe I should stop asking questions, Freddie. She's gone and I can't do anything about that."

He touched my shoulder. "I may argue with my sister,

but I would do anything to help her. That's what families are about—loving and protecting each other. I'm sure you'll do what you have to do to find peace."

A horn tooted and I looked up to see his mother's car in the driveway. She shouted, "I'm sorry I have to kidnap him so fast, but we have to get back to our house to prepare for a picnic later today!"

He walked down the porch steps. At the bottom, he stopped and dribbled the ball a few more times. Then he turned to me. "Remember, families stick together even when they're apart."

A tear trickled down my cheek. Out of the mouths of babes comes wisdom.

3

Monday, March 20, 2000
5:15 a.m.

I left southern Georgia very early Monday morning before Steve or his sister woke up. The sky was clear with a smattering of stars and the moon was still visible through the trees. It was time to get back to work. I stopped by my place for a quick shower and a change of clothes and still managed to pull into my parking space before eight. The lot was full. Crest Glass was open for business and life was back to normal.

Almost.

I stopped by the administrative suite first for a cup of fresh-brewed coffee and a bit of detective work. Victoria Adams was busy keying in new orders on her desktop computer, and in the office behind her my brother sat at my father's desk chatting on the phone. He acknowledged me with a wave and swiveled his chair to look out the window. There wasn't much to look at except the parking lot and a row of five tall palm trees that lined the street like soldiers standing at attention. He was probably talking to my father.

I shut the door to his office and sipped my steaming drink as Vicky continued to type. A few minutes later, a slew of orders spit out of the printer and she finally glanced up, looking somewhat staggered. "Oh, Marlene! I didn't see you there. How are you feeling?"

"Not too bad, considering—"

She interrupted, "Are you looking for your father?"

I shook my head. "I'm waiting for Matt."

She gathered the orders, snapped them apart, and sped out of the room. "I'll be back in a few minutes," she promised. "We can chat then."

I didn't want to talk to her and I didn't need to see my brother. When she was out of view, I pulled a slip of paper from my pocket and busied myself at her terminal where I keyed in the order number Lenore had been working on. I was mystified when the message INVALID ENTRY popped up. I verified the numbers I had typed and entered them again but still had no success.

I cleared the screen and managed to look innocent when the door clicked open and Matthew walked into the reception area. "What'cha doing?" he asked. "Waiting for me?"

"Yep. Did they leave?"

"Who?"

"You know who I mean."

He snickered. "Why? Did you want to go with them?"

I managed a weak laugh. "You know the answer to that, little brother. I guess I'm asking you if it's safe to be here."

"Sure, you're safe, but you don't need to be here. He gave you the week off."

I was skeptical. "You must be kidding."

"You're off."

I spun around and walked with determination toward the Custom Glass Department. "I don't want to be off." Matt edged up beside me, keeping up with my fast pace. He touched my arm to stop me just before I reached my work area, but it was too late. Michele Barton sat on my stool and Andrew Litton was working the flame at Lenore's station. I was furious. "What's going on here? Am I being forced to take time off?"

His eyes were apologetic. "I'm sorry, Sis. Dad insists and I have to do what he says. You know that."

I did, but it didn't make it any easier to accept.

"This stinks!" I roared.

I looked around and saw a room full of dazed faces—friends who looked away to avoid embarrassing me more. It was pointless to debate the issue.

I pushed my brother out of the way and left the building without arguing or bothering to look back.

As usual, my father had managed to gain the upper hand.

❧

I stayed home the next three days, most of that time in bed. I slept, ate cold cereal, watched soap operas, and slept some more. The phone rang incessantly. I knew it was either my parents or my brother and I refused to answer. I turned off the ringer to silence their calls.

By the fourth day, every bone in my body ached. Pain forced me out of bed and into the kitchen where I binged on cookie dough and baked dozens of cookies.

Monica appeared on my doorstep Friday morning. "Leave me alone," I fumed, taking my frustrations out on my sister-in-law. "And take these with you!" I shoved a brown paper sack of warm chocolate chip cookies into her hands. I knew my two nieces and their little brother would appreciate Auntie Marlene's donation. As she drove away, I was miserable.

Saturday, I went back to Crest Glass.

The building was locked tight, as was the office, but I had a key to both doors. My heart beat fast and furious as I approached the entrance. I craved a torch in my hands, and I also wanted to snoop around some more.

I checked the file cabinet beside Vicky's desk but it was secured by a combination lock. I played with it a while, imagining I could somehow stumble upon the right numbers like a professional safe-cracker. I guess I watch too many movies. Eventually I gave up.

In my department, I scanned the shelves to determine what Andrew and Michele had produced in my absence. There was still no sign of any item on Lenore's list. Instead, they had worked on a large order that the two of us had begun two weeks before—a variety of unicorns, dragons, and wizards for a fantasy convention in Orlando. Each piece was designed exclusively for Drayton Wilson, the owner of Count Drayton's Glass Menagerie. He provided the ideas, but it was up to us—the hotworkers—to melt, shape and spin the finest glass tubing into works of seamless beauty. I scanned his purchase order and selected a fairy sitting on a bed of mushrooms—something fun to create.

Just before I fired up the oxygen-propane torch, Matthew arrived. I wasn't surprised. He often works on weekends, especially when he is filling my father's shoes.

"I knew I would find you here!" He was much too cheery. "Come with me. You can help me out back."

I followed him to the heart of our business—Building

Two, where three furnaces burn around the clock. Each oven holds 330 pounds of clear liquid glass, the starting point for every piece we make. Several times a week Tony shovels raw materials into the ovens: a blend of silica sand, borax, ash, lime and soda. Each batch must cook at a temperature of 2300 degrees Fahrenheit for at least twelve hours. To say the building is sweltering is an understatement.

"You wanna talk?" he invited as he donned his apron.

"Nah." I put on my apron. "Not now."

I was still hurt and annoyed and I didn't want to get into all the things that were bothering me, but I always welcome the chance to work in front of a furnace.

Matthew is a master of his craft and a great teacher. I admire him immensely and learn from him every time I visit his hot glass studio. He thrives on refining the complexities of glassmaking, and he's enthralled by the infinite possibilities, always experimenting with surface tension, working temperatures and thickness of wall. He refines his methods almost daily. In turn he challenges me to cultivate and improve my own technique.

I had always wanted to join his team but Lenore had begged me to stay with her. As I look back, I realize it was my years in the Custom Glass Department that provided me with an unequalled opportunity to bond with my younger sister as an adult.

That Saturday I helped my brother was the first time we really connected. Working in rhythm, attuned to each other's moves, we were silent except when Matt barked an order. Only the roar of the furnace and the sound of our work filled the air.

I forgot my anger as we both pulled down our protective

glasses. Matt picked up a four-foot stainless steel rod, stared directly into the furnace, and slowly pushed it into the glory hole. He dipped the blowpipe into the white-hot honey, spun it a few times and then gingerly removed the orange-sized fireball adhering to it. He swiftly stepped over to the marver—a waist-high table—chilling and rolling the glass on the smooth, cool metal, using just enough pressure to form it into the shape of a cylinder.

When working with molten glass, a glassblower must think and act very promptly. Working at the furnace is completely different from the solitary world of the torchworker. I had to concentrate on Matt and pay close attention to his movements. If not, I'd pay the price for not staying on guard. Using a water-soaked cherrywood paddle, I helped him modify the shape of the glass. The glow faded in a few minutes and he guided the piece into the furnace for a second gather and reheated it to a temperature of about 1,500 degrees. Glass can't cool too much or it becomes difficult to work.

He withdrew it and rolled the emerging vase onto a layer of amber-gold glass granules to add color.

"Now!" he ordered.

He took a deep breath and blew into it, breathing life into his creation. He swung the bubble out to make it longer and I used metal tongs, called jacks, to manipulate the glass into an elongated blossom. It was a dance—a process of steady activity involving constant turning of the rod and multiple revisits to the glory hole.

He cued me with a nod and I necked the piece, creating a small groove just below the blowpipe where the final piece would break off. I then paddled the underside lightly to create a flat surface before he attached a punty to the bottom of the glass. He used a file and water to set a chill line then snapped it off at the base. When we were finished, we had given birth to a stunning multi-hued ginger jar.

We worked together as a synchronized team for several hours. When we were finished, both of us were drenched in perspiration but our smiles reflected the inner glow we felt as we admired a rainbow of ten swirled vases that sat side-by-side in an annealing oven, where they would slowly cool overnight.

Matt slapped my back heartily and announced, "Way to go!" I smiled, wiped my brow, and sat on the concrete floor. "Feel better?" I was too tired to respond. "Have you been drinking?"

I laughed. "Come on, Matt! Would you have let me work beside you if I was smashed?"

He wiped his face on his sleeve. "I'm not talking about today. Have you been drinking a lot since Lenore died?"

"Daddy told you to find out."

"Of course."

"I don't drink anymore. When will you all believe me? Do you want to smell my breath?"

"Nope." He started to walk to the rear of the studio where I knew he would grab a shower.

"Wait!" I shouted. "Can I come back? I need this place."

He stopped in his tracks and turned toward me. "Sorry. Dad gave you another week off."

"I don't want another stinkin' week off!"

"He says you need time to recover."

I was boiling mad. "Recover? How do I get over the death of our sister, Matt? How do you? Why didn't he make you take a leave of absence too?"

He walked back, standing tall beside me. "You know it's always been different between me and Dad. It's just the way it is. You work all the time, Marlene. You should think of this as a vacation."

I harnessed my rage and spoke slowly. "I don't want a vacation. I need to work. Blowing glass is all I have."

My brother gathered me in his arms and whispered in my ear, "I know."

My father knew also knew glass was my life. I didn't understand why he had taken it away from me.

Before he disappeared into the locker room, Matt offered a truce of sorts. "Meet me here Monday, after hours. You can assist again but don't tell the old man."

Later that evening, Matt and Monica hired a babysitter and treated me to my favorite meal: rare prime rib, a crisp salad with chunky blue cheese dressing, and a trucker sized baked potato heaped with sour cream and crumbled bacon. We dined at one of Jacksonville's best restaurants, the River City Brewing Company. It was worth the fifty-minute commute to the city for the delicious cuisine, the dynamite view of the St. John's River and the Jacksonville skyline, and because we finally had a chance to talk about Lenore.

On my late night drive home, I rehashed our conversation.

Monica had defended Lenore with exuberance, insisting, "She would never kill herself," when I made that suggestion.

Matt hadn't commented too much other than to say, "All I know is she is dead, and it doesn't matter how she died. She's gone and we can't change that fact. We have to get on with our lives." I was alarmed by his candor and disturbed by his lack of emotion. We definitely handled our grief in different ways. His parting words stung. "You analyze things too much. Let her go."

"I don't want to let go of Lenore!" I shouted in the privacy of my car. Her smiling face popped into my head and I was reminded yet again of how hard it would be to work without my sister beside me.

A vacation was a good suggestion but I still rejected that notion. The idea of running away from the situation, like my parents, made me nauseous. I was exasperated and my head ached as I drove North on I-95. If my father would just let me go back to my job, I could immerse myself in work. I was worried he would ban me from my job for an extended sabbatical. What would my next step be if that happened?

I never imagined that decision would be made for me when I arrived back at Sea Turtle Beach.

⁂

My house is a typical 1950's beach bungalow with weather-silvered cedar shake siding. It stands by itself at the end of a gravel road near the sand dunes. Normally I like the seclusion, but the hair on my neck bristled like a cat's when I pulled into my driveway and realized my place had been burglarized. The creeps hadn't bothered to close the front door. They'd tossed my house, leaving furniture overturned and the lights blazing.

"You should have called us from your cell phone." Floyd Bremmer, a STB cop, chastised me. "You could have walked in on a crime in progress, Marlene."

My cheeks became hot. Frankly, I'd charged into my

house without once considering the consequences. I was more embarrassed than scared by his statement.

Floyd was Steve's old high school buddy. I followed him around the house and realized nothing was missing, except for the rest of my cookies. At least the culprit had found something worthy of stealing.

"Must have been a woman," I joked. "PMS will make a female go to any lengths for chocolate."

Floyd, ever serious, cut his eyes at me but didn't smile. I, on the other hand, would have given anything for some chocolate at that moment. Bloody thieves! Stress always makes me grab for sweets and I was having an overwhelming urge to munch out on the chocolate chipped cookies they had appropriated.

Steve walked through the door and looked around anxiously until he saw my face. "It just gets worse, doesn't it, Marlene?" He grabbed my hand. "Are you okay?"

I freed my hand from his. "I think so."

I wondered how he knew about the burglary attempt until he thanked Floyd for calling him. I didn't realize they were still friends. "No problem," Floyd said as he sat down at my kitchen table to make a few notes. "I sort'a figured you'd want to know, it being Marlene. At least they didn't swipe nuthin'."

Steve stared at me, his eyes wide. "They didn't take anything?"

"Just some cookies." I giggled nervously. "Must have been hungry."

It was the second time I didn't earn a laugh. Apparently I'm the only one who tries to relieve tension with humor.

"Probably some kids," Floyd announced. "Bored teens

havin' a little fun at Marlene's expense."

I was angry. I went outside and paced the gravel road in front of my house. Why would anybody want to break in? As far as I was concerned, there wasn't anything valuable in my place except for a tabletop television that cost $299 plus tax at a local discount store, and they had left that behind.

I considered Floyd's suggestion that it was juvenile delinquents but I wasn't convinced. Nobody wanted chocolate chip cookies that much.

After I had cooled off, I went back inside. Floyd stayed about thirty minutes to complete paperwork and ask me a few questions. The typical stuff. Where had I been? When did I leave? Who was I with? Did I suspect anybody?

He finished his report around 1:20 and packed up to leave, saying, "Oh, by the way, I'm sorry about your sister. Rough month, huh?"

"Are you finished yet?" I snapped.

Flustered, Floyd hurried out the door without a goodbye.

After he was gone, Steve said, "Pack a few things and come back to St. Mary's with me." I almost laughed at his suggestion. I guess I looked amused because he added, "I'm not kidding, Marlene. Amy's worried sick about you, and she'll never forgive me for leaving you alone in this house tonight."

I knew the invitation was really from him, but he was afraid I would say no just to be obstinate. I gave him a passing hug. "I appreciate the offer but I'll stay at my parent's house. They're out of town."

He followed me around as I gathered a few belongings, locked up and walked out to my car. "Are you sure?"

"I'll call you tomorrow."

As I drove away, I glanced in my rearview mirror and saw him still watching me. It struck me as peculiar that my ex-husband was the one person who kept reappearing on my doorstep. I wasn't sure if it was because he still cared, or because he knew more than he was willing to admit.

᙮

I realized the minute I turned into my parent's driveway that something was wrong. Déjà vu. The house lights were on, the door open wide, and when I went inside I saw Mama's perfect living room had been ransacked.

Whatever they were looking for, they meant business and it was apparent the culprits were losing patience. I picked up the place, put back the red-checked cushions on my mother's sofa and closed drawers and doors on her valuable vintage oak credenza. What had started as a fairly decent day had turned into a flat-out bust.

"The place doesn't look too bad," Matt remarked upon entering the house twenty minutes later.

"I cleaned up a bit," I admitted. "They tossed this room."

He looked at me, a question mark plastered on his face. "You cleaned up?"

Suddenly I realized the mistake I had made. "I guess I shouldn't have, huh?"

"Well, if there was any evidence, I'm sure you added your fingerprints to the mix."

He gave me the 'look what she's done now' expression that he reserves for me, his older sister. Any other time I would have punched him in the arm but I was feeling stupid again, so I stood down and said nothing.

We investigated each room together—Matt with a portable phone, me yawning. He called our father and assured him that zilch was missing, at least nothing that we noticed at two in the morning. After much discussion, and after he told my father that I had cleaned up the mess in the living room, they opted to keep the matter private. No cops this time. I wasn't sure it was a wise decision, but I didn't comment since it wasn't my house.

I walked outside and waited on the front porch to avoid a phone conversation with my father. I decided not to tell either of them about the previous break-in at my place. I needed sleep, not a lecture about security.

My house and my parent's home had been burglarized, so I decided to drive to Lenore's place to be alone.

It took about eighty minutes to drive to Mayport since the ferry wasn't operating, but I didn't mind. I often take the long route around the river because I love to drive over the Dames Point Bridge. The two-mile long suspension bridge spans the St. John's and connects Northern Duval County with the beaches and the southern part of the county. I could see its graceful diagonal cables—illuminated like giant clipper sails—from miles away. As I crossed the river, Jacksonville beckoned to me, a jewel sparkling in the night.

It was 4:27 when I arrived at her townhouse. It looked safe enough so I went inside without a tinge of fear.

When I turned on the kitchen light, I gasped.

I collapsed in the middle of Lenore's beige living room carpet and sat there, thinking about what had transpired over the previous twenty-four hours. Up until that moment, I had figured the break-ins were a coincidence, or like Floyd had said, teenagers up to no good.

I didn't know what was happening but I wasn't scared. Not sad, not morose, not even angry—completely drained of emotion.

I felt empty, like Lenore's apartment.

4

Sunday, March 26, 2000
10:46 a.m.

The maid pounded on my door the next morning. I sent her away and slept another hour. When I was fully awake, I grabbed a quick shower and notified the front desk that I'd be staying another night in Jacksonville Beach.

Less than thirty minutes later, I walked beneath a flapping banner that advertised FIRST MONTH FREE and into the leasing office for Seacoast Townhouse Apartments, where I found the assistant manager waiting for potential tenants. A hefty woman, she greeted me with a welcoming smile and a robust hug.

"Marlene! I'm so sorry about your sister. I meant to send you a note but I couldn't find your new address."

Her embrace was overpowering and took my breath away.

"It's been a rough two weeks, as you can imagine," I said, stifling a groan. I escaped to the opposite side of the room where I stared at my sister's vacant townhouse across the street. "Did you see anybody over there this week? Perhaps a moving van?"

"I just opened the office," Maggie replied. "I haven't noticed any activity since I've been here today."

"How about earlier in the week?"

"Why do you ask?"

"Lenore's belongings are gone. Did you find a key in the night depository?"

"Nope. Nobody turned in the key. What do you intend to do about that?"

"What do you mean?"

"You'll need to turn in the key or I'll have to get the locks re-keyed."

"Shouldn't you do that anyway for security?"

"Well, um…" she stammered, "we do change the locks, but the lease says you turn in the key and clean the apartment or you lose the deposit."

I cringed. "You're acting ridiculous! I've cleaned the apartment. Considering the circumstances, I'd think you could make an exception about the key. My sister didn't move out in the middle of the night and she didn't break the lease. She died. Did you forget that?"

Maggie moved to the other side of her desk. "I don't make the rules," she said with a voice that had changed from friendly to authoritarian. "I just enforce them. This complex is operated by Coastal Management Group. I'm their employee and I just do my job."

She flinched as I reached toward her and grabbed a notepad where I scribbled my name and phone number. "Call me if you see any action over there. Otherwise, forget you know me."

"What about the key?"

"The apartment is spotless," I answered curtly. "Keep the deposit. All I want is a phone call if you find out who moved her stuff." Deep down I supposed that would never happen.

Livid with rage and frustration, I stormed out the door with new resolve. I was becoming more and more confused about my sister's life and the circumstances surrounding her death.

Now somebody was messing with me. I wasn't going to let that happen without a fight.

❧

My second floor hotel room faced the Atlantic. The ocean always calms me. I sat on the balcony eating dinner and the seagulls squawked and floated on the evening breeze as they begged for food. I was famished and put away a burger and fries before I went inside and phoned my answering machine. Matt had called three times, my parents twice, and even Steve had checked in to ask if I was safe. I wanted to go home but stuck with my decision to lay low one more night.

I fell asleep before eleven but the television aroused me just a few hours later. I switched it off and tossed around for the next sixty minutes or so, trying to keep my eyes closed. My foot itched, my shoulder popped, a motorcycle outside backfired, and the obnoxious drunks in the neighboring room were having a grand party on their balcony.

After another fifteen minutes of rolling around on the hard mattress and listening to their stupid stories and insufferable guffaws, I realized I was making a worthless effort. I slipped out of bed, eased my patio door shut and turned on the two o'clock repeat of the local evening news.

That's when I saw Jonathan Lucas.

I stared at the screen. I'm not politically inclined and I don't watch much television, so I had managed to avoid most of his campaign advertising. I turned up the volume and listened to him talk, not really paying full attention to the rhetoric he spewed. An attractive blonde stood in the background, obviously admiring him. I guessed she was his wife or an aide. I laughed because she flashed a toothy smile like the Cheshire Cat every time he made a point, and her head bobbled when the crowd applauded. Women like that make me squirm.

Jonathan Lucas made me fume. I still couldn't forgive him for breaking Lenore's heart a decade before when he'd called off their engagement without an explanation. I figured I'd never see him again, yet there he was on the television, still looking debonair with the same curly black hair I remembered from high school. He expounded his so-called convictions and made promises I was certain he would never keep.

"Run!" I shouted to the young woman cheering behind him. I thought Jonathan was a snake but as I listened to his perfectly choreographed responses to reporters' questions, I doubted anybody else had a clue.

Sickened by my memories of the senatorial candidate, I turned off the television again and made myself go back to sleep.

❧

The front desk clerk called me promptly at 10:00 a.m., as requested. I stretched and yawned. "No place to go," I mumbled to myself, turning over for a few extra minutes of sleep. No work. No house. No sister to meet for a luncheon rendezvous.

I sat straight up in bed, flailing my arms and kicking my feet in a proper tantrum. "I can't stop thinking about you!"

Lenore wasn't going to allow me any rest.

I didn't look too bad as I examined my face in the bathroom mirror, but I was tired of wearing the same clothes. I rinsed my mouth, splashed some water on my face, and headed back to the island to face the world and get on with my life.

When I arrived, Steve stood behind a police cruiser in my driveway, talking with my brother. Tony was helping Floyd Bremmer check the perimeter of my property.

I parked on the gravel road at the edge of the dunes and realized I was in trouble when they approached my car with scowling faces. I took the offensive, hopping out and slamming the door shut with a loud thud. "Before you say anything," I ranted to Steve, "you are not my husband!"

I turned to Matt and added, "And you are not my boss today, so you can't tell me what to do, who I can see, or where I can go!"

"Did I say anything?" he asked.

"No, but—"

"BUT," he emphasized, "I am your brother and I was nervous when you didn't answer your phone. Then we couldn't find you." He gestured to the posse of men who had surrounded us and they all nodded in unison.

"We all were," chimed in Tony, Steve and Floyd in perfect harmony, like a boys' choir.

I marched across the lawn with purpose, waving them off. "Well, I'm home now so you can stop fretting."

Floyd came up behind me at a trot. "Where were you?"

"In Jacksonville."

"Humph!" he grunted. "After your incident the other night, we were concerned that somebody had hurt you. You shouldn't disappear like that, Marlene." He gestured over his shoulder with a waggle of his head. "They were worried about you, especially after what happened to your sister."

I bristled. "What happened to my sister?"

Floyd glanced anxiously at Matt, over to me again to study my expression, and then back to Matt with a look of exasperation.

Chill bumps covered my arms. "How did she die?"

"Ask your brother."

"What doesn't she know?" Steve asked.

That's when Tony asked Floyd for a ride and they made a hasty retreat.

Matthew invited me into my house and Steve followed dutifully behind and settled on my sofa. Normally, I would have asked him to leave, but that afternoon I felt comforted by his presence. I paced back and forth in front of him.

"So?" I demanded, fixing my eyes on my brother.

Matt settled into a chair. "Are you sure you want to hear this?"

That's when I erupted. "Stop treating me like I'll shatter. I'm tired of losing sleep, sick of sneaking around, and I'm extremely angry that you and Daddy are keeping me in the dark!"

"Where were you the past two nights?"

"You're avoiding my question."

"Like you avoided telling me that this place was burglarized?" I looked away. "How about Lenore's place? Tony went to Mayport yesterday to move her things into storage but her apartment was empty. Did you take her belongings?"

I leaned over and faced him down, nose-to-nose. "No. Did you?"

He pushed me away and went into my kitchen for a drink of water.

I glanced at Steve. "Did he answer me?"

He shrugged.

When Matt came back into the room a few minutes later, he was more composed but I was trembling.

"You won't like what I'm about to tell you," he warned me as he sat down again.

"I don't like that our sister died at all." I tried to remain calm. "I need to know why she is gone." As far as I was concerned, there was nothing he could tell me that would change my opinion of my sister.

How do I describe Lenore? She was very talented and extremely naïve. She expected the best from people but rarely got it. She was also a hopeless romantic and remained ever optimistic that she would one day meet the man of her dreams.

The bond between women can be very special, but the affection between sisters who love and respect each other is indescribable. That kind of devotion defies words. For Lenore and me, our relationship started when we were children sharing the same bed, lying side by side, sometimes cuddled in each other's arms. Even then, I felt an instinctive urge to shield my younger sister from the world. I would play with her, protect her, and guide her. At night, we would whisper secrets and chatter until we fell asleep.

We grew even closer as adults, especially after my divorce. Lenore understood me more than most people. We shared all our secrets.

I was the only person she told about her pregnancy after Jon abandoned her. She didn't even tell him. Instead, Lenore transferred from Jacksonville University to Franklin Pierce University in New Hampshire, another private college that offers glass blowing as part of their Fine Arts program. My parents assumed it was her need for a change of scenery. At 19-years-old, she was a broken woman and didn't feel prepared to care for a child by herself. After much thoughtful consideration, she decided to carry the baby to full-term, and her infant daughter was adopted by a devoted couple in Boston. I promised not to reveal her secret.

I also knew she had been on antidepressants after that experience. She was a survivor, which was exactly why she was able to help me recover from my miscarriage and subsequent addiction to alcohol.

That's why I didn't believe my brother when he told me about the coroner's report.

"Lenore was a doper."

"Like I'm going to believe that story," I said. "Tell me the truth."

"I just did." He stared at me and waited for me to grasp his words.

Steve eased himself to the edge of the couch. "What did the autopsy say?"

My brother leaned closer and whispered, "Are you sure you want him to hear this?" I nodded. "There was cocaine in her blood."

I glanced at Steve. "Was she doing drugs?"

"Not that I know about."

Matt looked at Steve then back at me. "How would he

know?"

"They were friends," I replied matter-of-factly.

Steve leaned toward me and spoke in a composed manner. "She was a good kid, Marlene. Don't forget that, no matter what you hear."

I turned things over in my head. Had I noticed any signs that Lenore was addicted to anything? Were her eyes glassy? Did she have a runny nose? Had she acted jittery? I couldn't think of one indication that she was doing drugs. In fact, the night she called my house she sounded sober despite the anxiety I heard in her voice.

"Does Mama know?"

"Dad protects her the same way he tries to protect you, Marlene. She knows when to stop asking questions, but you never give up."

I had imagined many possibilities surrounding Lenore's death, but I had never considered a drug overdose. She'd been hooked on prescription pills ten years before, but the image of Lenore doing a line of white powder sent me to the bathroom to throw up.

❧

Before he went home, I assured my brother that I was finished delving into the circumstances of our sister's death, but I knew I couldn't stop. I don't give up easily when something bothers me. His agenda was to protect Mama from the truth, but I was infinitely more interested in verifying the story he'd just told me.

When he was gone, I leisurely strolled through the dunes behind my house, taking a long winding path through a natural garden of prickly pear and sea oats. I chose a soft sandy mound fifty feet from the breaking water as a place to meditate and clear out the thoughts that were nagging at me. I hadn't been there for months—not since late August when the sea turtles were still nesting along our shoreline.

Every summer, I help watch over the nests when the eggs hatch. Volunteers, like me, mark their locations to ensure the new babies are undisturbed. You'd think that would be my favorite time of year, but I actually prefer the winter months when the island is essentially abandoned and I have the beach to myself—like that day.

It was a glorious afternoon with temperatures in the high seventies. In the distance, a shrimp boat glided across the horizon with its forty foot booms spread parallel to the water like two long arms. Its nets, cast beneath it like an enormous web, trawled the ocean floor for the day's catch.

A flock of white seagulls followed so closely behind the vessel that they looked like a waving streamer fluttering in the air. A pleasant breeze blew in from the Atlantic and the sun warmed my face as I closed my eyes and cleared my mind. I was startled when I heard movement behind me. A sandpiper flew out of a thick clump of sea grass and he landed in the shallow water down shore where he foraged in the muddy sand, probing with his bill until he found a tasty sand crab for lunch.

I sloshed ankle-deep in the icy surf, pacing up and down the shoreline. My solitary house stood in the distance. It was almost hidden by a sandbank, but I could see Steve watching me from the deck. He waved and I invited him to join me by waving back.

He hit the beach at a full run a few minutes later and

deposited two towels and a surfboard at my spot. Then he charged by me and dove beneath a white-capped wave. He's a Florida boy to the core, always traveling with a board and a wet suit in the back of his truck. I, on the other hand, had no desire to go deeper into the cold water. It would be at least another month before the Atlantic would be warm enough for me. I trudged back across the hard sand and sat on a towel, where I watched him toss his body into the churning salty broth.

He returned to the shore long enough to claim his prized board. He and the surfboard sliced through the water. About 200 yards out, he stopped. Bobbing up and down, he studied the horizon and waited. A promising wave unfurled. He plastered his body to the board and began to paddle with his hands. Atlantic waves are nowhere near the size of the Pacific surf. Still, they provide a nice ride, especially in the winter. Steve caught the choice wave and easily rode it to the shore. He waved his arms at me, turned around, and paddled back out to wait for his next ride.

Steven Wagner belongs to the sea. He is a master diver and rescue swimmer, and at that time he was assigned to the USS John F. Kennedy. He is a great guy. I made the right decision when I married him.

It's not his fault that I didn't hold up my part of our vows. If it had been his choice, we would have never split up, but my life changed when I miscarried his baby. He did his best to be supportive, but I shunned his attentions. I divorced Steve to protect him from my all-too-frequent alcohol-induced tantrums. After seven good years together and one year of misery, I left him. I didn't want Steve to end up hating me. I could never hate him.

Unexpected tears welled up. I didn't know why I was upset except that it wasn't about our failed marriage. I had accepted my decision and was accustomed to life as a divorcée. We were both doing very well separately. I wondered why he was still alone, why he was spending his days off with me, and more than that, I was unsettled by his relationship with my sister.

I needed a drink.

I went back to my house and threw together a gallon of Florida Essence, my own mixture of orange and grapefruit juices blended with fresh strawberries. I chugged two glasses full of the tangy-sweet concoction before Steve walked through the door with the two towels I'd left on the beach draped over his right shoulder. I filled a tall glass and pushed it to him. "Tell me more about your relationship with Lenore."

He looked startled, standing there with water dripping from his hair and a puddle forming at his feet. "Mind if we talk about this after I take a hot shower?" He walked out of the room.

I busied myself by making a salad while I waited for a large pepperoni pizza to arrive at my door. I was surprisingly at ease preparing dinner for my former housemate—like old times. Realizing that made me edgy and more apprehensive when he walked back into the room a few minutes later, wearing the khaki shorts and black muscle-hugging shirt that I'd stashed away in my closet.

"Look what I found!"

"You might find a few more of your things around here if you search hard enough," I said, trying to mask my discomfort. About that time the pizza guy showed up, saving me from further embarrassment. I gave him a generous tip.

"You remembered my anchovies!" Steve stuffed the first slice in his mouth.

I hate those salty little fish so I'd added them to just half of the pizza. "Why would I forget?"

"Thanks anyway." He took another slice. "You took Matt's news amazingly well."

"Not really. Do you believe Lenore did cocaine?"

"You'd be amazed by who uses drugs these days, Marlene."

"I worked beside her, for heaven's sake. I would have noticed something."

Steve shook his head. "Not really. I've worked with cokeheads in the past. They still managed to do their jobs."

I tried to imagine Lenore flameworking while she was on a high, but it didn't seem feasible.

"Well, it's a little late to prove otherwise," he said. "Besides, the Coroner's Report—"

"The Coroner's Report doesn't mean squat to me," I snapped. "I haven't seen it."

"Sisters aren't always perfect, Marlene."

"Did you ever see her do cocaine?"

"No."

"Then shut up."

Unfazed, he finished eating his last piece of pizza in silence.

"Have you ever tried it?" I had to ask.

"No." He wiped his mouth and stared at the pizza. "You gonna eat yours?" Before I could answer, he grabbed another piece and covered it with grated Romano cheese and a sprinkle of crushed red peppers. "I know you're upset about

Lenore's death." He looked up at me and his face reflected our mutual sorrow. "I don't think she ever did drugs but the evidence might prove otherwise. And since she is buried, it's pointless to argue about it—unless you plan to dig her up." He fixed his eyes on me.

I shuddered. "No. I don't want that." I deliberated for a moment and remembered the question I had asked before he took a bath. "Did you sleep with her?"

He studied me before responding. "That's an unfair question."

"How so?"

"If I say no, you won't believe me. If I say yes, you'll despise me."

"I just want the truth."

He shoved the pizza box away and pushed back from the table. "I never slept with your sister. We were just friends. Don't ask me that again, because if you can't accept my explanation, then you need to understand your sister would never betray you that way."

5

Tuesday, March 28, 2000
10:05 a.m.

The historic district of Sea Turtle Beach encompasses twenty blocks of Victorian homes dating back to the 19th century. Middle Avenue runs smack-dab through the heart of town. People leisurely stroll along the brick sidewalks beneath shady trees, passing gracious homes with turrets, bay windows and gingerbread trim. The shops near the old seaport are always bustling, which is why my mother insisted on a retail outlet in Old Towne.

The town is quiet most days, but that morning was different. Traffic was backed up and I couldn't get near the center square. I detoured through an alley, cut across Third Street, and parked in Mama's space behind the store. In the distance, I could hear the Mighty Marching Pirates—the high school band from nearby Fernandina Beach—tuning up. Loud shouts and cheers filled the air, coming from the direction of the courthouse.

The crowd lining both sides of Middle Avenue was thick. I pushed through, passing by Pop's Eatery, Second Chance Clothiers, and Beachcombers Antiques. I stopped by Jocelyn's Fudge Shoppe to satisfy my sweet tooth. She cut two generous squares of Peanut Butter Swirl—one for me, the other for Anita.

I can't tell you how many people stopped me on the way to the gallery. "Sorry about your loss," said one woman I didn't know. "Nice to see your shop is open again. I'll miss seeing Lenore's smiling face," lamented an old school chum. I couldn't wait to get off the street.

It was still early but Anita was already busy with a customer. The store was crowded and I wondered why Mama hadn't scheduled in more help. I shouted over the milling crowd. "What's going on?"

"Didn't you see the posters?" she yelled back.

Before I could answer, a customer stepped up to the register and asked me to ring up a pair of exquisite imported candlesticks she pointed to in a showcase behind me. They were very expensive amethyst mosaic tapers. As I carefully wrapped them in tissue paper, she said, "Jonathan Lucas is in town and he just gave a wonderful speech. In a few minutes the parade will be passing by your shop."

"How nice," I said through clinched teeth.

A parade to show off Jon Lucas—just what I needed to brighten my day.

Business was brisk until the parade rounded the corner at Saxton Street. In an instant, the gallery emptied. Anita and I watched out the front display window but we couldn't see a thing. Our view was blocked by a throng of people jostling for a spot to witness Jon's spectacle.

I handed her the little white sack from the candy store and said, "Go see the parade, then take the rest of the day off."

She looked bewildered. "You're not scheduled to work here today."

"I figured you might need a break since my mother is out of town."

"You can't handle this place alone," she protested.

"Don't worry, I'll be fine." I scooted her outside, locked the door, and hung the CLOSED sign in the window.

My curiosity piqued, I rushed upstairs and watched the procession pass down Middle Avenue from Mama's office window. The beat of the drums pounded in my chest as rows of pirates from a local high school marched by in unison, the horn section blaring. The band was followed by a squad of cheerleaders waving blue and white pompoms, two mammoth red fire trucks with flashing lights, Cub Scout pack #492—all of them wearing black patches over their right eyes—and a caravan of cars provided by a local automobile dealer. The mayor was in the first car, Miss Sea Turtle Beach was in car two, and in the third car sat Thomas French. I had to laugh. The last time I'd seen him, he was hobnobbing with Senator Wythe. Jon's rival. Apparently our banker has learned to cover all bets.

Next came the floats. The men from the local VFW, Elks and Moose had each produced monstrosities covered with flowers, crepe paper, balloons and smiling wives. Miss Ellen's Pink Posies happily tapped their way down the street. And at the very end of the parade, posed on the back of a white convertible, Jonathan Lucas waved at the crowd, obviously delighted by the turnout.

But I barely saw him. My attention was focused on his driver—my brother, Matthew Terhune.

❧

I positioned a rod over a blue flame and slowly warmed it to a workable temperature, gently shaping the glass into a rotund little body—the beginning of an angel. I glanced up when I heard the bells tinkle on the front door. Anita was back. She locked the door and walked down the hall to join me in the back work room, but she remained silent as I continued to fashion Lenore's cherub, meticulously adjusting the heat of the burner, turning, drawing and tweezing the hot glass as I added legs, feet, arms and hands to the angel's torso.

Anita waited patiently but bubbled over the minute I paused to study my creation, having stifled her excitement far too long. "He sure is cute!" she exploded with all the enthusiasm an 18-year-old girl can muster.

"Thanks, but how can you tell this one is a little boy?"

"Not the angel. Mr. Lucas." She held up a flyer. "He autographed this for me!"

Unimpressed, I mumbled, "He's not a celebrity. He's a politician."

"Well, he sure has my vote!"

"He's old enough to be your father."

She giggled. "You don't have to worry about me, silly. He's practically a married man."

Working the flame is almost hypnotizing, but it is important to stay on task. One wrong move and the angel would be ruined, or worse, I'd be injured. I readjusted my bench burner and peered at the angel's head through my safety glasses as I added facial features. It was obvious I wasn't going to get much work done with Anita in chatty mode. "Oh, really? I didn't know that."

"He's marrying Sylvia Wilkins on Saturday. Don't you

read the newspaper?"

Sylvia Wilkins. So that was the name of the woman with the toothy smile. "I never pay attention to anything written about Jonathan Lucas."

She settled into an overstuffed chair in the corner of the room. It's hidden from the view of the public, and so comfy that I've grabbed a nap in it a time or two. "Why is that?"

"I don't like him."

"You actually know him?"

"He went to high school with Lenore," I replied tersely. "Now stop asking questions and let me get back to work." I heard the testiness in my voice and tried to force a smile. Anita had recently graduated from Sabal Palm Island High School in June. She was young, eager, and curious about everything.

Her eyes clouded over. "Lenore never mentioned that to me. I miss her a lot."

That hurt. "Me too."

"He came in here once."

"Who?"

"Mr. Lucas. Lenore was helping me one weekend and she waited on him. They were cordial, but they didn't act like old friends."

"They weren't friends." I tweezed the hot glass above the cupid's face, creating tufts of curly hair. "Now go home."

"I can take a hint," she said, smiling just a little. "You don't like to talk about Lenore."

I looked up. "I don't like to talk about Jon Lucas."

She laughed nervously and gathered her belongings.

I shut off the torch. "Do you remember what Mr. Lucas purchased?"

Anita shook her head. "He didn't buy anything. They talked to each other for about twenty minutes and then he left."

She uncurled from the chair and stood in front of me. "Do you want to reopen the shop?"

"Nope. Take the day off. I'm almost finished here, and I'll be leaving soon."

As she walked out the back door to the parking lot, I withdrew a fractured wing from my tote bag and studied its design closely. Two more just like it would be added to my angel and then the piece would be complete.

❦

What was on my mind made no more sense to me than having dinner with Steve at Morehead's Fish Camp. Yet, there I was watching him eat fried gator tail while I indulged myself with a plate of blackened grouper and crisp apple fritters. I wondered if my brother had sicced him on me, or if he was there for his own purposes. Either way, I was stuck with him, and he really wasn't such bad company. After an afternoon at the gallery, I was more relaxed.

I was compelled to test my newest theory on Steve. "I think Lenore was seeing Jon Lucas again." Remembering her tear stained face and the years she had wasted recovering from their failed relationship made that possibility seem remote. Still, it was an idea worth investigating.

"I don't believe that," Steve said after swallowing another heaping spoonful of grits. "Jon hurt her too much. Besides, she would've told me."

"Why would she tell you?"

"How many times do I have to say we were friends? We corresponded by e-mail almost daily. She was my one quick link to home since Amy doesn't have a computer." I lost my appetite. Our waitress wrapped up my fish and fries while I continued to watch Steve chow down. He took a swig of dark beer and licked the foam from his lips. "Besides, she was involved with some other guy."

"She told you that?"

"Yes."

My stomach twisted. "She never told me." Why had she confided in Steve instead of me?

"Why are you surprised by that?"

"What was his name?"

"Don't know. Not sure she even told me."

"What do you know?"

He laughed. "He was a sailor, but this one was attached."

"Married?"

"I didn't press for details."

The restaurant was bustling and noisy. I stared out the window at the river where it was more tranquil. The boats and camping trailers in the fish camp were silhouetted against a magnificent red sky as the sun dipped below the pink and gold western horizon. I turned back to Steve. "Why are you doing this?"

He stopped eating. "What?"

"We're divorced. If this isn't a date, what is it?"

He popped a golden brown hushpuppy into his mouth and chewed slowly, studying me until I became uncomfortable. I thought he would never respond. He eventually answered with a question. "We're still friends, right?"

"I guess."

"Well, friends look out for friends, Marlene. It's as simple as that. We may not understand each other, and you may drive me crazy but I'll always check your six." He looked down at his empty plate and pushed it away. "I just wish I'd been here to watch Lenore's back."

Guilt makes a person do a lot of things. It made me reach out and touch his hand. It was the first time in years that I had made a gesture of friendship toward my former love. When he smiled, I withdrew. I didn't want to mislead him. He must have read my mind because he skipped the Key Lime Pie and asked for our check.

We sat in his truck for a while with the sounds of the night to keep us company. A chorus of crickets and tree frogs droned in the bushes that lined the river banks. I don't know what he was thinking about, but I couldn't get Lenore out of my mind. I rehashed the day's events, still wondering what had happened to the rest of the glass she had created. I had already searched the gallery, the studio, and Lenore's apartment. I'd even snooped around my parents' place.

And then I remembered one spot I still hadn't investigated. I turned to Steve and said, "I need to go home."

Tony was sitting on my porch swing, waiting for my return. "What's he doing here?" Steve grumbled. The set of his jaw, the glare in his eyes, and the sound of spinning gravel beneath his tires tipped me off that he was a little miffed by my uninvited visitor.

"What's his problem?" Tony asked as Steve sped away. I

didn't know, but Tony is always welcome in my house.

"Fix yourself a snack." I tossed him the television remote. "Find a good movie."

Steve's frustration could have been the result of the 'you need to quit smoking' sermon he had just preached to me on the way home. It came after he congratulated me on staying sober and with a reminder that Lenore wouldn't approve of my recently rekindled pack-a-day habit. "I only take a couple puffs," I'd told him, but he wasn't going for it. I knew he wouldn't let up until I quit again. He may have been uneasy because I'd asked to see his correspondence from Lenore. I wanted to know more about the mystery man she'd been dating. But I think Tony's unannounced visit had changed his mood. Either way, it didn't matter to me. I had something much more imperative on my mind.

"What are you up to?" He followed me through the living room. "Are you going back out?"

"Nah, make yourself at home." I disappeared into my bedroom and assumed he wouldn't follow.

I pulled a pillowcase from beneath my bed along with thick dust balls and emptied its contents onto the floor for inspection.

I placed Lenore's Bible on the table beside my bed. Her address book was useless. In it I found addresses, phone numbers and birthdays for our family and a few friends.

An elegant abalone jewelry box was my favorite keepsake. It hid a crushed blue velvet pouch, and inside that was a diamond ring on a golden chain. Was it the engagement ring Jon had given my sister a decade before he promised his heart to another gullible woman?

Next, I pulled out an almost empty box of feminine

napkins. Since we'd been teens, Lenore and I had stashed our secrets where we figured they'd least likely be discovered. As expected, I found booty in the bottom of the cardboard container. Most of it was worthless but there was one item of extreme interest to me: a receipt for a lock box at the Mayport Post Office.

The last item I picked up was the hardback book I'd taken from her bedroom.

"Do you need some help?" Steve's voice startled me. I don't know how long he and Tony had stood there watching me in silence, like the Ninjas in the martial arts flick that was on the television behind them.

"You came back."

"Never left. I went to the store for some brew."

Tony leaned up against the door frame. "I didn't think you'd mind my letting him in." He pointed to the book in my hand. "Are you going to read that tonight?"

I casually tossed it to the center of my bed and went back to the living room, closing the door behind me. "Nope, I promised you we'd watch a movie together."

I sandwiched myself in between them on the couch, but as they lost themselves in the non-stop Kung Fu action, my mind wandered. I couldn't wipe the book's title out of my head: *Getting Rid of That Man You Don't Really Need.*

I was glad for the company. My good friend, Tony, often came over to watch movies with me on cable television, but I had forgotten how funny Steve could be when he let down his guard. A couple of beers and a bowl of buttered popcorn mellowed him out. It was the first decent evening I'd had in recent memory. It reminded me of when Steve and I were still married. We joked, laughed, and had fun times. For a few hours, I actually put Lenore in the back of my mind.

Midway through the movie, Steve leaned his head on the back of my sofa and fell asleep. That's when Tony spoke up. "Why does he drink in front of you? In fact, why don't you tell him it bothers you?"

I was taken aback. "Because it really doesn't bug me and because he asked me if he could drink a beer at the restaurant."

Tony shrugged. "Well, one brewskie with dinner is different than going to a store and coming back with enough beer to make him pass out."

I was a little bothered by his words. "He only had two," I said nonchalantly. "The rest of the six-pack is in the fridge."

"Don't forget the one he had with dinner." Tony gathered the empties and strode into the kitchen. "I held my tongue out of respect for you. This is your house. I figured you would say something but you didn't." As he came back into the room, he glanced at his watch. "It's late. Do you want me to drive him home?"

"To Georgia?" I chuckled. "Look at him. He'll be there all night."

"Are you sure?"

"Yep." I gave him a hug and said, "Thanks a bunch. I know you worry but I'll be okay."

After I watched Tony drive away, I locked the door and turned around to see Steve sprawled all over my sofa.

I walked in the kitchen and opened the refrigerator door, staring in at four sparkling bottles of amber ale. Beer had never been my drink of choice, but I'd consumed enough for a lifetime. I had actually been partial to rum or bourbon served with any kind of soft drink because I had convinced myself that alcohol was relatively harmless when served that way.

With my sister's support, I had eventually given up liquor after our divorce, but I'd replaced that habit with cigarettes, and now Steve wanted me to give that up too.

I closed the door and walked back into the living room. Steve looked so tranquil. I doubted he was drunk. He was probably just dog-tired, like me. I lifted his legs to the top of the cushions and the rest of his body slid easily into a reclining position.

I couldn't help myself as I touched his cheeks—the face I had cherished for years.

6

Wednesday, March 29, 2000
8:45 a.m.

Since Steve was still on leave, I figured I'd let him sleep late. I intended to grab a few extra Z's myself. That changed when Centurion Security showed up promptly at eight. After the break-ins, Daddy had bought and paid for an alarm system for my house. Too bad he didn't let me know. Because he didn't, I greeted Ronnie Walker at the door in my pajamas.

When he went to his van to gather his tools, I changed clothes and shook Steve awake. "What's up?" he grumbled. He glanced around the room, still groggy from a beer-induced coma, and looked shocked to discover he had slept on my couch.

"I need to go out for awhile," I said, already heading out the door. "Help yourself to my groceries. Ronnie Walker's here to install a security system. If you don't mind, I'd like you to stay here while I'm gone." I trusted him to oversee the drilling, hammering and stringing of wire throughout my house.

"Sure thing." He tried to sit up, but fell back against the sofa cushion. "I'll be here when you get back."

❧

It was time to welcome my parents home. Ronnie had said his next appointment was at their place. I was sure my father would be there to supervise the work. Just a few minutes later, Daddy greeted me with a cup of coffee and a big hug.

"I was expecting you," he said with a welcoming smile. "You're late."

"Late?" I held back a laugh. He was covered nose to toes in flour.

"Yep. Time to eat! I've got scrambled eggs and buttermilk biscuits ready." The house smelled of maple-cured bacon, a familiar homey aroma.

Mama greeted us in the kitchen, which was, as expected, dusted in flour from top to bottom. "Just look at this mess, Mason!" She scolded him as she swept the floor, but she was grinning and I knew she wasn't really peeved. Believe me, after almost forty years together, she's accustomed to my father's chaotic breakfast routine. She glanced up at me. "Care to set the table?"

I pulled three dishes from the cabinct. "How was your trip?"

"Too brief," my father complained. "I wasn't ready to come back but your mother insisted."

"Now, Mason, it was time to come home." Mama lovingly patted his back. "You know we have a commitment this weekend."

"Saturday, Saturday, Saturday. Why do you keep reminding me?"

"Of what?" I glanced at them both, but Daddy took two of the plates into the dining room.

"We have a social engagement." She didn't elaborate.

I looked at my father as he returned to the kitchen,

imagining he would provide a more interesting answer. "You don't want to know." He waved his hand in the air. "It's just one of those things. There are times I have to make an appearance just so the higher ups will remember who I am if I need to call in a favor."

"Oh, Mason, you make it sound like such a chore." Mama winked at me. "You know he likes to dress up."

That statement reminded me of Lenore. She was the social whirlwind in our family, and before her death she had attended community affairs with my parents. It was obvious that my mother was thinking the same thing because the smile dissolved from her face. She sobbed and ran from the kitchen.

I felt awful.

Daddy dished up the biscuits, eggs and bacon and invited me to join him at the table. "She's been teetering on the brink of tears for a couple of days." He loaded a fist-sized biscuit with a dollop of orange marmalade. "A good cry will make her feel better. You just wait and see. She'll be back for breakfast in just a minute."

He tried to look cheerful, but there was an invisible black cloud over his head. I could hear the strain in his voice and wondered when he would break. As a businessman, he has been through plenty of hard times but I'm sure Lenore's death is the most devastating event he has ever faced. I know this not just because of the haunted look in his hazel eyes, but also because I've been through the same turmoil—the loss of my child.

His face brightened when Mama came back to the table. He stood up and pulled out a chair for her. When she was seated, they both told me about their trip to Key West.

Tears wiped away, my mother made a valiant effort to appear carefree but she still looked mournful. When she laughed at my father's stories, it was obvious that her indulgence was forced. They were both animated, handing off parts of the conversation to each other like a well-oiled comedy act. He'd set up the story and she'd kick in with the punch line. Mason and Trudy delivered their usual award-winning performance and I made sure to laugh at all the right spots, but I'm wise to their ways, and I know when my parents go into their George Burns and Gracie Allen shtick they are really covering up.

I jumped at the chance to interrupt their routine when Daddy paused to eat his last piece of salty-sweet bacon.

"So how are you?"

"Same as you." He sipped the last drop of orange juice from his glass.

Mama cleared the table of everything but my father's plate. With her out of the room, I bowed toward him and whispered, "How's she really handling all of this?"

He looked toward the kitchen door, checking to see if she was nearby before answering. "Not well. You saw her a few minutes ago. She's devastated."

"So the trip was a bust."

"No. The trip was worthwhile."

"I don't know how you can say that," I said testily. "You two always run away when there's a crisis, but when you come back the problem is still here. You can't make it go away by ignoring it, Daddy. You're not going to wake up from a bad dream and find out Lenore's still here."

I wish I had controlled my frustration better, but the words flew out before I could stop them.

My father's face reddened. His fork clattered against his plate as he dropped it and wiped his mouth on a linen napkin. I knew I had pushed him beyond his limits. "Do you think we're oblivious to the gut-wrenching reality that our daughter is dead?"

His look chilled me to the bone.

"Not really, but—"

"You are not our only child, Marlene." He stood up stiffly. "Our lives do not revolve solely around you, although you seem to think otherwise. We needed time alone to recuperate without playing nursemaid to our other children."

My stomach knotted. "But you invited me—"

"Your mother wanted you to accompany us. I knew you wouldn't come along, but I figured I'd invite you if she needed your companionship." With unbridled malice, he added, "Obviously you didn't think she needed you, because you disappeared quicker than a jack rabbit fleeing from a fox."

My throat tightened as I fought back tears, especially when Mama walked back into the room. She stood in the doorway for a moment, stared at the two of us, and left again without speaking.

"You're mad at me and you're trying to make me feel guilty," I insisted when she was out of range.

He glared at me. "Any guilt you feel comes from your gut, not from me."

My father is an expert at making me feel selfish. There's always friction between us and we always question each other's motives. "If you aren't angry with me, why are you punishing me?"

"Punishing you?" He looked puzzled. "Why would I

punish you?"

"I don't know," I said, my voice cracking. "You tell me."

"Do you doubt that I love you?"

Tears welled in my eyes. "I know you love me, but do you understand how much I love blowing glass? Why won't you let me work?"

He pushed away from the table, the chair legs screeching against the hardwood floor.

"What I know is that your sister has died and you are in pain. You have experienced a personal tragedy and even though Matt thinks I should allow you to return to your job, I can see that it's still too early."

He stormed outside. "Take a month off—more if you need it—because I won't let you work for me until I know you can do it safely. I've just lost one of my children and I don't want to attend your funeral this year too." Dismissing me, he marched toward the dock.

My father and I have been sparring on a regular basis since my teens. I think the dynamics of our relationship—the heated debates, protracted arguments, and eventual ceasefires—help us learn more about each other than if we simply communicated with cursory hugs and the occasional so-so conversation over dinner. We have gritty conversations about real issues. We don't pull punches. And even though we may occasionally offend each other, he would do anything to help me tackle a crisis.

I watched him from the kitchen doorway. It was a pleasant morning, the kind of day that should inspire serenity, certainly not animosity. I'm accustomed to finding my father sitting on the pier with his feet dangling off the sides as he trawls for blue crabs, but that day he paced the deck, looking forlorn. As I studied him, I felt responsible for his pensive mood and I realized he was forcing me to deal with my sorrow instead of wallowing in self-pity and misery.

I figured we both needed a break.

He always keeps bait in the garage freezer for impromptu fishing trips. I threw a block of frozen shrimp in a washtub and ran tepid water from a garden hose over it to wash away most of the ice. A few minutes later, I stood beside him with a tackle box in one hand and a bucket of brine shrimp at my feet. When he looked into my eyes, I handed him his favorite rod and reel.

"Ready?"

He crawled into his old aluminum boat and chuckled. "What took you so long?"

I joined him and we stood there, balancing precariously, locked in an embrace.

My mother came out of the house with an ice chest and a bag lunch packed for both of us. She kissed his cheek. "Dinner's at six."

"We'll be back before the security company shows up," he promised. He winked and blew her a farewell kiss. Mama waved and threw kisses back to both of us as he steered into the channel and headed out to deeper water.

High tide was coming in and with it schools of bait-sized fish fluttered just below the surface. The outboard motor hummed and the water sloshed against the sides of the boat. A great blue heron glided over us, dipping into the water for an early lunch—a good sign.

We traveled several knots before I broke our silence. "You should buy a new boat."

"What's wrong with this one?"

"It's old, too small, way slow, and just plain ugly. And besides, you can afford the best—something sleek and fast."

He shook his head. "I don't want fast, and I don't need sleek." He patted the side of the little skiff affectionately. "This old gal's just right for me."

I moaned. "That's not the point, Daddy."

"Well, I don't want one and that is the point."

A few minutes later, we pulled into our favorite fishing cove. "It's been a long time since we did this together," he said as he baited a hook. "With a little luck, maybe we'll have catfish for supper."

I cast my line. "The way my luck's running, I'm betting on mullet."

He gave me a patient smile. "Don't be such a pessimist."

"Me?"

"You."

I was astonished. "I'm the most positive person you know—" And then I heard myself and stopped mid-sentence. "I guess…well, I guess that's changed. It's hard to be upbeat when all I really want to do is scream."

"So scream."

"What?"

The boat rocked as he stood, offering me a hand. "Stand up."

I stood up awkwardly.

"Scream," he repeated.

I stared at him, feeling rather foolish.

"You can do it, Baby. Nobody's out here but the two of us. By gosh, I'll yell with you." Then he let out the loudest ear-splitting screech this earth's ever heard. Surrendering to the moment, I joined in and it felt good letting loose. We yelled loud enough to shoo away every marsh critter within two miles.

"I guess we can forget fishing, huh?" I was hoarse and completely drained of that day's anger.

"Yep. Time to head for the ocean." He chuckled as he reached into a brown paper bag and fished out a tuna sandwich. "Better chow down. Looks like this is the only fish we'll be eating today."

※

There's nothing better than a mess of fresh fish fried up in a black iron skillet. While Daddy iced down another big one, I conjured the smell of hot grease and my mouth watered as I thought about my mother's red and blue coleslaw and sweet jalapeño cornbread. My watch said 1:23. We were late. I felt guilty that Mama would have to deal with the security company on her own.

"Time to go back." Daddy started stowing away our fishing gear.

"Don't be nervous," I said. "Dee Walker's son, Ronnie, works for Centurion. Mama will be safe with him."

He steered back into the channel. "Eight's enough, don't you think?"

I wordlessly began to stow our gear away.

We had enjoyed two great hours together, and lots of good fishing once we'd moved the boat to a cove upstream. He had protested every time I tossed a brim back into the river, but we had iced down plenty of catfish and our limit of red fish.

As I stowed my gear, I asked him the question that had

been on my mind all day. "After all these years, why are you installing a security system now?"

"As a precaution."

"Against what?"

"Nothing in particular."

I took out a cigarette.

He protested. "Throw those things away."

"You know that's not the way to make me stop."

"You don't need them. What you need is—"

I struck a match and he stopped talking. "You didn't answer me," I said after taking a drag. "Why are you beefing up security?"

"Why not?"

"Because you always say this island is the safest place on earth, and because you've always insisted that we don't need a security system. What's changed?"

"The world."

I felt uneasy. "That's rather ominous."

He didn't respond.

"You're doing this because some stupid teenagers have been having fun at our expense."

"That's part of it."

I reached across the boat and squeezed his forearm. "Are you holding back something that I should know? If you aren't telling me everything, you're being completely unfair to me."

He looked at me intensely. "Do you trust me?"

Unfair question. "Is it safe for me to return to my house? If it isn't, tell me now."

He paused and considered his answer before pronouncing, "You are not in danger."

I wasn't convinced.

I crushed the butt of my cigarette in the boat bottom. I didn't want it. I didn't even crave a drink. I just wished the nightmare would stop.

※

As we approached the pier, I noticed Ronnie's van was parked in the driveway. Daddy was about thirty minutes late for his two o'clock appointment. He cut the motor, climbed out, and tied up the boat before I got out of my seat. He's quite agile for his age and a lot more limber than me.

Ronnie appeared from the north corner of the house. Seeing me wrestle with the ice chest, he broke into a jog and ran to the side of the boat. "Glad to see you two," he said as he helped me hoist the chest full of fish to the deck. He extended his hand and pulled me to his side. Then he politely shook my father's hand. "Mr. Terhune, I'm Ronnie Walker from Centurion. Looks like you've had a good day! I'll unload a few things from my van while you unpack your catch. Then we can go inside to discuss the installation."

They exchanged a few pleasantries and my father proudly showed off our bounty before he walked toward the garage to stash the day's catch in the refrigerator.

I walked with Ronnie to his van. "I've been waiting for you," he said.

"Waiting for me?" I was a little apprehensive. Ronnie is extremely handsome and very married. "I know we're late, but why did you think I'd be here?"

"Well, I didn't actually mean you, Marlene. I was just waiting for somebody to let me in the house."

A chill of apprehension swept over me. "Didn't my mother answer the door?"

Ronnie shook his head. "Nope. I rang the doorbell several times and I tried knocking." He held up his phone. "I tried calling but nobody answered. Honestly, I was about to leave when—"

I panicked and broke into a trot before he finished his sentence.

The entry door was still locked and I fumbled with my keys. Once inside, I zoomed to the kitchen and shouted, "Mama! Mama?" But she didn't answer. Still yelling, I made a circuit around the first floor, through the dining room, into the living room and up the stairs to the bedroom level.

Mama was cowering on the floor beside Lenore's bed, clutching a stuffed teddy bear against her chest.

My heart practically burst out of my body, but she didn't notice. I sat on the floor beside her and she took my trembling hand in hers. "Be very quiet," she whispered. "A strange man is wandering around outside." I felt like a little girl again, hiding behind the couch with my mother when a door-to-door salesman knocked at our door.

"It's okay, Mama. You know him. Ronnie is Dee Walker's son. He's here to install the security system."

"That's not who I saw."

"Did you see a white van in the driveway?"

"No."

"Ronnie says he's been outside about thirty minutes. He's been ringing the doorbell and knocking on the door. He even tried to call you but you didn't answer."

She shook her head vehemently. "I've been hiding up here for more than an hour. The man I saw never rang the doorbell and I don't know him. He was wandering around outside so I went upstairs and watched out the window. The last time I saw him, he was traipsing through the woods toward your father's storage shed."

My mother's fear was palpable and her chin trembled when she spoke. Her beautiful dark brown eyes were bloodshot from grief-stricken tears. "When the doorbell rang again, and then the knocking—well, I figured he was back. I sat here quietly and hoped he would just go away."

"Why didn't you call the police? Why didn't you call me?" I felt guilty. Why hadn't I called my mother from the boat?

"There's no telephone in this room."

Her answer may not seem sensible since she could have gone to another room, but to my mother it was logical. She went to a place where she felt safe and waited for help.

"What did he look like?"

"He might have been a salesman, but I don't think so. He was dressed rather nicely in trousers and a button-down shirt. His hair was brown and short and he was somewhat tall and broad at the shoulders. I didn't recognize his face, but I didn't stand in the window and stare at him either."

Her description could have fit many men I know, and a thousand I've never met.

I gave her an enormous hug. "You're okay now. I promise. Daddy is downstairs."

Her frightened face softened into a bright smile. She sprung to her feet and walked toward the bathroom. "I'll be down in a minute. I need to freshen up."

I joined my father outside. "Was your mother napping?"

"She's awake but she'll tell you what she's been doing."

Ronnie was busy erecting a ladder up to the roof, so we had a few minutes to converse privately.

"Do you need me to help you move Lenore's belongings out of her apartment?" I was still fishing and hoping to get a catch.

"No, Tony did that for Matt when we were away."

Apparently they hadn't talked since my parents returned to the island.

I pretended that I had no knowledge of what had transpired at my sister's place. "That's good." Then I waited a few moments before I asked what I really wanted to know. "Are you expecting anybody else to visit today?"

"Not unless your mother has some friends coming over."

"Do you have anything here that belonged to Lenore—an article that somebody might be searching for?"

He gave me a curious look then my father's expression became dour. "If you're asking about drugs, you won't find anything like that here. What did Matthew tell you?"

"He said she was using cocaine."

"I don't believe that. Do you?"

I spoke softly so Ronnie wouldn't hear our discussion. "I don't know what to believe."

"She was the good—um, she was—" He averted his eyes from me.

"I know, Daddy. She was the good one."

Still looking away, he said, "I'm sorry. I didn't mean to say that."

"Sure you did." I touched his arm. "Let's not worry about words you've said or things I've done. We're beyond that now."

He managed a tepid smile. "I guess we're starting over,

aren't we?"

"I don't think we need to start over, Daddy. What we need is to learn how to cope and go on without her. It's going to be hard."

"That's for sure." He ran his fingers through his tousled hair and studied the house, the ladder, and Ronnie on the roof.

"Her car!"

"Her car?"

"Yes. Lenore brought it here and parked it in the shed the weekend before she died." He was referring to a pre-fabricated metal building hidden out of view on the other side of his property. It's where he stores his classic 1964 Mustang and the yard tractor, and apparently where Lenore stashed her orphaned Mazda Miata.

"Did she say why she wanted to leave it here?"

"No. She just asked to borrow your mother's SUV for a couple of days. I never gave it a thought."

"Is it locked up?"

Ronnie began descending the ladder and my father tossed me a key to the shed. "Go ahead—take a look."

I gave him a quick hug and anxiously threaded my way through the trees. I called back to him, "Thanks! I'll give it back to you before I leave."

Crime is almost non-existent on Sabal Palm Island, so my father's definition of the word 'safe' meant 'safe from the weather'. I'm sure he never thought somebody would break into his house or his shed, but he was wrong. I had no use for the key because the padlock was already broken and the doors were wide open.

Inside, the Miata was still parked beside his tarp-covered

Mustang. The windows and soft-top convertible roof were intact. That meant the intruder hadn't been searching for drugs. Otherwise, the car seats and carpet would have been in shreds. In fact, the car was undamaged except for the trunk lock that had been popped to open the lid. Because the thief had only broken into the trunk, I had to deduce that he was looking for something big that wouldn't fit into the two-seater passenger compartment. Whatever it was, it was gone because the trunk appeared to be empty.

I grabbed a flashlight from the glove box and peered inside the trunk again. A crystal flower with a chipped petal had been left behind in the far right corner. That's when I concluded that the person who had invaded my house, my parent's house, and Lenore's apartment and automobile had been searching for the same boxes of custom blown glass that I had been trying to recover.

Why had Lenore stashed them in her car, and why was the collection so valuable that someone was willing to risk arrest for stealing them?

I felt sick, but mostly I dreaded telling my father that his property had been burglarized again.

People die. Under normal circumstances, families grieve together, sharing fond memories of their deceased loved-one and bolstering each other through difficult times. But the way my family responded to Lenore's death made me feel very alone.

Instead of talking about my sister, my parents avoided speaking her name. When my mother was overcome with emotion, she'd run away from me to seek solace in Lenore's room. My father had banned me from his business, which meant he didn't have to converse with me on a daily basis. And Matt was so cool and collected that he acted like nothing traumatic had happened to our family. I suspected he was mad at Lenore for dying from a cocaine overdose, but that wasn't fair because she couldn't speak for herself and tell us what had really happened.

There was no time and no place for me to even begin recovering from the shock I felt when my sister died. Strangers broke into our homes and our lives, and nobody wanted to do anything about it. Except for me.

When I told my father about Lenore's car and the missing glass, he barely raised an eyebrow. "It's just stuff," he said, sounding relieved. "At least your mother wasn't harmed."

'Yes, but what about the glass?' The glass my sister had secretly created. The last thing she had touched. The glass that was missing.

I kept that thought to myself because I knew he would think I was being sarcastic. Worse, he might imagine I had no empathy for my mother, and I couldn't let either of them think that.

He was right. At least Mama was safe.

But if she was safe—if we were safe, like my father told me in the boat—then what was going on?

I felt trapped in a maze of conflicting stories and events that kept me perpetually on edge. I was overwhelmed with anger because something was happening that I couldn't understand. I was emotionally drained, my nerves were raw, and I didn't know who I could turn to for help.

I considered Steve. Could he help me? If so, how much more involved in my life did I really want him to be?

When I got back to my place, his truck was gone.

That was my answer. I realized I couldn't depend on Steve or anybody I knew. I felt the urge to throw things like I had when Steve lived with me. I picked up an ashtray and considered sending it into the wall, but I took a deep breath and threw it into the kitchen trash can instead.

I felt like there wasn't a single soul I could confide in, nobody that would help me sift through my questions, and no one that would show me how I could protect my dead sister's reputation.

I had convinced myself that nobody cared enough or had the fortitude to get more involved in what I perceived as my final duty to my sister—to prove that she was the angel my parents always thought she was.

But I was wrong. That's when Sherry Hill came into my life.

❧

Lenore was the official spokesperson and goodwill ambassador for Crest Glass. She had introduced me to Sherry Hill once when she was touring our factory to research an article about an elaborate chandelier that our company created for a famous cathedral in California.

Sherry is a reporter for the Beach Informer. They're the local newspaper on the island, but since there's not too much going on around our community, they only print a Sunday edition featuring articles about high school sports, community events, local businesses and personalities. I was sure that week's lead story would be about Jonathan Lucas's appearance in his hometown and his impending wedding, which was the only reason Sea Turtle Beach would be worthy of a visit from a senatorial candidate.

When I saw her business card had been slipped beneath my front door, I suspected she wanted to talk to me about Jon. Everybody knew he had been engaged to my sister, and everybody knew Lenore had recently died. I imagined she was eager for a story that would move her up in the newspaper hierarchy. That's why I didn't call her, even though she had scribbled URGENTLY NEED TO SPEAK TO YOU on the back of the card.

I had skipped the fish dinner at my parent's house, so I put a frozen entrée in the microwave and went to my bedroom to change into comfy loungewear. I was exhausted and planned to spend the evening doing absolutely nothing.

After eating, I turned on the television, laid down on the couch, and promptly fell asleep.

Steve called me around seven o'clock. "I'll be there in about an hour," he announced, without an invitation.

"For what?" I mumbled, still half-asleep.

"I don't want you to stay there alone. Too many weird things have been going on around you recently."

"And you're going to protect me?"

"Yes, I am."

"Did you forget I have a new burglar alarm?"

"No, but I have to show you how to use it. Only I know the current security code. I'll need to show you how to change it."

I was still irritated that he had left my house before I returned. I replied, "Not tonight," and hung up.

I dialed up Tony but he didn't answer his phone.

By then it was dark. I rolled off the couch and walked over to the sliding glass doors at my kitchen. The new moon was invisible and the ocean melted into the black sky. Normally, I would walk out on my deck to listen to the soothing sloshing of the surf, but that night I stayed inside in case another creep was sneaking around the island. I slammed my hand against the glass, angry that strangers had made me feel so insecure.

The front door knocker rapped almost imperceptibly. I didn't expect company, and while it could have been an unexpected visit from a friend, I was uncertain about what to do next. I had no way to look outside without parting the curtains and that put me on edge.

I walked to the door. "Steve?"

Nobody replied.

"Tony?"

Still no reply.

I raised my voice and put my mouth closer to the door. "Who is it?"

"It's Sherry Hill. Sorry I'm here so late, but I need to talk to you."

I opened the door slowly to catch a glimpse of her face but she didn't look familiar at all. Her blonde hair had been cut to shoulder length, and she wore more make-up than a circus clown. I recognized her only when she introduced herself again. Her pitchy voice was particularly distinctive—unforgettable—even though I hadn't seen her since she and Lenore walked across the commencement stage at graduation.

"I'm here to talk about your sister."

No surprise to me. I invited her inside.

I imagine men swoon over Sherry. She has a fashion-doll figure and a calculated aura of naïvety that I'm sure she uses often to cultivate and harvest the articles she writes. She'll do well at a bigger urban newspaper some day. I was prepared for her questions and I had no intention of exposing my family or my sister to Sherry or her readers.

I showed her to a chair and examined the card she had just handed me as if I had never seen one like it before.

"I don't talk about my sister." I hoped my lack of participation might chase her away.

"I can understand that, especially in light of recent events." She placed her purse beside her feet and sat back in the chair. "You don't have to talk. Just listen to what I have to say."

I sat in silence on the couch beside her.

She fixed her eyes on mine. "Do you ever read *The American Interrogator*?"

"I don't indulge in gossip, not even in print."

"Marlene, I have a good friend who works for them. She called me yesterday to ask a few questions about Jonathan Lucas and your sister. They're planning to print an exposé about him on his wedding day."

Nice people. "What does my sister have to do with his wedding?"

"According to my friend, that scandal sheet has evidence that they were having an affair."

I felt like I had just taken a punch to the gut and it rendered me speechless. She allowed me time to digest what she had just revealed. She walked into my kitchen and brought back a cold glass of water that I accepted with gratitude. I took a few sips and watched her watching me.

Finding my voice, I asked, "Why should I believe you or your friend? And how can I change anything that rag wants to publish?"

She frowned. "What you need to know first is that we're on your side. You may not know it, but I went to college with your sister. We were sorority sisters, as was my reporter-friend, Donna.

"And you're right...we can't stop publication of that article, but we certainly can gather our own information to refute their claims. Donna and I both know what Lenore went through with Jon Lucas and we can't believe she was seeing him again. I would enjoy writing an exposé about Jon, but not at Lenore's expense. Neither one of us wants to see her reputation smeared."

Already tired from a long day and an interrupted nap, it was too much information for me to grasp that evening. We agreed to meet for lunch the next day. When I showed her out the door, Steve was sitting on my porch steps. I waited for Sherry to drive away before I spoke.

"I guess you're determined to stand guard tonight."

"Yep."

I pushed the screened door open. "You can sleep on the couch again. Just don't wake me up unless it's an emergency."

Steve came inside, locked up, and set the burglar alarm. "Who was that?"

I threw him a pillow and blanket. "One of Lenore's friends." I closed the door between us, snuggled into my bed, and felt a bit safer with Steve in the house a second night.

Around eleven o'clock the next morning, I pulled into the paved lot beside the Museum of Science and History on Jacksonville's Southbank and parked in a shady spot at the edge of Friendship Park. A picnic lunch wasn't exactly what I had expected when I called Sherry that morning, but she had a business appointment downtown and I figured a meeting away from the island might be a good idea. I arrived a good thirty minutes early, even after stopping by a deli to purchase lunch for both of us.

The squirrels played tag beneath a cluster of multi-colored azaleas that were already in full bloom. It was a mild day, sunny but not too hot with a pleasant breeze that delivered the aroma of fresh roasted coffee beans from the nearby Maxwell House plant.

I decided to get out of the car to stretch my legs and strolled over to the railing that surrounds the center fountain. I was mesmerized by more than sixty nozzles that were shooting water into the air in an elaborately choreographed routine. I love to watch the water dance. It's even more spectacular at night when the performance is lit by a rainbow of colored lights. I couldn't remember the last time I'd been there. Certainly it had been several years.

A cold spray misted my face as the water fell into a shallow pool, refreshing me and my memory. I recalled a wintry evening, carols broadcast through speakers around the park, and sharing hot cocoa with Steve as we watched a flotilla of boats decorated for the Christmas holidays sail between the two banks of the St. John's River in the city's annual light parade.

I doubt Steve ever reminisces about that night because that was around the time I decided to end our marriage. He did everything he could think of to put me into the holiday mood, but I had sunk into such a deep depression that it was impossible to lift my spirits. Parties provided endless opportunities to drink alcoholic beverages, but my husband never complained.

On Christmas morning, I smiled and graciously accepted gifts from beneath the tree, convincing him that I was doing okay. It was just an illusion because inside I felt dead. Despite his efforts, Steve couldn't save me from myself or from the memory of our precious daughter we had lost in May.

I walked away from our marriage on New Year's Day.

How could I do that to him? How could he ever forgive me? Yet, he was staying at my house, taking care of me as usual.

I selected a picnic table close to the river and watched tourists and office workers from nearby hotels and office buildings amble along the Riverwalk. A bicyclist cut a path across the park and two skateboarding teenagers did a few tricks before being sent away by a park employee. The river was also bustling with activity. A sail boat skimmed by a water taxi that was taking commuters to the opposite shore, and the Annabelle Lee paddle-wheeler steamed by as her luncheon passengers waved to me from the top deck. A freight train even made an appearance as it crossed the river and sounded a blast from its horn. Despite the squeal from the train's wheels and the noisy automobile traffic on the Main Street Bridge, and regardless of the endless procession of pedestrians meandering by my table, an afternoon at Friendship Park was just as delightful as a day at the shore.

"Thanks for meeting me. Have you been here long?"

I turned to see Sherry approaching and stood to greet her. She gave me a huge hug, like we had been friends forever.

"Not too long. This park is so beautiful I could sit here all day." She admired the city skyline behind me and agreed.

I unpacked our lunches and we sat down to talk.

"First, I apologize for barging in on you last night," she started. "You have my condolences. I don't think I told you how sorry I am about Lenore's death."

I watched another River Taxi shuttle people from the opposite shore to Friendship Park. I'm not sure I even replied.

She reached for my hand across the table and stopped just short of touching mine. "Can we talk about your sister? Or is it too soon?"

"I'll talk, but I want some information from you as well." I rewrapped my pastrami sandwich and put it back into the bag.

"Of course I'll share what I know with you." She pulled a small recorder out of her purse and placed it on the table.

"Do you really need that?"

"It helps me remember details, but if you don't want it, I can put it away." She reached to return it to her bag. "I'll just take notes."

"I'm being silly. It makes no difference to me. It's just hard—"

"I know it's difficult to discuss painful things with an outsider, but sometimes it helps to talk."

I couldn't imagine how it could help me. "What evidence do they have linking Lenore to Jonathan?"

"Photos. I haven't seen them but Donna has."

"What are they doing in those photos?"

"She said they were standing close to each other, but none of the pictures show any kissing or touching."

"Then they have nothing."

"They have enough to make it seem like something. That's all it takes to plant the seed of suspicion, which is an excellent opportunity for one candidate to smear another. Think about it—infidelity with an ex-fiancée just before a wedding. If a man is capable of cheating on his future wife, can he be trusted to represent his constituents? Once the story hits the shelves, people will spin the story to suit their needs and it will eventually morph into something you won't recognize at all."

I felt ill.

"Do you think they were having an affair?"

"I'm not sure what I believe. So much has happened since Lenore died that my head is spinning."

"Like what?"

"I don't even know how she died."

Sherry looked at me in disbelief. "Haven't you seen her death certificate?"

"No. I haven't even seen her obituary. I guess I avoided reading it."

She fished into her purse again and pulled a clipping out of her wallet. "Read this."

Woman Dies At Glass Factory

Police are investigating the death of a woman whose body was discovered at

*Crest Glass Tuesday morning, a
Sheriff's Office report said.*

*About 6:30 a.m., Sea Turtle Beach
police were called by Anthony
Gilman, an employee of Crest, when
he found Ms. Lenore Terhune
unconscious and non-responsive. She
was pronounced dead by paramedics
at the scene.*

*The Medical Examiner's Office in
Jacksonville has been asked to
determine the cause of death.
Authorities said there were no
obvious signs of foul play.*

I looked up at Sherry. "That's it?"

"Do you know more?"

I told her what Tony had said about how he found her
and that we initially thought she had died of carbon
monoxide poisoning. I also told her that my brother
suggested she had died from an overdose of cocaine.

"Was she a user?"

"I'm not sure." I paused and reconsidered my answer.
"No. I spent a lot of time with her and I really don't believe
she ever did cocaine."

"How about other drugs?"

"She was a prescription abuser for a little while—after her
break-up with Jon—but she's been clean for years." I couldn't
tell her about the adoption, or the guilt Lenore felt until she

fully realized that her decision had been the best one for her child.

Sherry scribbled a few notes. "I doubt she was using any drugs, in particular cocaine. If that had been the case, you would have noticed something."

Not according to Steve. "Like what?"

"Had she lost a lot of weight recently? Did you see any needle marks? Was her nose red or did she have the sniffles? Were her eyes glassy? Did she exhibit any remarkable change in personality?"

"No on all counts."

"I have to tell you, Marlene. I don't think she was doing cocaine, and if she was, it wasn't on a regular basis. Having said that, I would tell you that if she was stupid enough to use it at her job, I doubt she would have fallen asleep at all. In fact, I think she would have been hyperactive, not lethargic."

"Then my brother is lying to me."

"Why do you say that?"

"He told me the coroner found cocaine in her blood."

"What have your parents told you?"

"Next to nothing—my father is determined to protect me and my mother. I guess he figures the less we know, the better we'll handle Lenore's death."

"Do you know if OSHA or the EPA paid a visit to your father's business after the incident?"

"I'm sure they didn't. Somebody at Crest would have told me if that had happened."

"Curious."

"What's that mean?"

"If Lenore's death was a work-related accident, it's standard procedure that they would conduct an investigation."

Why hadn't that occurred to me? Adrenalin pulsed through me as my suspicions increased ten-fold.

"Again, I haven't been working. Maybe they were there. I just don't know."

That's when I realized that an impending investigation from the EPA, OSHA and the police might be a plausible reason for my father and brother to keep me out of the building, but it still made no sense to me.

Sherry took one last bite of her sandwich and threw the rest in the trash. "Let me do some investigating. I'll get a copy of the medical examiner's report."

As I followed Sherry's black Thunderbird out of the park, I was glad I had enlisted her help without divulging too much of my family's private affairs, but I was more baffled than ever about why my brother was misleading me.

7

My original intention was to finish the custom glass Lenore had been creating when she died. I didn't care who it belonged to, because it wasn't about the client or even the reputation of Crest Glass. It was about completing and delivering an order for my sister because she was always proud of her work.

My original plan had evolved into something completely different. I never imagined my personal tribute to Lenore would become a clandestine investigation. I had been angry with her for dying because of a stupid mistake, but now I wasn't even sure how she had died. The police, three burglars, two reporters, and the Medical Examiner had squeezed themselves into my life, not to mention an ex-husband, two grieving parents, and one lying brother. The only thing missing was the hand-blown glass that my sister had hidden in her car for no apparent reason.

Matt wasn't at work when I called, but when I stopped by his house, his youngest daughter, Sophie, told me where to find him. I headed for the golf course at Amelia Island. Since my father was back, I imagined my brother was taking a few days off to play a few rounds of golf and recuperate from two hellish weeks filling in for him at the office.

In the past, I would have parked myself at the bar where I could smoke and drink Chocolate Martinis all afternoon while I watched the golfers finish their games through an enormous window that had a magnificent view of the 18th hole. I knew better than to tempt myself, especially since I was feeling so scattered. Instead, I wandered through the elegant lobby of the country club and down the hall toward the banquet rooms.

I ducked into the Ladies' Room on the way. After I freshened up, I stepped back into the hallway and found myself face-to-face with Tony's mother, Eloise Gilman.

"How nice to see you," she exclaimed, rushing to me before I could even speak. "What lured you off the island?"

We embraced. "I could ask you the same thing." The last time we had conversed was at the anniversary bash. She owns *Tantalizing Events*. It's a catering company located at Sea Turtle Beach.

"I'm catering the reception for Jonathan Lucas and his lovely fiancée, Sylvia."

"Good gig."

She smiled. "It's a great opportunity. If Mr. Lucas wins the election, perhaps he'll remember what I did for him here. I'd love to cater his celebration party when he wins the election and whatever other event he'd like to toss my way."

I forced a smile that I'm sure looked more like a smirk. "Perhaps a baby shower looms in the future."

"Oh, yes. I could handle that too," she cooed.

"Is the happy couple around?" If they were, I needed to make a quick exit.

"I haven't seen the bride today, but Mr. Lucas said he'd

stop by to see how things looked after he finishes a round of golf. I saw your brother too. I'm sure you'll run into him."

I had a light bulb moment. Matthew was playing golf with Jon.

I followed her into the largest banquet room. The champagne walls were draped in luxurious ivory satin, and overhead were six elegant chandeliers with prisms that glittered like diamonds. We walked between a maze of tables that were swathed in expensive lavender linens and intricate lace that flowed to the floor.

"Jonathan preferred to hold the event on our island, but they can handle 500 guests in this room. There's no venue on Sabal Palm Island that can accommodate that many people. Besides, it's more convenient for the guests since most of them will be overnighting at The Plantation."

She called out to one of her employees. "Barbara, make sure they put ten pillar candles in the middle of each table."

Eloise turned back to me. "As you can see, we're in the middle of decorating."

Two men in starched-white uniforms stood on ladders, crisscrossing white lace streamers from one side of the room to the other. Another employee—a hefty man with a long, full beard—walked by me with strings of sparkling butterflies draped over his shoulders. I stifled a laugh when I saw the word TANTALIZING embroidered on his shirt pocket.

The atmosphere was very elegant, I suppose, but too frilly and overstated for my taste.

While Eloise explained how she wanted him to hang the butterflies from the ceiling, I wandered over to several long tables along the west wall. They were covered with wedding decorations, but four large stacked boxes caught my eye.

Each one had the Crest Glass logo stamped on the side. I turned around just in time to see Eloise exit the room. It was the perfect opportunity to peek inside one of the opened boxes.

What I discovered was exactly what I had hoped to find. Under the top of the first box, beneath several sheets of bubble wrap, was a layer of ten beautiful pink glass seashells in assorted sizes and shapes.

A young lady walked through the door on my left.

"What are these?" I feigned naïvety.

"Aren't they beautiful?" She reached into another box and withdrew a clear glass dove with violet wings that sparkled when she held it up to the lights overhead. "They're going to give these to each of the guests as a wedding favor. Each place setting will have one of these in the middle of a dinner plate." She replaced the dove into its bubble wrap nest in the box and walked away.

Lenore, were you really that gullible?

Back in the corridor, I found Eloise chatting with the county's preeminent Wedding Planner, Mavis Clarke, and I instantly knew who was providing the wedding cake.

I silently walked by them and left the country club without questioning my brother or confronting Jon.

By that time, my brain was rattling with confusing questions. I sped back to my house to center myself again.

❧

"It's darn foolish, if you ask me," Steve ranted after I told him where I'd been and what I had found out.

"Explain that remark." I bristled at his tone.

"First, you left without telling me where you were going. Then you met some strange chick in Jacksonville, and after that you went to that highfalutin country club alone."

"What's so alarming about any of that?"

"You've just told me that not only your house and your parents' place were vandalized, but you also neglected to mention that your sister's apartment was emptied out. Now you tell me her car was vandalized and you found the glass order—the one you have been hunting for since she died—at this ritzy private ballroom where Jon Lucas is hosting his wedding party."

I remained calm and let him complain, my hands resting on my hips in a defensive stance. When I didn't respond, he added, "Aren't you afraid that somebody is going to off you?"

"Off me?" I was a little taken back by that idea. "Why would anybody want to kill me over a few hundred pieces of hand-blown glass?"

"Ask that same question again, but this time replace 'me' with Lenore's name. There's something wicked going on here."

Chills swept over me because his words clarified my suspicions. My sister was dead, someone was stalking our family, and it was becoming very clear that all of the ominous events of recent weeks were somehow connected.

"What do you think about Matt being one of Jon's buddies?"

"You didn't see them together today," he reminded me.

"Not today, but I saw my brother chauffeuring Jon in a parade a few days ago."

Steve's eyes widened. "You forgot to tell me that as well?"

"I haven't forgotten to tell you anything because none of

it seemed connected until now. I just wanted to finish Lenore's order but I couldn't find it. I had no tangible reason to think there was something sinister about how she died, except that she may have committed suicide. I didn't expect the lies, and I never imagined an order of hand-blown glass could cause such turmoil. Now I find myself worrying about what will happen next."

I stormed into the kitchen to find something to shove into my mouth. I felt like I was losing control and food had replaced liquor and cigarettes as my favorite way to comfort myself. I looked through all the cabinets and stared into the refrigerator.

Steve walked up beside me. "I'm sorry." He leaned over my shoulder and whispered, "None of it makes sense yet, but we'll figure this out. I'll stay here until this mess is over."

"How can you do that?"

"I'm getting out of the Navy. You didn't ask me where I was the other day, but I went to Mayport to finish the paperwork. Lenore knew I was a short-timer. She had offered to treat me to a celebratory dinner when I got back, but I was a few days too late."

I got brave. "And you still say there was nothing between the two of you?"

He stared into my eyes. "I never said that."

My hand clinched tightly around the door handle as I waited for him to finally tell me the truth—that he and my sister had been having an affair.

"Lenore was my best friend," he announced, his gaze still fixed on my face. "She was the one friend I could talk to about important stuff. She never turned me away."

"Like I did."

"I didn't say that either."

He placed his hand on my shoulder and I leaned into the refrigerator, effectively extricating myself from his uninvited, and unexpected, touch.

"I'm looking for something sweet," I announced.

He spun around and walked back into the living room. "Yeah, you need that."

It was evident that we were still testing each other, like old times, but this time was different because I didn't run away to my bedroom and he didn't leave the house.

I sat beside him on the couch. "You've been very patient with me." I reached over to his hand. "Don't give up on me, Steve. Lenore's death has been hard on me, and you know I don't handle bad times gracefully. I guess I'm depressed."

He leaned over and kissed the top of my head. "You are depressed, Sweetie. You've been depressed for a very long time, even if you won't admit that to yourself."

Nobody had ever spoken those words to me. I suppose they'd hinted at it, but when my parents or my brother brought it up, I'd change the subject. When Steve broached the subject before, I divorced him.

"You're just like your dad."

"I am not."

"You know I'm right. You two are cast from the same mold."

I bristled and fought the urge to argue with him. "How can you even suggest that? My parents run away from setbacks. I deal with them. When our baby died, I went right back to my job. How can you say I handled it badly when I got right back to work, and my life went on just the way it was before my miscarriage?"

"When our baby died, that wasn't a setback, Marlene. That was a crisis. It was a life-changing event for both of us, but you buried yourself in work and ignored me. You stopped living your life and just existed. You divorced me and sent me on my way without an explanation."

I slammed my hand on the couch. "This isn't about our divorce!"

He slipped his hand over mine. "No it isn't. It's about so much more than that, Marlene. It is actually about you and the possibility that you are going to self-destruct if you don't manage your emotions. This is not about you hurting others, although your actions usually do have a tendency to cause turbulence in the lives of everybody around you. I'm trying to make you slow down and think about your actions. Lenore wouldn't want you to use her death as an excuse to withdraw from others again."

I stared at him through tears that stung my eyes. "Am I doing that?"

"You've been doing that for a very long time. You are definitely not the woman I married. Marlene Terhune was a woman who loved a challenge. She was excited to try new things and she always stayed busy. She was my best friend and she was surrounded by friends. The woman I see before me right now is self-limiting. You stay home, go to work, come back home, and repeat the same mundane tasks every single day. You don't even go to church anymore."

"And you do?" I asked accusingly.

"Yes, in fact, I do," he said, with a reflecting smile. "I just returned from the Arabian Gulf. I need God in my life, especially when I see what happens in other parts of the world."

I felt guilty that I'd asked, realizing I had insinuated that he'd left the church as well.

"I've changed recently," I admitted. "I've been getting out and about. Or haven't you noticed?"

Steve chuckled softly. "Yes, I've noticed, and I will admit that I like seeing you get out more. But you aren't doing it for you, Marlene. You are doing it for your sister."

I stood up and marched into the kitchen, using a glass of water as an excuse to escape Steve for a moment.

When I returned to the room, I said, "I've always taken care of my sister. She is my best friend."

"She's no longer here, Sweetie."

I stood stiffly in the middle of the room and said nothing.

"Lenore and I talked about this quite often."

"About what?"

"About you. About how you had changed, about how you depended upon her, and about how your actions limited her life."

"I did that?" I felt sick. Had I been a burden to my sister?

Steve approached me. He took me by the shoulders and asked, "When was the last time you went to a movie?"

"I don't recall."

"When was the last time you did something with your sister, besides work?"

I couldn't remember; it had been so long.

"When was the last time you took a vacation?"

"With you...before I got pregnant."

"How often do you visit your parents?"

"I've seen them recently."

"How about before your sister died?"

"Not so much."

The conversation was disconcerting. I escaped from his grasp and walked toward my bedroom.

"Time for sleep," I announced.

Steve remained silent, standing in the same spot as I disappeared from his sight. I'm sure he expected me to walk away. After all, I am a master of avoiding confrontations, just like my father.

8

Friday, March 31, 2000
2:17 a.m.

After more than two weeks of insomnia, I don't know why I imagined I could sleep all night. I slept for a few fitful hours, but Lenore kept asking me for help and that eventually woke me up. I laid in the dark for awhile but I couldn't get back to sleep so I sat on the edge of the bed. I sometimes wander through the house when I can't sleep, but I made myself stay in my bedroom so Steve could rest.

I missed Lenore. She was the one I could always call, no matter what the time. Once, when I was so sick with a bad cold that I couldn't sleep, she showed up at my door with canned chicken noodle soup, tissue for my nose, a variety of cough and cold medicines, and movie videos that she watched with me throughout the night. The next morning when I finally went to sleep, she snuck out of the house and went to work, only to return a few hours later to make more soup for lunch. How could I not miss a sister like that?

That's the kind of husband Steve had been to me. I missed him, even though I never told him. He had always looked out for me, taken care of me, and offered me only love and attention. I divorced him, yet here he was protecting me again and sleeping on the couch when I had the comfort of a nice warm bed.

The urge to take a look at him was so overwhelming that I became agitated. I began pacing the floor. "Leave him alone. He needs to sleep," I admonished myself. I cracked open the door and peeked into the living room, but it was hard to see him through the dark. I returned to my pacing. My mind raced with questions. Why is he here? Is he really worried about me, or does he have some other motive?

After ten minutes, I was forced out of my bedroom.

He looked content enough, lying on his back with his left leg thrown over the back of the couch. I snuck into the kitchen for a sip of water and stood in the doorway admiring Steve's ability to sleep throughout the night despite everything that had happened recently. I picked up the blanket from the floor and gently covered him.

My eyes had adjusted to the darkness and I easily navigated over to the sliding glass doors where I tried to catch a glimpse of the ocean, but it was so foggy outside that I couldn't see beyond the chairs on the deck. When I turned around, Steve was sitting in the middle of the sofa watching me.

"Oh! Did I disturb you?"

"I wasn't really asleep. I was just resting with my eyes closed. Thanks for the blanket."

"I woke you up."

He turned on a lamp and I was greeted by Steve's drowsy eyes. "Can't sleep, huh?"

"Sorry. I didn't mean to bother you."

He pushed the coffee table away with his foot. "Come sit by my feet."

"Huh?"

"Come on, Marlene. You know I have magic hands. Let me give you a neck rub. A massage always relaxes you. Before you know it, you'll be ready to hit the rack again."

"I don't think so."

"Have it your way." He curled up, put a pillow beneath his head and closed his eyes. "You might be up for the night but I could sure use some more Z's."

"Would you like some coffee?"

He opened one eye. "That would thwart my plan."

"Plan?"

"I like sleep. Sleep is good. It's one of my favorite things to do when somebody else isn't trying to prevent me from pursuing my dreams."

"Never mind." I turned and went to the kitchen. "Go ahead. I'll just make me a cup of coffee and then I'll take it to my room and leave you alone."

Steve moaned. "Why don't you just forego the caffeine, get back into bed and stay there until you drift off to la-la land?"

"Easy for you to say." I filled my coffee maker with just enough water and coffee to brew two cups. "Are you sure you don't want any?"

He hid his head beneath the pillow, but I wasn't ready to be ignored. I needed to talk. A few minutes later, I pulled the pillow back, poked his nose with my finger, and offered up a cup of steaming brew."

"You're a problem child. You know that, don't you? A problem with a capital P."

I lowered myself to the floor between the coffee table and couch and grinned mischievously. "You knew that when you married me."

He sat up again, took a swig of coffee and placed the flowered cup on its saucer with a clank. "We're not married."

"That's a technicality. Besides, you keep coming back."

"For more insanity."

"Ouch!" That hurt. I suddenly felt uncomfortable in my own home.

He touched my shoulder. "I didn't mean it that way, Marlene. I was just trying to bug you back and the wrong word popped out." He took another swig of coffee and winked. "You're just a little overwhelming in the middle of the night."

I swallowed down the rest of my drink. That way I didn't have to respond.

"Stop acting that way. Don't play the victim."

I reared back. "Why do you always do that?"

"Do what?"

"You're always humiliating me. Like that day at your sister's house. You said people are always protecting me, and then you told Amy to hide the liquor."

"Yeah, I'm sorry for that. I was upset about Lenore, and I was a little mad at you."

"No kidding."

"Besides, you do play the victim."

"There you go again!" The more he talked, the more offended I was. "When you demean me, I am the victim." I started to get up, but he gently pushed me back down to the floor.

"That's what I'm talking about. You get mad, you stop talking and you walk away from your problems. Ignoring them won't make them go away."

"Pay attention, Steve. I'm not ignoring the problem. I'm walking away from you." I collected the empty cups and took them to the sink, put together two peanut butter sandwiches, and returned to the living room with two tall glasses of cold milk. "I've changed. If you'd pay a little more attention to me instead of getting stuck in our past, you'd notice that I'm more self-sufficient, more resilient, and I am certainly capable of protecting myself from your stinging remarks."

We sat in silence, eyeing each other as we ate overstuffed sandwiches.

"Thanks for that," he said, after swallowing his last bite.

"For the food or for the speech?"

"Both."

"I couldn't make a snack for me without giving you something."

He chuckled.

I got up to return to my bedroom.

"Don't go." Steve patted the cushion beside him. "We can talk."

I sat on the floor instead, where I felt more in control of the situation. "What do you want to chat about?"

"All of this is about Lenore, isn't it?"

"Well, yeah."

He rolled over on his side and stared directly into my eyes. "Then let's hash it out. What, in particular, is bothering you tonight?"

My stomach churned. I had wanted to talk but now that the opportunity presented itself, I didn't know what to say or where to begin. "You've got it all wrong about me avoiding problems. That's the rest of my family. My parents just came back from a vacation that was designed to avoid talking about my sister, and Matt is the real Artful Dodger. He says we should just get on with our lives and stop thinking about her."

"What do you think?"

"When has anybody ever cared about what I think?"

"I do."

"Well, besides my sister, you're the only one who has ever shown any genuine concern for me, and right now I am a bit muddled about why you still care. You don't owe me anything. I've caused you all kinds of trouble, and yet you're here listening to me when you should be sleeping."

He sat up. "I'll always be in your corner. I promised you that when we first got together. I meant it then, and I mean it now. That hasn't changed." He walked around the room and came back with a note pad he'd grabbed from the kitchen counter.

"What's that for?"

"Just start talking about what's bugging you."

"Everything is bothering me. I'm feeling guilty that I couldn't help Lenore. I don't understand what happened to her. My family won't tell me what's going on, and now I'm starting to think they're hiding the truth from me."

"Give me names. Tell me who you think may be lying to you."

"Gosh, I wonder if I'm being paranoid."

"Are you?"

"I don't think so."

He prompted me again. "Names…"

"Matt."

Steve scribbled his name, "Why are you suspicious of your brother?"

"He avoids my questions. He says Lenore was on drugs, and he's hanging out with Jon."

When he'd finished writing, he said, "Who else, and why?"

"Well, I guess I have to say Tony. He's the one who found her body."

"Tony." He wrote down his name. "Next?"

"Jon, for obvious reasons. His girlfriend too."

"Have you met her?"

"Not yet."

"More?"

"My father. I don't know why, but since he always protects me, why would I think he isn't hiding something from me now?"

"How about your mother?"

"Definitely not."

"Anybody else?"

"You said somebody was dating Lenore. Whoever it was, I think we need to talk to him."

Steve agreed.

"Do you think I'm being unreasonable?"

He looked up and stared into my eyes. "The only thing that really matters is that you want to know why your sister died. I don't think that's unreasonable. Honestly, I'm not comfortable with the things you've told me, and I think you are entitled to ask questions."

I touched his hand. "Thank you."

"Just remember one thing while you're trying to figure things out, Marlene."

"What would that be?"

"It is very possible that none of those people are responsible for Lenore's death. Her death may be from natural causes…or perhaps an accident. The M.E. will tell us that eventually."

"I realize that, Steve. But I can't stop myself from investigating every possibility—"

His smile broadened as he grasped my hand. "I know, Marlene. Your need to feel in control is always a priority."

I chuckled uncomfortably, realizing he was right.

He clapped his hands together. "Now turn around, sit down, and I'll massage your neck so we both can get back to sleep."

Without any hesitation, I turned my back to him and surrendered to his powerful hands as he massaged my head, my neck, my arms and my back. I closed my eyes and cleared my mind, giving in to relaxation. It took a few minutes to relinquish myself to the warmth of his strong hands, but when I did, I became less tense and calm enough for sleep.

"That's enough, thank you. It's time for bed." I granted him a quick kiss on his forehead, excused myself, and returned to my bedroom, leaving the door open. After a few minutes, I realized the living room lamp was still on. I shouted "Good night!" but there was no response, except for a loud snore.

With a thick comforter pulled up to my neck and my eyes closed, I thought about the list we'd just created together. I had given him six names. Four I knew, two I'd never met. One name was missing. Although I was grateful for Steve's help, I knew his name belonged at the top of the list because I was still bothered by his relationship with Lenore.

I laid there doing what I do best when things aren't going my way—I felt sorry for myself. I looked up at the ceiling, although the room was so dark I couldn't see a thing, and I said out loud, "Now what are you going to do?"

I'd never felt more miserable, more lonely, or as useless as I felt in that moment. Tears slid down my cheeks. What I really knew how to do well was torchwork, but my father had taken that away from me, and it didn't look like he was going to relent in the near future. I still didn't know why, and I'd turned that question around in my head so often that it made me sick.

He had said he wasn't protecting me, and even though I doubted his words, I doubted myself more. Wasn't I a good daughter? As soon as the thought crossed my mind, I knew the answer. He was probably right in removing me from my position. I had failed him and Mama before, and I hadn't shown him any signs that I was worthy of their trust by the way I had acted the past several years.

After I lost their first grandchild, I'd divorced their beloved son-in-law, and become a drunk. Who in their right mind would trust their business to a person like me? Even though I was their daughter, and even though Daddy had let me keep working as I sorted myself out, I didn't blame him for suspending me while he decided whether I could work without Lenore supervising me. He trusted Lenore.

And then my mind spun to another scenario. Had I failed Lenore as well?

"Why God?" I asked through anguished sobs. "Why did you take Lenore and leave me behind? She was the good one!" I buried my face in a pillow. I didn't want Steve to hear me.

I cried for what seemed like endless minutes, until my pillow was soaked and my tears drained. I dabbed away my tears and turned over, facing toward Heaven again. I felt empty.

"Please help me," I whispered. "Help me get through this. Help me find my way."

❧

When my eyes popped open, it was still gray outside and the sun was just beginning to make its first appearance of the day. I closed the door to the living room and slipped into the shower. As I lathered up, I thought about my strategy for the morning. I intended to get out of the house early. It was the day before Jon's wedding and I had plenty to accomplish.

I combed my damp hair, brushed my teeth, then dressed quietly so I wouldn't disturb Steve. About that time, I smelled a delightful aroma wafting in from the other side of the house.

I opened the door and Steve greeted me with a loud, "Good morning!" He stood at the stove, vigorously stirring eggs in a skillet. He was already dressed to leave.

"What are you doing? I thought you'd still be asleep!"

He looked at me proudly, as if he'd just accomplished a coup d'état in my kitchen. "Wherever you're going today, I'm going with you. But before you leave, you're going to have a hearty breakfast. I've got pancakes and sausage prepared, and when these scrambled eggs are finished cooking, we can eat. You wanna set the table?"

"I'll do that after I dry my hair."

I slipped back into my bathroom and turned on the hair dryer, which drowned out the radio Steve had just turned on in the living room. I know I should have been more appreciative of his efforts, but taking him with me was his idea, not mine. He'd just get in my way. I would have snuck out, but I couldn't make an escape without getting caught.

When I stepped into the dining room, the table was already set with two full glasses of orange juice, two cups of hot coffee, two full plates of tempting food, and one ex-husband who was sitting on the opposite side of the table with a contented smile on his face. It was hard not to laugh at his ridiculous pose. "Thanks," I said as I sat down. We ate in utter silence, but his expression conveyed self-satisfaction throughout the meal.

He finished before me and began to clear the table. When I was full, I joined him in the kitchen and began to rinse the dishes. "Just leave those in the sink," he offered. "I'll get them when we return later."

"It won't take long to clean up," I said, but he handed me a towel to wipe my hands, and my jacket to keep me warm as he pressed me out the door into the morning coolness. I watched as he armed the new alarm system.

He walked to the car.

I double locked the front door, remembering my previous uninvited guests. "Are you driving?"

"Nah! I'll leave that to you." He stood beside the passenger door and waited for me to let him in. "I'm just going along for the ride and to give you some moral support. I haven't a clue where we're going, but I'm sure this is going to be an interesting day."

"I never said I was going anywhere today."

"Marlene, I know you too well. Don't try to bamboozle me. Based on the past couple of days, I know you have an agenda. Let's hit the road. Where are we off to this time?"

"That's for me to figure out. Just relax."

I didn't have a well thought out plan for the day. I'm more impulsive than that. While my time in the glass shop is always organized and methodical, the rest of my life can be described as being spontaneous and a little chaotic. That's what keeps my days interesting, and it's also why I tend to find myself at the brink of trouble more times than I care to admit.

I headed down the gravel road in front of my house. About a half-a-mile down the road, I made a left turn on the spur of the moment and headed toward the ferry, with Mayport as my target; still no plan in mind, but it seemed like a good place to begin my mission.

Mayport Post Office was bustling with activity at half-past nine because Friday was the last day of March. It was time for last minute bills to be paid, and end-of-month invoices were ready to be mailed out. I stood in line while Steve remained in the car. It took more than fifteen minutes for me to get my turn at the counter, but the clerk was finished with me the moment I told her what I needed.

"I can't do that," she said with a scowl that told me she was already wishing for the end of her shift. "Your sister needs to come in here in person or you'll need to get her key."

I had shown her my sister's receipt for a lock box, along with my Florida State Driver's License for identification. "That will be difficult since she died recently." I hoped she would feel sorry for me and cave in.

"Sorry, I can't help you. There are regulations we are required to follow. Forms to fill out." It was practically the same conversation I'd had with the assistant manager at Lenore's apartment complex. Apparently all keys come with invisible rules attached to them. "Can I help you with anything else?" She flipped her stringy black bangs out of her eyes.

"No." I stood there in disbelief, unable to make my legs move.

"Then you'll have to clear the way for the next customer. Next!"

I held up a finger. "Wait. Is there somebody else I can talk to about this?"

"You can ask the postmaster, but he'll tell you the same thing."

I didn't move an inch, "He can make that decision. I'd like to speak with him, please."

She stood there a few moments, glaring at me with some degree of unspoken hostility that I didn't think I'd earned. I fixed my sight on her and stood my ground.

That's when I felt a presence looming beside me. I looked up into the menacing face of the next person in line, a robust man who must have been a professional wrestler. "Hey, lady, move along. I've gotta get to my job."

"You'll be back to work soon enough," I said. "But first, be patient and use the manners your mother taught you. Get back in line and that kind gentleman over there will assist you when he's finished with his current client." I pointed to the unwary clerk at the next window. "I'm still in line before you, and I won't be moving until I've been assisted in a satisfactory manner by this nice young lady." I glued on the biggest smile I could muster and fluttered my eyelashes at my own clerk, realizing that I had just become the most memorable nuisance of her day.

The livid postal worker huffed, spun around, and disappeared into the heart of the building. When she returned a few minutes later, an older gentleman with silver hair and wire-framed glasses followed her. She was still visibly upset but her supervisor remained calm and quite civil.

"If you'd be so kind as to meet me over at the doorway to your left, I'll entertain you there," he said poetically. Who talks like that? I'm sure my mouth dropped open, but I obediently followed his instructions.

"You're next, sir," he said respectfully to my former adversary. The hefty guy stood tall, puffed out his chest and strutted to the window as if he'd just won a coveted prize belt. The clerk rolled her eyes and shook her head, glad to be rid of me. Once everybody was satisfied, the postmaster unlocked the door marked EMPLOYEES ONLY and joined me in the corner of the crowded lobby. "How can I help you today?"

I unfolded my sister's tattered receipt and explained my dilemma in a professional yet sincere manner, trying not to sound too desperate.

"This presents an unfortunate predicament," he said as he examined the paper. "Have you searched for the key?"

"Everywhere." I fibbed a little. I had explored my parents' house and Lenore's apartment, but I didn't have any idea where else I could check.

He shook his head as if to say 'no', but instead he said, "Stay here. Let me see if there's any mail in her box."

I waited for his return with the kind of anticipation usually reserved for a holiday gift, my heart pattering from a fresh dose of adrenalin. When he came back, he held a handful of letter-sized envelopes. "I can't give these to you," he said in a calculated whisper. He stood with his back toward his employees, blocking their view of our conversation. "But I can look at them, and if perchance you should be watching while I'm inspecting these pieces of correspondence, you might commit an address to memory that will help you decide if you should pursue this request any further." He looked at me expectantly. I glanced fleetingly at the counter, but the employees and postal customers had lost interest in us.

I turned back to him. "That will work," I whispered.

As he shuffled through the envelopes, I took in as much information as possible. Ever gallant and stone quiet, he took his time and paused each time I nodded. When he reached the bottom of the small pile of envelopes, he winked, walked back into the sorting room, and returned empty-handed. To capture the attention of those around us, he cleared his throat with an unexpected "Ahem!" that was so vigorous I cringed. "I'm sorry I couldn't help you," he said too loudly. "Perhaps you can return later with the key."

There are times when saying nothing is the wisest choice. I turned around and walked toward the exit without speaking. Behind me, the familiar voice of the vexed clerk spit out, "How rude!"

Pleased with the results of my diligence, I snickered to myself as I walked back to my vehicle. I felt obliged to thank the older gentleman for his award-winning performance but I couldn't do that without revealing that he'd just ignored bureaucratic guidelines to make my life less problematic.

Steve was slumped against the side window. I slipped inside the car unnoticed and reached into the glove box for a stash of paper napkins that I collected from fast food chains. Using one for note paper, I scribbled what I could remember from my quick study of Lenore's unclaimed mail.

Each envelope had been marked 'Return to Sender', and all of them came from the same person—A. J. Fleming—at an APO address. I sensed that I was at the beginning and ending of the same trail, with no hope for further exploration. When I was finished writing, I absent-mindedly frayed the napkin edges while I considered my next step.

Just five days before, I had promised the assistant manager that I would never return to Lenore's abandoned townhouse, but idle threats are worthless when you require information from the person you're trying to intimidate. When I arrived at Seacoast Apartments, I had a box of donuts ready to offer Maggie as a truce. Steve was still napping so I trudged up the steps alone.

A slender woman with a blonde pageboy haircut greeted me at the doorway. She wore a red power jacket over a blue knee-length skirt and a name tag on her lapel that introduced Jackie Wilson to me without a word being spoken.

"Welcome home," she said, offering her right hand in greeting. In her other hand, she held a ring of keys. "Would you like to tour our models?" She handed me a slick brochure and I noticed that the apartment complex had magically transformed into Ocean Cay Condominiums since Sunday afternoon. With that knowledge, I suddenly felt disoriented.

"No, thanks. Is Maggie here?" I searched the office for a familiar face.

"She no longer works here but I can help you. I'm the new sales manager, Jackie Wilson." She offered her hand to me again, forgetting that my hand was freshly shaken. In fact, I could still feel the dampness of her lotioned palm on my fingers.

I walked over to Maggie's old desk, placed the box of donuts on top, and began to fill out a check. "I owe you money for a key. Do I make this out to Ocean Cay or Seacoast?"

"Oh! No, no, no..." She took me by both shoulders and gave me another little shake. "You must be Lenore's sister."

"I am. Did you know Lenore?"

"Yes, I knew your sister well. I've recently been promoted, but I've worked here a few years. I was the leasing assistant, but now I'm the newly appointed sales manager."

I'm sure Maggie was ecstatic that she'd been passed over for the lead job. "Well, Maggie said I owe you—"

Jackie put her finger to her lips to hush me. "Forget about the key. We're remodeling each unit as it becomes empty, and that includes new door hardware and locks. In fact, I just signed a refund check for Lenore's deposit yesterday." She shuffled through disheveled paperwork on the top of a corner desk and presented me with an envelope. "Since she took over your original lease, I made the check out to you."

I was extremely pleased by the surprising announcement and accepted the check graciously. To my utter astonishment, two strangers—the sales manager and the postmaster—had shown me more empathy in the past thirty minutes than anybody I'd encountered over the course of three weeks of excruciating sorrow.

Jackie brewed a fresh pot of coffee and I offered her the first choice from the aromatic box of pastries.

"Did you ever meet my sister's boyfriend?" I figured that was a good place to start the conversation.

She nibbled a chocolate cake donut and tried to catch its crumbled bits in the palm of her hand. After taking a loud slurp of coffee, she wiped her mouth with a paper napkin and attempted to answer my question. "I didn't see your sister often. She was gone all day when I was at work, and she didn't return until after I went home for the evening."

"How about weekends? Didn't you see her then?"

"I'm sorry I'm not much help, but I had just started working weekends when I was promoted."

"Did you see any men coming or going from her apartment?"

She took another bite from the donut, shook her head and mulled over my question. "You might want to visit her neighbors. She seemed friendly enough on those rare occasions when I did see her." She took out a file folder and paged through its contents. "Nobody ever registered a complaint with us. I'd say she was the ideal tenant."

That was my sister. She was a pleasant, easy to get along with, caring woman that didn't have an enemy. Lenore was happy, and that's why it was so hard to accept her death.

I gathered my belongings. "Do you mind if I take a walk around the neighborhood?"

"Not at all."

I thanked her and headed outside with no particular course of action in mind, as usual.

I reached inside my pocket and fingered Lenore's not-so-missing key; the one I'd kept just in case I needed access to her apartment again for further investigation.

Perhaps I would return later, after Jackie left the premises.

9

That's how, after just a five-minute conversation, Jackie Wilson's name was added to an ever-expanding cast of suspicious characters that populated Lenore's too short life. She initially professed to know my sister well, but I was baffled when Jackie changed her story before she even finished a cup of coffee. I couldn't imagine why she would exaggerate or lie, but I didn't intend to waste my time listening to any more of her deceitful rhetoric. I'd had more than enough of that from people I knew.

I started up the Jeep without disturbing Steve and felt a little guilty that I'd kept the poor man awake most of the previous night. At the mini-market across the street, I parked behind the dumpster where we wouldn't be noticed. After purchasing two cups of steaming hot cocoa and another dozen donuts, I hid behind a tower of two liter sodas and watched out the enormous front window. Within minutes, I was rewarded for my newly acquired sleuthing skills.

Jackie Wilson sped out of Ocean Cay Condominiums in a brand new BMW Z8 Roadster. Apparently sales of renovated apartments were fattening her purse as fast as she could drive her shiny black sports car out of Mayport.

Although I had wondered what she would do once I left the premises, I didn't expect her to leave the property that fast. Still, I felt reasonably certain that she wouldn't be returning quickly. I felt safe enough to abandon my secret spot and stood beside my road-dusty Wrangler while I finished off a glazed donut and my lukewarm drink. When I was finished, I shouted, "Open your eyes, sleepy head!" through Steve's closed window.

Jolted awake, he was startled to see me standing outside the car. He rubbed his eyes before he swung open the door to accept his cup of hot chocolate and a box of donuts. "Thanks," he grumbled. "I didn't mean to doze off."

I went to the other side and climbed in beside him. He looked around to determine our location. "Where are we?" he asked. I understood his confusion because all dumpsters look alike.

While he finished off two donuts, I drove over to our old apartment complex. "You do recognize this place now, don't you?" Without answering, he bit into his third donut, filling his mouth to bulging. After I parked, I reached over and wiped the powdered sugar off his chin and white-dusted collar. "What would you do without me?" I asked without thinking first.

He stopped chewing and gave me such an unsettling glare from those piercing blue eyes that I felt uneasy and very aware that I'd misspoken.

Steve closed the lid on the leftover donuts and placed the box on the floor behind my seat. I watched awkwardly as he brushed a dusting of white powder from his shirt, and worried about his impending response. His prolonged silence made me even more uncomfortable and I felt myself becoming annoyed. I hate reacting that way, but I have no control over my response mechanism when I feel nervous or anxious. I transform from defensive to offensive stance in an instant.

Just before I exploded with words that Steve didn't deserve and that I would regret later, he said, "With a little help from the Navy, I've become quite competent at taking care of myself."

It's amazing how he can turn a potentially bad situation around so easily. That's how he had handled me throughout out entire marriage, and although I admired him for his conciliatory talents, I also found those same skills to be quite annoying. Simply put, I was resentful of his ability to put me in my place with just a few well-spoken words.

He looked at the new Ocean Cay signboard. "So, when did they turn this place into condominiums?"

"Over night," I said, still feeling a bit unsettled by the impending transformation. Why would anybody want to turn an apartment development in Mayport into condominiums? Sailors and their families are often temporary residents of a region, unless they are lifers and choose to retire in a particular town. Still, I doubted most retirees would select Ocean Cay as their final residence. Fleet Landing, a well-known gated retirement neighborhood in Mayport, is located just a few miles away. It is more like a resort than a community, with heated swimming pools, tennis courts, and a variety of outstanding facilities that outclass anything Ocean Cay advertised in the glossy promotional pamphlet Jackie had given me.

"What are we doing here, Marlene?" Steve got out of the car, stretching and yawning after his hour-long nap.

"Snooping around." I locked the car and aimed for Lenore's apartment.

"Isn't it empty?"

"Yep, but maybe I missed something."

I didn't really expect to find anything, but I hoped there was still a clue inside that had not been discovered by me or somebody else. As I inserted the key into the knob, I held my breath and prayed for a revelation. When the cylinder clicked and the door opened, I felt instant gratification and heaved a sigh of relief.

Steve pushed past me and into the main room, looking around in astonishment. The wall-to-wall carpet had been removed, revealing a concrete slab. Holes in the walls had been spackled, and in the far corner several unopened buckets of daffodil tinted latex paint stood ready for application. All that was left of the obsolete kitchen appliances were empty niches waiting to be filled. Ugly decades old laminated countertops had been yanked up, and all of the natural oak cabinets were now replaced by low end particle board prefabricated units that were covered with a standard white veneer.

Anxiety washed over me and I hurried into Lenore's former bedroom. The new carpeting had not yet been installed, but the walls had been sprayed the same color as the canned paint in the living room. I went to the closet. When I opened the door, my knees buckled and I collapsed on the cold concrete floor. The single clothes rod and warped wooden shelf had been upgraded to a vinyl-coated wire shelving system. Steve discovered the same closet organizing kit had been installed in the bathroom. I swallowed back tears and tried to mask my disappointment, but when he stooped down to comfort me, I dissolved into ugly sobs. He stroked my hair and whispered, "What did you expect to find?"

I straightened up and coughed to clear my throat, but it took awhile before I could speak clearly. "In a dream last night, Lenore said she had hidden a note for me on top of the shelf. It was so vivid that I was sure I would find the note here. I imagined it would reveal everything about her death." I choked on my words and paused again to regain my composure. When I recovered, I went to the bathroom sink for a sip of copper flavored tap water, using the palms of my hands as a cup. After I splashed cool water on my face, Steve offered his shirt sleeve to dry my eyes.

With a hoarse voice, I asked him, "Don't you think she would leave a note for me if she intended to commit suicide?"

"I don't know, Marlene." He pulled me close to him, pressing my right cheek against his chest.

"If she were addicted to drugs, wouldn't she come to me for help?" I looked up into his face for an answer.

"Sweetie, I'm sorry I can't help you, but I don't think we'll find your answers here. This place has been stripped to its bare bones."

He pulled me out of the bathroom and led me through the apartment and out the front door. I followed him without protest, but I grimaced as the bright sunlight amplified a throbbing pain behind my eyes.

As we walked from one side of the property to the other, Steve and I paused a couple of times to chat with a few residents. Most of them weren't familiar with my sister, and none of them offered a clue regarding her personal life. One middle-aged man that I didn't recognize greeted us as Mr. and Mrs. Wagner. Neither one of us mentioned that we were divorced.

There were at least seven empty apartments, but it looked like only Lenore's unit was in the process of renovation.

Just as we arrived at my vehicle, Jackie Wilson returned from her impromptu errand. I pretended to remove an item from my purse.

"Look what I found!" I walked toward her, holding Lenore's key in the air. "I'm sorry for the confusion, but I came back to give you this. My mother found it in a box of Lenore's stuff."

I hate liars so you can imagine my discomfort over making up one of my own, but it was the fastest justification I could conjure up for our return.

Jackie politely accepted the key that I no longer needed or wanted. I still had loads of unanswered questions, but based on our recent tour, I figured I wasn't going to get any viable information from her or the residents of the complex.

By mid-day, the skies had cleared and the temperature had warmed to a pleasant 70 degrees. It was a perfect day for a stroll on the beach or, better yet, to borrow my father's little boat for an afternoon of total relaxation. Steve and I would just have to be content with another quick ride on the ferry, but there were still a few more loose ends to tie up on the southern shore of the St. John's River.

Even after a big breakfast and two totally unnecessary donuts, I was starved. We returned to the market where we both purchased bottled water and two pre-packaged egg salad sandwiches. I handed the man behind the counter the same photo of Lenore that I had just shown her oblivious neighbors.

"Do you recognize her?"

"Sure, that's Lenore." He looked over at my lunch companion and smiled. "Hey, dude! I haven't seen you in months."

Steve looked mystified as the clerk offered his hand for a friendly shake.

"Been out of town," Steve mumbled in a voice so low I could barely understand his words. He reached into his pocket and pulled out a few bills with some coins to pay for both of our ready-made meals. We opened our triangular shaped sandwiches and ate them on the spot. Mine was very cold, tasted bland, and wasn't worth the price Steve had just paid, but at least it stopped my stomach from growling.

The cashier sorted the money into the register drawer. "You don't remember me, do you?"

Steve stepped back and cocked his head. "Sorry, buddy. I don't recognize you."

It was easy to guess he was ex-Navy because his hair was still buzzed short, and his right bicep sported a huge tattoo of an anchor.

The man laughed good-naturedly. "Imagine me standing behind a bar pouring drinks." When Steve still didn't respond, he added, "I'm Harry. I was the bartender at that little pub just outside the main gate."

"Aha!" Steve managed a smile, but his vacant eyes told me he still didn't recognize the man. "Put a few brews in front of me and I'll either remember you forever, or I'll forget you ever existed, depending on what kind of day I've had. You caught me on one of my bad ones."

Both men chuckled, but I didn't get the joke and I was restless.

"Sorry to interrupt the party, fellas, but we have to get going." I picked up Lenore's photo from the countertop and slipped it back in my wallet. "How did you know my sister, Harry—from here or from the bar?"

With no apparent reason, he laughed again. "Neither. She dated a guy I knew."

I practically leapt over the counter to give the guy a smack on the lips, but I managed to keep myself in check.

"What was his name?"

"Josh something. He shipped out a few weeks ago and said he wouldn't be back after this tour. Nice guy though. He was kind of a loner."

Josh something. Big help. "How did you know him?"

"He was a friend of a friend of a friend. You know how it goes. People come and go. I don't remember how we met, but I liked him a lot. I'd see him from time to time, here and there. He always treated me right and the dude seemed to like your sister. Tell her I said hello, will you?"

"Sure." I gave Steve a little nudge at the ankle to shut him up before he had a chance to speak. "Harry, would you happen to have the phone book nearby?"

He stooped beneath the counter and came up with a ragged edition of the Yellow Pages. "Do'ya need some paper?" Without waiting for my response, he handed me Steve's receipt from the register along with a pencil.

I opened the book, located the business I was searching for, and jotted down the address as well as *JOSH*

SOMETHING on the back of the curled up paper.

After we both made a pit stop in the restrooms, Steve and I met at the car where we sat talking for nearly ten minutes.

"That was interesting," I said as I slid behind the steering wheel.

"I'm going to quit drinking." Steve sat in his seat so stiffly that he looked like a statue. If the top of the Jeep had been removed, pigeons would have landed on his head.

"Where'd that come from?"

"I just thought you'd want to know."

"When did you make this decision?"

"The morning I woke up on your couch. I couldn't remember how I'd ended up sleeping there."

I gave him a playful punch in the shoulder. "Yeah, and I'll stop smoking!"

"I'm being serious," he said. "I'm really going to stop buying beer."

"I've already smoked my last cigarette. I was stuck in a dilapidated boat with my father for several hours on Wednesday. He made it clear that my smoking bothers him."

"I kind of hoped you quit because I asked you to stop." Steve stuck out his lip and pretended to pout. "When have you ever done something simply because your father asked you to do it?"

"Lenore's gone. He said he's afraid of losing me too. I think he meant that."

"Of course, he did."

I started the car, checked the address I'd written on the receipt, and steered out of the parking lot.

Steve rolled down his window. "Where are we heading off to now, kiddo?"

I always liked that about Steve. He knew when to change the subject. "Just a few miles up the road to a place that rents moving trucks."

"I assume you're trying to figure out who swiped your sister's stuff?"

"Yep."

"What makes you think they'd use a small truck?"

I turned right on Mayport Road and aimed for a truck dealer just South of Hanna Park.

"Lenore didn't own much furniture, and people don't usually pay attention to trucks like that around here. There's always somebody using a rental truck to move their belongings back and forth from storage units." I pointed to a box truck in front of an old repurposed gasoline station just as we turned into the parking lot. "If a huge moving van had pulled in front of Lenore's place, somebody in that complex would have noticed."

"Makes sense to me," Steve said.

I parked next to a smaller truck. "I know you want to go inside with me, but just stay here while I check this place out. If there's a guy in there, he may be more willing to answer my questions if I'm alone." I don't know why I thought that would work, but based on my recent luck with the postmaster, and after being chewed up by his female employee, I knew I had to change my approach.

"The old flirt and beg routine, eh?"

"Exactly." Steve understood me perfectly. I'd forgotten about that.

I pasted on my best smile and marched into the office where I was greeted by a balding truck-rental guy who chomped on a smelly cigar as he spit out a speech he'd recited often.

"If you need one of those babies, it'll cost you twenty bucks for a local move, provided you bring it back the same day. Gas is on you. If you need a bigger box, or if you're planning a long distance move, then the cost goes up. Got a credit card? You'll need that, too."

Instead of pulling plastic out of my wallet, I took out the photo of Lenore. "Do you know her?"

"Nope. Should I?"

"Probably not, but I do need a favor. She may have rented a truck from you."

"Listen lady, I see lots of people and I can't be expected to remember all of them."

Against my better judgment, I reached across the counter and touched the top of his hairy hand. "I really didn't think you'd remember her face. Let's start over. If you could just show me your invoices for the past couple of weeks, maybe I'll recognize somebody's name. I'm trying to figure out who helped her move."

"Then ask her. I can't help you."

Before I could stop myself, I said, "She died. I can't ask her."

"Are you a cop?"

"No, I'm her sister."

He stubbed the nub of his cigar into an ashtray and ran his palm over a head that I'm sure once had plenty of hair. Now, most of it was gone.

"Sorry, but I still can't help you. Our company policy states—"

"Never mind." I stormed out because I didn't need to hear the same words over and over again. I climbed into my seat and stewed as Steve studied me quietly.

"No luck, huh?"

"Nope."

"Are you going to explode?"

"Maybe."

We watched as the store clerk came outside, leaned into one of the trucks, and recorded something on a clipboard.

"I know him!" Steve jumped out of the Jeep and shouted at the object of my fury. "Say, Chief! Do you remember me?"

They came together in the middle of the lot, embracing each other with giant man hugs, sturdy pats on the back, and loud guffaws that signaled male bonding was occurring before my thunderstruck eyes.

I wanted to melt into the seat when Steve moved the reunion to my open window. "Chief, you remember my wife, Marlene, don't you?"

He apologized for not recognizing me. "I've been retired awhile, little lady. I've forgotten a lot of faces, but this guy will always be a buddy—even if he's not much of a sailor!" He slapped Steve's back so hard that I winced. "Right, Steve-O?"

Again, I listened to laughter I couldn't understand. Why would Steve laugh with a man who was insulting his integrity? Steve cut his eyes at me, sending me the same kind of wordless message I'd given him earlier when I'd nudged his foot. Clearly he knew he was being belittled but he wanted me to lock my lips.

Chief waggled his head toward the building. "Come back in the office with me. Maybe I can help you just a little bit. For old time's sake, you know?"

I pursed my lips shut, grinned and followed him obediently. Steve locked his arm around mine and gave it a little squeeze, as if to say things would turn out okay.

Imagine how I felt when the ruler of truck rental land gave us complete access to his files. The only thing that would have made the experience more satisfying was if we had discovered a single name that we recognized. Of course, we didn't.

"How many more dealers are in this area?" Steve asked when we'd returned all the folders to the rusty file cabinet.

"There are four of our franchises within a five mile radius on this side of the river," Chief replied. "More if you go to truck dealers run by that other outfit. And if they got the truck from across the river, you can figure you'll find at least another three or four over on the island."

My stomach twisted. "Thanks for your help," I offered, giving him a light thump on the back. I meant what I said. He didn't have to give us complete access to his files, but he did. A Navy man being loyal to another sailor is a custom I can understand.

That's the kind of loyalty I felt toward my sister.

We said our goodbyes and headed back to the ferry terminal. It was almost two o'clock and I had one more place to go before we returned to my house to prepare for the evening.

I was already exhausted. It was going to be a very long day.

10

I slouched in my seat as the noisy diesel engine revved and the aging ferry began to steer a course across the river to the opposite shore.

"Marlene, I'm tired. How about you?"

"I just want to go home."

"We can do that."

I shook my head. "Nope. We're facing a deadline and we have a few more places to visit before we can head back to my place."

His thick eyebrows furrowed and his forehead creased with apprehension. "What are you talking about?"

Before I could answer, a member of the crew appeared at my side window and startled me. I'd forgotten I had to pay a toll for the services of the ferry.

"Just a minute," I said. I hastily took a few dollars out of my wallet. "Here you go!" I looked up and was surprised to see a familiar face. "Oh, Donna! I forgot about your new job!"

My cousin's oldest daughter smiled as she took the toll from me. "I'll be back to chat after I collect from the other cars," she promised. When she walked away, I got out of the Wrangler and squeezed between two rows of cars until I made my way to the railing, leaving Steve behind without an invitation to join us. I'm not sure he'd ever met Donna before that day, but he wouldn't recognize her anyway. She was still a perky high school cheerleader when we'd last met.

A few moments later, Donna joined me. "Nice to see you, cuz!" She gave me a quick hug, but not anything like the enormous bear hug Steve had shared with his former Chief.

"I can't believe you're all grown up!" How long had it had been since I'd last seen her?

She kissed my cheek. "I'm so sorry about Lenore. I thought I'd see you at her memorial service."

"I couldn't go through that." I should have gone. I'd told myself that over and over again since that morning when my father and I cried together, but it was too late. I realized that I didn't attend the wake because I felt sorry for myself, and that wasn't a good enough reason for me to miss my last chance to tell the world about how wonderful my sister was.

"Lenore would understand. You two were so close."

True, and I'd never appreciated how close we were until she was gone from my life forever.

"I miss seeing her."

"Did you see her often?"

"Just about every morning, when she was going to work...not so much at night."

I perked up. "I guess you were off shift by then, huh?"

"Not always. I just figured she took the long way around, or went to your parent's house, or worked late. She always seemed so busy."

Why hadn't I noticed how busy Lenore was? "Did you ever see anybody with her?"

"Sometimes, but not too often. Let me think." She pondered for a moment then added, "I saw her on weekends.

I work every other Saturday. That's when I would have seen her with a friend."

"She had a lot of friends." I realized that I didn't really know any of her companions outside of the circle of business associates we both worked with at Crest Glass.

"I saw one guy with her. She never introduced me to him, and I never asked any questions. I figured Lenore would tell me if he was someone special."

A man. Maybe a man named Josh something. "Was he blonde?" I was fishing, but I didn't want her to realize I didn't have a clue about who Lenore was seeing. After all, we were supposed to be the closest of sisters.

"He was a tallish guy. Not thin, but not fat. Nice looking, with dark wavy hair. Does that sound familiar?"

Her description sounded like a lot of men.

"Was she driving her car?"

"They were in his car once but I can't remember what kind. I see hundreds of vehicles every day." The diesel engine slowed and Donna excused herself to perform her duties. As she walked away, she turned and shouted above the engine's roar, "Hey, it's good to see you and Steve are a couple again!"

Like everybody else, Donna had just enough information to make me antsy but not enough to help. By the time I walked a few feet back to the car, I was frustrated. Steve was sitting behind the steering wheel. I waggled my finger at him.

"That's awfully presumptuous of you."

"Simmer down," he said, not bothered in the least by my change of mood. "Get in, put your head back and take a nap. But first, tell me where we're going."

I looked at his sly grin and felt the aggravation melt away. When he did thoughtful things like that, it was impossible not to like him. I told him where to go then climbed into the passenger seat, closed my eyes, emptied my mind and dozed off before the boat was moored at the terminal.

I'm familiar with most of the residents on Sabal Palm Island. After all, the majority of us have grown up there. When I strolled into Christine's Fabulous Cake Emporium and Bakery, I knew all but one person in line and every employee in the front waved and smiled at me.

Even though I'd asked Steve to stay in the car, he was attached to me like the shadow Wendy stitched to Peter Pan.

"Hey, Marla! It's been ages since we've talked," I said to the lady in front of me.

That invitation to talk resulted in a five minute narrative about how she admired Lenore and how much she missed seeing her. I just stood there and pretended to listen attentively because I knew from recent experience that I wouldn't get a chance to add anything to the conversation. I'd been the audience of the same one-sided discussion for weeks. Every acquaintance I encountered said they loved my sister, but they rarely asked me how I felt. I wasn't jealous of Lenore, but they all made it rather obvious who the favorite sister had been.

I saw their prying eyes examining me and a chill swept over me. More and more, I felt like I was living in a glass bowl with everybody watching me. What were they saying as they whispered to each other?

Without Lenore, I was just plain Marlene, the Terhune's oldest daughter. That's why I loved Lenore so much. She loved me for being me, not because I was Mason and Trudy Terhune's daughter or Steve Wagner's wife, and not because I created pretty pieces of custom blown glass that people could present as chic designer gifts.

Lenore had been the only person in my life that made me think anything was possible. She was the little sister that looked to me for support and advice, and the one who thought her big sister walked on water. She saw beauty in everything and challenged me to do the same. I was disheartened that I would never experience her enthusiastic passion for life again.

Christine seemed to appear out of nowhere to rescue me from Marla and the other benevolent looks that acknowledged me from the long line of bakery patrons. Steve dutifully followed us through heavy swinging doors into the back area. I think we both felt the same relief when we were hidden from their prying eyes. There is only so much pain and mourning any one person can tolerate in the length of a day, especially the magnified sorrow shared by well-meaning yet tactless acquaintances who want to examine and explain their grief as if it were being viewed by a microscope. They imagine that sharing their sadness will somehow make you feel better, but I can tell you that listening to their stories didn't diminish my grief at all.

Christine broke into my self-induced stupor. "I bet you're here to see the wedding cake," she said with enthusiasm.

"How did you guess?" I wondered why she would think I was the slightest bit interested in Jon's impending wedding, even though I really was there to check on the cake.

"Well, you and Lenore were partners in most things, so I just assumed you were involved in the great surprise."

"You guessed right. I'm sorry I didn't come by to take a look before today."

She was right on track because I was truly amazed that Jonathan had brought his wedding to Sabal Palm Island and lassoed my sister and the rest of my family into being a part of the ceremony. I'd figured out that Matt was in some way involved in the matrimonial ritual and that my parents were planning to attend the wedding, which meant I was the only member of the family excluded from the island's biggest social event of the year. That didn't bother me because it gave me an opportunity to snoop around, including checking out the wedding cake.

We paraded behind her, winding by busy bakers who were pulling trays of savory breads and aromatic pies out of hot ovens, stacking trays of pastries on rolling carts, and frying gooey donuts in sizzling grease. I was amazed by the size of the kitchen as we walked into another wing where we were shown tables covered with miniature wedding cakes in various stages of decoration.

"Are these for Jon's wedding?"

"Yes, there are more than 500 of these little beauties." She pointed to four busy decorators—one man and three women. "They'll be here until every tiny cake is decorated and packed for delivery in the morning. I doubt they'll finish before midnight."

"Look at this!" Steve said with wide-eyed pleasure. He leaned over with his hands folded behind his back and scrutinized a two-layered lavender frosted mini cake. "The detail is remarkable. Did you see these tiny flowers, Marlene?"

We continued to walk down a hallway into a larger kitchen in the back. "I never knew this place was so enormous!" I marveled. I had never been past the front section of the store until that day. The unpretentious canopied entrance and ordinary lobby had concealed the larger operation behind the retail store.

Christine said, "I rent out this back space to a local caterer. They take care of the cuisine for wedding receptions while we handle just the baked goods, like the dinner rolls and cakes. We expanded into this facility for Jon's wedding. In fact, this kitchen is being used exclusively for their wedding cake and the little babies you just saw."

I gasped as I looked around the room. There were eight stainless steel tables, each of them holding at least one white-frosted layer. "This is all for one cake?"

"Eleven layers."

"How do you stack eleven layers?"

"I won't. The main part of the cake is five-tiers, then the other six layers wind around the cake on top of pillars, each standing at a different height."

"And those mini-cakes in there—what happens with those?"

"They're party favors. Each guest and member of the wedding party will take home a small palm-sized wedding cake to commemorate this extraordinary occasion. I dare say most people will freeze their cake as a treasured souvenir," she added. "After all, how many people have the opportunity to attend the wedding of a United States Senator?"

"He's not a senator yet," I protested, but she didn't acknowledge my sarcastic commentary.

Two young ladies sat at a smaller table in the corner of the room. "This is Katy and Anne. They're interns from the culinary program at our community college, and today they are meticulously wrapping each little cake in an individual favor box that gets tied with a silver ribbon and bow." Beside them sat a rolling cart with ten layers of trays, each containing a dozen unpackaged frosted cakes. A twin cart beside it held trays that were jam-packed with an abundance of wrapped keepsakes.

"This must have cost Jonathan a ton of money!"

Christine winked and I knew she was delighted with the windfall revenue the senatorial candidate had contributed to her small town establishment. "Don't ask!"

He'd obviously earned her vote.

That's when Steve sauntered in from the other kitchen. "What flavor is the big cake?" he asked.

"The center layers are our signature cake—a delectable butter sponge cake paired with cream custard and homemade raspberry between the layers."

She toured around the room with Steve and me following close behind her. "Each of the six satellite cakes has a different personality." We paused by every table as she introduced the individual cakes like they were treasured friends.

"This is a Spanish Almond Torte. It has a subtle almond flavor, with a hint of orange zest, and a filling of custard and toasted almonds. It's my favorite."

At the next table, she told us, "The next cake was requested by the bride in honor of her parents. They served it at their wedding, and I'm using her grandmother's recipe. It's an Italian Coconut Cake. It has a cream custard filling and the icing is flavored with strawberry puree."

It smelled like it was created in heaven.

"The third cake is our Carrot Hazelnut. It's made with grated carrots, chopped hazelnuts, orange zest and brown sugar. The over-all flavor is accented with cream cheese icing."

We crossed to the opposite side of the room.

"Number four was baked at the groom's request. It's a sponge cake that is soaked with an aged dark Rum that Jon special-ordered from the islands. The inside is filled with white chocolate custard." The fifth cake sat beside it on the same table. "And this is a very traditional English cake that has been flavored with mint ganache."

At the end of the room we found the final layer. "The last cake is a moist butter sponge cake with a filling of fresh blueberries, sliced peaches and Bavarian Cream."

She turned to Steve and grinned. "I believe that answers your question."

"Oh."

My former husband was unimpressed.

"Steve thinks chocolate is the only flavor," I explained.

She patted him on the back. "Don't worry, Honey. When you get married again, I'll create a very special chocolate wedding cake just for you." She winked at me again and I wished I could dissolve into a giant vat of icing.

Christine nudged his side. "We make several kinds of chocolate cake, Steve. One is Chocolate Cappuccino, another is Peanut Butter Truffle, and still another is—"

"Chocolate. Just plain chocolate."

"That would be the Chocolate Fudge Cake I was going to tell you about before you interrupted me. It's a Devil's Food Cake frosted with Fudge Icing."

"That's the one!"

"You'd better make that a birthday cake, Christine, because we're not getting married," I said as I turned away from both of them and stared at one of the heart-shaped center layers.

"Who said I was marrying you?" he protested.

Christine joined me while I admired a cake like no other I'd seen before.

"Notice anything missing?"

I studied each of the main layers and tried to imagine what she was talking about. The white fondant icing was perfect and the lacy lavender decoration was exquisite. I looked at her, saying nothing.

"The surprise," she hinted.

I didn't blink.

"Think harder, Marlene. This is the top layer."

"Oh, that!" Suddenly, I knew exactly what she was talking about, but I'd intended to keep that revelation to myself. I tossed my keys to Steve. "Can you go to my car and bring back a box that I've stored in the trunk?"

He caught my keys and said, "Sure thing!"

When he'd disappeared from our sight, Christine wrapped me in a protective hug. "You are an amazing woman, Marlene."

I reciprocated her hug and backed away. "What makes me amazing?"

"Lenore would thank you, and I'm sure the bride and groom will be appreciative of your efforts."

Steve returned to the room and placed a brown box in my hands. They both watched attentively as I gingerly unpacked its contents.

"Let me remind both of you that this was intended to be a secret until tomorrow," I said. "I don't want anybody to know about this until the cake is revealed at the reception."

They both concurred.

"Voila!" I presented Christine with the intricate blown glass cake topper that I'd worked on in the privacy of my mother's store. They both gasped. I knew Christine imagined the sparkling art glass was my sister's wedding present for the couple, but in my gut I felt it was much more than a handmade gift.

Based on their incredulous facial expressions, I couldn't wait to see how the bride, groom and all of their guests would react to the cake topper that may have cost my sister her life.

❧

We arrived at my place just short of six o'clock with just enough time to get showers and change into something more appropriate for dinner. While I got ready, Steve called ahead to make reservations.

When I came out of my bedroom, he asked, "Are you wearing that tonight?"

His question annoyed me. "Of course, I am. Do you have a problem with this dress?"

"No. I guess I don't."

We didn't have time to run up to Amy's house in Georgia for him to change clothes or to a local store to select dressier attire. Nevertheless, he looked fine in a white button-down shirt and a pair of dark blue pants he'd left in the back of my closet.

As we drove to Amelia Island, he said, "Remind me why we're doing this."

"Because we're hungry."

"And the other reason?"

"To snoop around some more."

He snickered. "Ah, yes! That's what I thought you would say."

Steve pulled into the parking lot and up to the curb beside the front door. I was amused when he turned his keys over to a valet. The young man wore a dark blue jacket with the country club's gold monogram embroidered on its pocket. Watching Steve tip the valet for parking his truck made me chuckle. Still, his vehicle was polished and clean, which was why we'd left behind my dusty Jeep.

We walked directly to the dining room upstairs, passing by the bar and the banquet hall where the wedding reception would be held the next day. The doors were closed but that didn't stop me from pausing to peek inside. Just as I'd thought, Eloise and a few of her employees were still busy decorating the monstrous room.

Steve took me by the arm and led me away before I was noticed. "Eat now, poke around later."

The Maître d' took one look at my escort and disappeared. He returned a moment later with a dark blue jacket, similar to the valet's but without the stitched insignia. When he was satisfied the jacket fit Steve properly, he escorted us to our secluded corner table.

The view was spectacular with the sun setting over the manicured lawns of the golf course. After a few minutes, the lights around the swimming pool turned on and we were treated to another beautiful picture of the clubhouse surroundings.

At precisely 7:30, just after we'd finished our Tuna Tartar appetizers, the wedding party appeared at the podium. We watched as the guests were efficiently marched into an adjoining private room for what I imagined would be an elaborate rehearsal dinner. As expected, my brother was at the head of the line, but I was staggered and a little hurt to see his wife, Monica, by his side.

At that point, our waiter delivered Steve's Bison Rib Eye Steak. He slammed into his dinner with gusto, but I just sat there and admired my Wild Salmon with Sweet Potato Raviolis.

Half-way through his meal, Steve realized I hadn't taken a single bite. "Eat." He reached over with his fork, broke off a piece of salmon, and fed me like a child. "Forget about what you just saw. I knew we shouldn't have come here."

"You're right," I heard a familiar voice announce. I looked up into the eyes of Matt, who had left Monica behind in the other dining room. "What are you doing here?"

Steve sliced into his juicy steak. "We're eating. You should try this!"

Matt gestured toward me. "She knows what I'm talking about. She picked out that dress to make a point. Marlene, I didn't think you would stoop that low."

I glanced down at my dress but didn't get his meaning. "What's wrong with this?"

"You knew they were having the rehearsal dinner here tonight, and you showed up in a black mourning dress."

I took a taste of the tasty ravioli and set my fork on the edge of my plate. "I am in mourning."

"So am I," Matt said, putting his hand on my shoulder. "But this is a festive occasion and you're making a point of wearing black to show Jon you don't approve of his wedding."

I stood up and boldly faced my brother, both of us taking our usual argumentative pose. "He didn't see me, and neither did his fiancée. Go eat your dinner and leave me alone to enjoy this fine meal."

Matthew shrugged his shoulders, turned around, and walked out of the room.

When I sat down, Steve looked at me and said, "Touché!"

"I can eat now," I declared, and together we finished off every morsel on our plates.

At 8:15, we stood outside waiting for the valet to deliver the shiny truck. "Did you get what you came here for, Marlene?"

"I suppose I did," I admitted. "But tomorrow is the day I'm anticipating the most."

11

Friday, March 31, 2000
8:42 p.m.

Steve drove me home, which was a good decision on his part. At first, I sat in silence as images of the wedding party replayed in my head. Jon's fiancée had been flashing her ultra-white teeth and television smile as usual, while she entertained her entourage of bridesmaids.

It was obvious where she had been while Jon played a round of golf with my brother.

Sylvia's blonde hair fell over her shoulders in long twisting ringlets. A stylist had weaved in long strands of hair, which lengthened her tresses at least six inches, and he'd also given her a fresh perm to make it curlier.

As the crowd made their way to the private dining room, the younger women paired off, giggling like schoolgirls telling hushed secrets. A line of less conspicuous groomsmen trailed behind them.

There was still something about Jon's fiancée that made me uneasy, but I didn't have a legitimate reason for disliking his future wife, except that she was about to marry the man who had broken my sister's heart.

I exploded. "Matthew wasn't even fazed that I'm not invited to the wedding!"

Steve is used to my outbursts so he didn't flinch as he turned onto the road that leads to my place. "Probably because he knew you'd react like this."

He parked in front of my house and I stormed out of the car, still ranting and yelling with each step. "I'm his sister! Where is his sense of loyalty?"

"Maybe he doesn't know you weren't invited to the wedding."

"Oh, he knows! You can count on that! You saw how he acted in there tonight! My brother practically ran us out of the restaurant. He tried his best to shame me!"

"But he didn't."

"No, he didn't. I have rights to eat where I want to eat, when I want to eat, and to select who I dine with."

Steve stifled a laugh. "Well, this evening you chose to eat with me and that didn't seem to bother him in the least."

I stopped in my tracks and studied him. "Why is that?"

"Because I'm a good guy?"

I turned back around and unlocked the house. "Nah, that can't be it." We both laughed and I held the door open to invite him inside. He unarmed the alarm system and joined me in the living room.

"Matt didn't react at all. Everybody on the island has had something to say about us hanging out again, but my brother didn't act like he even saw you."

"Should I feel insulted?

"Get serious."

It was too late to lock him outside, so I left him behind and went into my bedroom to change clothes. When I returned, he had changed back into the same outfit he'd been wearing all day.

"I do have a washing machine and even a dryer." That was my way of telling him he could make himself at home. When I heard those words come out of my mouth, I wondered why it was so hard to tell him how much I appreciated his help, and that I enjoyed having him around again. Before he could respond, I added, "But why don't you go home?" He gave me a questioning look.

I wanted him to stay, but my practical side realized he needed to at least pack a bag with a few clothes and essentials if he planned to babysit me for any length of time.

"Are you sure?"

"Just go there long enough to pack an overnight bag." I handed him the key to my front door. "Let yourself in because I'll probably be asleep by the time you get back from St. Mary's. And don't forget a suit for tomorrow."

Steve tossed the key into the air and caught it. "Yeah. Tomorrow. I wouldn't want to miss that fiasco." He gave me half-a-salute and headed to his truck.

My insides twisted as he drove off. I was disappointed and a little afraid of being alone. I didn't like that feeling.

Just as I closed the door, my phone rang. I answered, "So soon?"

"Don't forget to turn on the alarm system before you hit the sack."

I laughed but I was very grateful that he was concerned about my welfare. "Yes, sir, and you take it easy on the roads. Don't speed."

"I'll be back tonight. Go to bed early, Marlene. Tomorrow is going to be a whirlwind of activity, even if you behave yourself."

Going to bed at 9:00 was way too early, no matter what I had planned for the next day. And I certainly didn't intend to behave myself, at least not in the way Steve was alluding to with his snide comment.

I had a lot to think about and time was not only of the essence, but I had the increasing fear that time was about to catch up with me and plow me deep into the earth, where I'd never be seen again.

Why I felt that way, I can't explain. The events of that month had been so overwhelming—so completely time-consuming, soul-wrenching, and heart-breaking—and for what reason? I had no clue about what was propelling me to do things that I wouldn't normally do.

For the most part, I am a home body. I get up in the morning, go to work and do my due diligence, which is filling an order or doing what my father tells me to do, and then I go home to recover so I can face another day just like it the next day, and the next day, and the next...well, over and over again. That's the way my life has been since Steve and I parted ways.

Following our divorce, I had no inclination to do more than what life required of me, and that meant I simply had to exist. Other than Tony and my sister, I had no real friends. Amy lives up in Georgia, so we see each other occasionally. And other people that I care about have their own lives to lead—jobs to go to, children to take care of, bills to be paid, and aging parents to worry about. At my age, most people are attached either by marriage or by an invisible tether they call co-habitation, which might as well be marriage if they'd just sign a few documents and get on with their lives together. I had already failed as a wife, and even though I ended our relationship, I guess I was still stunned that our vows didn't last. I admit that was more my fault than Steve's, but I wasn't ready to take that giant leap again, and I didn't feel like dating a string of strangers just to appease the people who told me I should take a chance again. Nope. I wasn't going that route and I was content to stay home alone and take care of myself.

But now my sister had died and my best friend was gone forever. Life without Lenore would be…well, it just wouldn't be the life that I wanted to have. Despite what people saw on the outside, I was crushed and without hope on the inside.

So, having my former housemate around—even if it was just a temporary arrangement—was not only a surprise, but I was starting to realize Steve was what Mama would call a 'God Send'.

These were all the things I thought about as I grabbed a quick shower and changed again—this time into pajamas for the long night ahead. Without that exasperating man around to taunt me, what would I do?

I called Tony for the umpteenth time and he still didn't answer his phone. He doesn't have an answering machine, so I determined that I'd talk to him at the factory the next Monday. That's when I intended to face my father again and beg him to put me back to work right away.

I pulled out the stash of items I'd brought back from my parents' house and Lenore's apartment and sorted through them again. It was time to put away things she no longer needed. Lenore's jewelry box went into the top drawer of my dresser where I covered it with my lingerie. An empty shoe box became a place to store her combs and brushes. I'd never use them, but I couldn't stand the thought of throwing them away. The cans of assorted aerosol sprays, fragrant lotions, and a partially used box of feminine napkins went under my bathroom counter.

That left me with a small bundle of letters and greeting cards and the book I still hadn't read. I had also collected a Bible from her bedside table. I placed it on a pillow.

The phone rang. "What now?" I demanded, figuring it was Steve bugging me again.

"Excuse me?"

"Oh, Sherry!"

"You must have been expecting another caller," she apologized. "Why don't you just phone me back?"

"No, I've been hoping to hear from you. Did you find out anything from the coroner?"

"Yes, but also no. I'm calling to warn you about a few things. Can I come over for a few minutes to talk to you in person?"

Since I preferred not to be alone, and I was anxious to hear what she had to say, I welcomed the idea of having Sherry's companionship for the remainder of the evening. I looked at the clock. It was 9:39.

❦

By 11:15, I was worried. Sherry hadn't shown up and I still hadn't heard more from Steve. As much as I insist he annoys me, at that moment I needed to hear his voice.

I called Amy but was aggravated when her recorder answered. "Amy, pick up!" I waited but she didn't respond.

"Hey, have you seen Steve tonight? If you hear this, give me a call. It's Marlene." When I hung up, I shuddered as I thought about a similar phone call my sister had made to me the night she had died.

Anxiety swept through me as I paced the floor aimlessly. What did Sherry want to warn me about? How could I sleep? I walked to the front door, rechecked the security alarm to make sure it was still armed, and returned to my bedroom.

I untied the bow around Amy's letters and began reading, becoming oblivious to time ticking away as I analyzed each one meticulously, imagining that I might somehow find a clue. Most of the frayed pages were old love letters, worn-out from too many readings. I couldn't understand why Lenore would keep anything from Jonathan Lucas—including his ring—after that deceitful man had subjected her to so much despair. But try as I might, I couldn't find anything remarkable or devious in the letters that pointed me in his direction. I considered throwing them in the trash, where they belonged, but retied the bow around them instead and tucked them into the shoe box where they were joined a few minutes later by assorted greeting cards that had no worth to me. But if they were treasured by Lenore, they would remain in my safe-keeping.

The phone rang just as I shoved the box up on a closet shelf.

I glanced at the clock beside my bed and realized it was already half-past midnight. Stress again overtook me. I literally ran from the closet to grab the phone receiver.

The tragic loss of my sister had already taken a toll on my heart, my temper, and my mind and I imagined the worst scenario. I am a woman who likes to think I am in control of my life, but recent events had been consuming me in huge bites and that night there was very little left of my self-restraint. I was teetering on the brink of total despair, and if that happened, I was sure there would be very little left of me.

"Where are you?" I demanded. I didn't care if it was Steve, Sherry, Tony, or even Amy. I just wanted to hear from one of my missing friends. I needed to know that I was not alone and that they all were someplace safe.

"Marlene, please forgive me! I didn't mean to keep you awake this long, and I thought I'd be at your house by this time. I am so sorry!" Sherry apologized profusely. Her high-pitched voice was even more penetrating and alarming than I remembered, as she continued to spit out, "So much has happened since we last talked, and I'm still in the middle of a slew of phone calls with Donna, and I'm also talkin' with a police-friend, and I can't leave, but you need to know what's going on to stay out of trouble...so, sit down and just listen...and don't tell anybody what I'm telling you tonight!"

I sat down and waited nervously but said nothing, as directed.

"You still there?" she asked.

"Yes, Sherry. Please take a deep breath and slow down so I can understand you."

"Okay." I heard her take in a long, deep breath. When she exhaled, her breath blew noisily into the receiver. Hearing her voice and sensing her unsettled but passionate behavior, I realized the story she was about to divulge was probably the most exciting event she had ever covered as a small town reporter. That meant the information would pertain to Jon, and that made me even more uneasy.

"You're planning to go to the wedding tomorrow. Right?"

"Yes."

"Did you get an invitation?"

"No."

"No matter…I knew you'd be there."

I was becoming impatient. "Just spit it out, Sherry. You're killing me."

"I'll start at the beginning. I chatted with an acquaintance at the Medical Examiner's office. He said they hadn't made a final determination yet, but that Lenore's death is an ongoing investigation and that results are pending test results coming back. What that means to us is that Lenore did not die from natural causes. That also means they are conducting an investigation to determine the cause and manner of death, including suicide and foul-play."

I gasped.

Sherry added, "I asked him if drugs were involved, but he declined to comment. I know they sent lab work out. That can mean many things, but based on what you've told me, I'm assuming it is drug-related."

"Marlene, you'll have to be extremely patient. It can take 90 days to get the test results back. If foul play is suspected, it can take up to 9 months before a final report is released."

"What you are saying is that we still don't know anything, and we don't have any more information than we had before."

"Well, yes…but, no. We're talking about one roadblock, girl. Just listen, because I have more to tell you."

I perked up a bit, but remained wary. "You said you had to warn me—"

"Yes, I need to warn you about tomorrow because big things are about to happen. To quote my cop-friend, 'Big as in capital B, capital I, capital G…BIG things are going down tomorrow.' He didn't tell me what or when, but he said I will be rewarded with a story if I show up at the wedding."

"I wonder what that means." Apprehension was replaced by anticipation as I tried to envision what the new day would bring. "Do you have any ideas?"

Sherry laughed. "Aha! I can hear the little wheels in your brain spinning. I've been trying to figure it out too, but the only thing I know for sure is that the press will be there."

"The press?"

"Um…let me re-word that. And please, please don't repeat this to anybody. I will be there. But this information was leaked to me by Donna. As you know, *The American Interrogator* planned to do a story about the so-called relationship between Jonathan Lucas and Lenore. They were going to run the story before the couple got married, but then they decided they would hold the story because it would become even more sensational if the marriage took place before the story goes public."

"Sleezeballs."

"Yes, I agree. But I'm glad Donna works for them because without Donna, we wouldn't have any information at all. So, Donna called me earlier today to say they were rethinking their approach. She's been calling me with updates all day. About forty minutes ago, they sent a crew on the road to cover the story. Mind you, not just a reporter and photographer. They are sending a crew of several reporters and two cameras to cover this story, so that must mean they have a tip and something newsworthy is in the works. It might mean it is even bigger than their original story, so we both need to be prepared, keep our eyes wide, our ears tuned in, and our heads turned down while we follow any clues we see. You may have all of your answers when the day is over, or you may just have a piece of the puzzle. Whatever happens, you will know more tomorrow night than you know right now."

❧

At 1:18 a.m., Steve unlocked the front door, reset the alarm, and made his way to the couch to sleep. I remained still, studying the face of my digital clock, and concentrated on my conversation with Sherry. I was dead tired but sleep was still out of reach.

I clicked on the lamp and stared at the ceiling. What time was the wedding? I couldn't remember ever hearing the time, and I was perturbed that I had missed that vital piece of information. And where were they going to be married? I had assumed it would be at a church, but maybe they would just have the ceremony at the country club.

I reached over and set the clock alarm to 7:00 a.m. I'd call Matt or my mother in the morning. Either one of them would know the time and place for the best performance of the year. But if I called them, they would be alerted that I planned to show up. No, I couldn't call them. I wasn't too worried because I had faith that with just one phone call to Sherry, I'd have the schedule for all the day's events.

"Here I am again, God," I said to the ceiling. "I'm a bit apprehensive about tomorrow, but I'm also eager to get on with it. I don't know what to expect, and that does bother me somewhat. I'd appreciate if you would give me a few minutes of sleep before this whole debacle begins. And I'd really appreciate if you will look out for me and my family. We're hurting. Please let me figure everything out so I can get right with my family again. Thank you…uh…Amen."

It wasn't much of a prayer, but I said what was on my heart. I turned over and on top of the pillow beside me laid Lenore's Bible. I sat up, placed it in my lap, and studied its soft leather cover. The inscription on the first page indicated she had received the Bible just a few years before when she had joined a singles group for a weekly Bible study. I always figured she'd done that to meet available men.

As I skimmed through the Bible, I soon realized the group had meant much more to her. Sentences throughout the book were highlighted in yellow, and in the columns, Lenore had jotted notes to explain what specific passages meant to her. Several bookmarks and scraps of note paper were scattered between the pages. Lenore obviously had a better understanding of the Bible than I had. I remembered her telling me about her 'personal relationship with God' and I wondered what that meant. How had God helped Lenore? And could he help me as well?

Just then, a yellow paper fell to the floor. On it, Lenore had scribbled:

> *The Lord is close to the broken-*
> *hearted; he rescues those who are*
> *crushed in spirit.*

12

Saturday, April 1, 2000
9:18 a.m.

It had been an eternity since I'd had such restful sleep, but my internal clock sent out a potent spurt of adrenalin that jump-started my entire body, taking me from zero to racing in mere seconds. I awakened with a seismic lurch, heaving forward and upright with barely a breath. My heart beat so vigorously that I could feel its forceful pounding in my chest and hear its rapid cadence in my ears.

Despite my first inclination to dart out of bed, I forced myself to sit still until my heartbeat settled into a more comfortable rhythm. I rubbed my eyes to clear away sleep and lethargically stared out my bedroom window at cloudless blue skies over the Atlantic.

A cargo ship, recently departed from the port in Jacksonville, became smaller as it cruised toward distant harbors beyond the eastern horizon. Beneath it, the deep ocean water was cerulean blue, but its color faded to a murky teal as it approached the shallow coastline and ended in persistent, crashing waves that churned and spit out frothy sea foam. High tide slowly covered the beach, but that didn't deter a solitary surfer nor assorted seabirds that dotted the shoreline in a last-ditch effort to claim a tasty morsel from the receding current and the outflowing sand.

I was irritated when I glanced at my bedside clock and realized I had turned it off earlier that morning without conscious thought. It was almost half-past nine. The sun had risen three hours before and had disappeared behind a tall cabbage palm tree. It was already so far above the horizon that the mid-morning shadows it cast against the ground were short and undefined.

"Wake-up, Babe!" I shouted to Steve, without realizing what I'd just said. I was in a hurry, absent-mindedly leaving my clothes in a heap on the floor as I rushed to take a quick shower. We had both overslept and wasted two whole hours, which meant we were running way late for the day ahead of us.

I jumped in the shower before the water was regulated, letting out a squeal as cool water slowly became tepid and suddenly turned hot. I made a hasty adjustment, passed a sudsy washcloth over my body, smeared shampoo on my hair, and stood under the spray to rinse all the suds down the drain. The whole process took less than five minutes.

With a towel wrapped around my body and another on my wet head, I yelled to Steve as I stepped into my bedroom. "Your turn! Water's still running, so hurry up!"

But there was no reply.

I cracked the door and looked into the living room. A pillow lay on top of a neatly folded blanket at the end of the sofa.

"Steve?"

When there was still no response, I tiptoed across the hardwood floor, leaving damp toe prints behind me. "Steve?" If he wasn't in the kitchen, where was he? That worrisome flutter in the pit of my stomach returned, but it was displaced fast by irritation when I peeked out the front window and realized his truck was missing.

"There's no time for this nonsense!" I yelled, even though I was the only one in the house. I returned to my bathroom where I dried and styled my hair as I considered the day's schedule, wondering where I could make cuts so that we'd get to the wedding on time. That's when I realized, again, that I still didn't know all the details. Why had I waited until the last moment to figure everything out?

I threw three outfits on my bed—two formal dresses and a casual sundress—and considered which one to wear as I dialed Sherry. This whole thing had transpired so fast, with me finding out about the wedding in just the past week. Was it any wonder that I was overwhelmed and ill-prepared?

No answer at Sherry's. No surprise.

When I heard the front door open, I threw on a robe and hurried into the living room. Steve, with his arms full of bags and one hanging from his teeth, pushed the door shut with a quick nudge from his foot and disappeared into the kitchen without so much as a nod. Intending to give him a taste of my anger, I rushed after him but shut up when I saw the booty he had brought back.

"I figured there's no time to make breakfast, but we'll sure need nourishment to get through this day," he said with a chuckle. The logos on the empty bags indicated he'd visited two different fast food restaurants. I watched as he methodically lined up a variety of goodies on the table, cafeteria-style. "Didn't know what you'd want, so I brought you a few things to choose from."

Orange juice, coffee, and iced tea were my beverage

choices. Sausage or chicken biscuits, a breakfast burrito, and an English muffin stacked with ham, egg and cheese were the breakfast selections, along with fried potato grease sponges or a healthier yogurt and fruit parfait. "Whatever we don't eat now, we can put in the fridge for later," he announced. "You get first choice."

With all of that to choose from, and knowing how much thought he'd put into the menu options, I felt a little guilty when I picked up the healthier parfait with iced tea. Truth is, my stomach was queasy as I anticipated the day ahead of us. I sat down beside the window, staring at the surf as I enjoyed the vanilla yogurt with mixed berries. When Steve flopped a newspaper in front of me, I grabbed the first section.

On the front page was a large photo of Jon Lucas and his future wife, one a photographer had snapped on the day they'd visited Jacksonville's mayor. On closer examination, I decided she was attractive despite the now familiar smile that overwhelmed the rest of her face. The article that accompanied the picture mentioned their upcoming nuptials but made no mention of the time or location for the ceremony.

"Why the frown?" he asked.

"I still don't know where they're getting married."

He squeezed mustard on the chicken, closed the biscuit, and took a gigantic bite, eating it as he studied my face. I threw my empties into the trash and stared at him irritably. "What?" His nose crinkled and his eyes squinted as he scrutinized me. "Are you angry with me? Because if you are, I wasn't gone that long, Marlene."

"I'm mad at myself. We might as well stay here today. I don't have a clue where to go. I don't even know what to wear!"

He laughed. "Well, that is serious."

"I am serious!"

He put some of the remaining food in the refrigerator and turned to me. "You're worrying too much, as usual, Honey."

"Don't 'Honey' me, Mr. Wagner." I was tempted to clobber him, but that wouldn't accomplish anything except to vent some of my anxiety.

"What's it worth to you?"

"What do you mean?"

"Is all of this fretting really necessary? You've got to get control of your anxiety, Sweetie. It's going to make you sick."

"I am sick of secrets! How many times do I have to say this? I thought you understood my problem. I just want to go to this stupid wedding and figure out what the big secret is."

"I do understand."

"You do? Well, you certainly don't seem to—"

He reached into the trash can and pulled out a discarded envelope that I'd tossed away with a slew of junk mail. He pulled open a drawer beneath the counter, found a pencil, and scribbled on the back of the envelope.

I picked it up and read: Wedding 2:00 p.m. at Sabal Palm Church.

"That's our church."

"Why is that such a shock? It's the church we all grew up in. It's the church we got married in."

I exploded, "And it's the same church he promised to marry Lenore in!"

"Yes. That would be true as well."

"How do you know this? It's not even in the newspaper."

"I have my ways."

"Steven Wagner— "

"I saw Tony's mother at the gas station this morning. I figured she would know."

Without thinking, I gave him a quick kiss on the lips and ran into my bedroom to finish dressing. "I'll turn on the shower for you. You'd better hurry." He entered the room behind me. "No need for a shower. I took one last night before I came back. I just need to freshen my shave and tug something on." He glanced at his watch. "It's just after ten. Am I dressing now for the wedding or are we coming back later to do that? We've got four hours."

I looked at the apparel on my bed. "Not sure. I think we should be ready in case we're running late."

"If we're not invited, how are we getting in, Marlene? Have you thought about that? He's not just Jon Lucas now. He's an important man."

"Pfft! Important! Certainly not important to me!"

"You know what I mean. He's surrounded by security. Do you remember when JFK's son got married on Cumberland Island?"

"Of course, I remember that. But he was a President's son and the Secret Service was involved."

"This isn't so far from the same thing. He's a candidate for the senate and, believe me, he has body guards."

"Yes, and when they got married, they did it privately. Not with all the media Jon has been inviting to follow him around. He has created a spectacle to gain attention for his campaign."

"No media here now."

"There will be." I pulled the sundress over my head.

He looked at me with a giant, unspoken question mark looming over the silence.

I returned one dress to my closet and took the other dress, still on a hanger, to the living room.

"What do you know that I don't know?"

"Nothing for sure. Just be prepared for anything today. Now get ready. You can wear something casual, but bring along what you'll be wearing for the ceremony. We'll find someplace to change before we get to the church. For now, we'll dress for comfort. We've gotta hurry!"

When I went outside, I was surprised to see a sleek white Toyota Celica waiting at the curb. "Is this yours?" Steve unlocked the power locks and I climbed into the cushy bucket seat on the passenger's side, while he stowed our clothing and shoes in the rear.

"This is Amy's new car. She offered and I accepted. It sure beats going to a wedding in your Jeep or my truck."

"This is so...sporty. I didn't know Amy had this in her. Look at that black hood scoop, and the instrument panel! Go, Amy!" We both laughed as we imagined her breezing through town, the center of attention in her flashy new car.

It was a lovely day for a drive along the shoreline, and it was also the perfect day for a wedding. The weather was mild, the skies clear, and the palms fluttered as a cool breeze came in from the ocean. I whiled away most Saturdays on my deck, sipping tea and reading a good book. But this wasn't a typical Saturday, and there hadn't been anything normal in the weeks since Lenore's death.

I glanced over at Steve and he looked relaxed and very pleased with his good fortune. He noticed my attentions and smiled. "Nice ride. Drives great. By the way, where are we heading?"

"First stop is Tony's house. I'm worried about him. I haven't heard from him recently."

Steve looked bewildered. "Are you sure that will fit into the day?"

"We'll just stop for a few minutes. After that, we'll go by the country club to see how the morning is progressing."

During the ten minute drive to Tony's place, Steve was mute. I knew he was perturbed, but I didn't have the stamina or inclination to explain or defend myself that morning. I sensed he was jealous about Tony being in my life, but we were just friends. I was sure Steve knew that. Besides, we weren't married and he didn't have the right to be jealous of any man in my life.

We pulled into the gravel driveway beside the house where Tony lived with his mother. The red brick and mortar building was older than mine, pre-dating it by a full decade. Steve hopped out before me. "Stay here. I'll see if he's home."

I watched with some trepidation as he pounded on the door. When no one answered, Steve strolled around the side of the house and disappeared into the backyard. I heard him pounding on the kitchen door, then watched as he went from window to window, trying to see inside. Concluding his tour, he walked to the garage and tried to look through the dirt-covered windows on the garage door.

"No luck," he announced as he slid into the seat beside me. "Do you think he's helping his mother today?"

"Perhaps." But I thought not.

"We'll come back later, Sweetie. Don't worry. We'll find all your answers. Just give us a little more time."

He drove toward the country club and I sat considering

our route. It wasn't even eleven o'clock yet, but as we approached our church, I made an impulsive decision. "Turn now," I spat out. Steve jerked the steering wheel.

"Where?"

"There!" I pointed at the church.

When he parked the car at the curb, I jumped out. "I won't be long. I promise." He shook his head, tilted the seat, and closed his eyes.

I stopped on a gamble, not a premonition. There was no reason to expect Pastor Williams to be there three hours prior to the service. The rear entry was unlocked, and I found him inside the sanctuary near the altar.

White roses were everywhere. They hung in ribbon-draped bouquets from the ends of old-fashioned oak pews, graced every arched entryway, and two magnificent arrangements stood at the front of the church on each side of the center aisle. But to my eye, the most exquisite decoration in the church was not the flowers or even the half-dozen stained glass windows, but will always be the resplendent classic Dutch-style polished brass chandelier overhead —the one my third-great grandfather designed with 30 candle lights and suspended from the ceiling when the church was erected in 1858.

My purpose for the visit was still unknown to me. I sat in a middle pew and watched the man pace from one side of the room to the other, speaking in hushed whispers. I decided he was spending time in prayer. It was not the proper moment to talk with him, so I knelt down, bowed my head, and asked God to be with me. I was afraid. That was something I hadn't spoken to anyone, except for Him.

When I approached the rear door to leave, I heard a

familiar booming voice. "Marlene Terhune Wagner! God does move in amazing ways!"

I turned to see the beloved face of the man who had baptized me. He walked toward me with outstretched arms. It had been years since I had seen him, but at that moment, he was the only person on earth I really needed to talk to about everything that was bothering me.

"I've missed seeing you in church," he said as he enveloped me in an enormous hug. "And I imagine you're here about Lenore."

"Yes, sir."

"I've been expecting you, but I didn't think it would take you so long to find me. Of course, this is a special day and that might have something to do with it. Am I correct?"

"Right again."

"So, tell me what's on your mind and how I can help."

"I don't know where to start." By then, my brain was so muddled with 'what ifs' and 'how comes' and the possibility that I could find even one answer was...well, it felt like everything was just beyond my grasp. I was beginning to wonder if I should do what my brother had told me to do over and over again. Just stop. Let her go. If I stopped asking questions then maybe that was for the best because maybe the answers were so awful that I'd be sorry when I knew the truth.

"I'm lost."

Pastor smiled at me. "No, you aren't." He swept both hands in the air. "Look where you are. This is God's house, and this is the place you can always come to when you can't find your way."

I didn't cry. By then, I had shed so many tears that my

tears ducts should have been dried up. I wasn't there to complain or whimper. I was feeling a sense of numbness, and I didn't like that feeling. So many things had happened recently that I was on the brink of disconnection from the rest of the world. If I turned off my feelings, nobody could hurt me anymore. Deep inside, I knew if I let that happened it would be a long way back to reality, and that was a scary possibility.

He patted my hand. "Just tell me what's on your heart. There's no right way or wrong way to approach a problem. And if you're worried about telling me something, let me assure you my ears have heard stories that would curl your toes."

"How can you let Jonathan Lucas get married in this church?"

He had assured me I could say anything, but the expression on his face indicated he was taken aback by my question. "Why wouldn't he get married here? He grew up in this church, just like you. His parents still go here, as do yours. And even though he doesn't come to services here anymore, he attends church in Tallahassee, and may I remind you that you no longer come to services in this church, but you are always welcome here."

I just stared at him, but I felt guilty because I knew he was right. Still, I asked, "Doesn't it bother you that he was supposed to marry Lenore here? Don't you remember how hurt she was? I'm sorry, but I just can't understand—"

He touched my hand. "It's very obvious that you haven't moved beyond that moment, but I can assure you that your sister had."

"You know that for a certainty?"

"I do."

"And how is that?"

"We had many long talks, your sister and I. She came to realize that God has a purpose for everything. Sometimes our Father in Heaven gives us a problem because he has other plans for us. Did you know that?"

I laughed cynically. "He sure is testing me."

He leaned closer to me and whispered, "Did you know she forgave Jonathan?"

I sat back in astonishment, and I felt like my throat was closing, so I said nothing.

"As she grew up, Lenore realized that she was part of their break-up. They were too young, too immature, and neither of them was ready for a full-life commitment. She told me she had written him a letter once, one that told him these things. They were no longer companions, but they did have a cordial relationship."

"Why didn't she tell me this?"

"We don't always tell our family members all of our secrets, do we?"

That brought up a giant lump in my throat. I was determined not to cry, but why wouldn't my sister tell me everything? Hadn't we always confided our deepest secrets to each other?

"Everything I thought I knew about my family turns out to be an enormous lie." Yes, I was beginning to feel sorry for myself and I felt entitled to a bit of whining.

He pursed his lips as he considered a response. "People change as they grow up. They create new bonds and new relationships, and sometimes they begin to confide in new people. Haven't you done that?"

"Not really."

"Oh, but I'm sure you have. Did you come here alone today?"

"Um. No."

He looked around. "I don't see anybody else here."

"He's outside."

"Do I know this person?"

"Yes."

"Can you tell me his name?"

"I'm figuring you already know it's Steve." I felt caught, but I laughed with him.

"So, I'm imagining you still confide in him. Would I be right?"

"Sometimes."

"Have you forgiven each other? I'm sure you felt some animosity toward Steve when you divorced."

"I did." Admitting that, speaking those words out loud, filled me with regret.

"You're spending time together. Doesn't that indicate you have moved beyond the pain?"

"I guess it does."

"Have you forgiven him?"

"Pastor, I'm not sure there was ever anything I needed to forgive him for. I was the one who ended our marriage and I am the one who needs forgiveness."

"Have you told him this?"

"No, I don't think I have, but I should. Shouldn't I?"

"Only you know the answer to that, Marlene. Contemplate this. If our Father in Heaven is willing to forgive our mistakes, shouldn't we do the same for each other?"

"I took his hand. "Thank you. I imagine you had this same conversation with my sister. Am I right?"

"Many times. Forgiving someone is not always easy, but when you finally think everything through and understand that none of us are perfect, then your heart is ready to heal. Forgiveness heals both parties. You cannot move on in life if you continue to nurse old wounds."

It was like a mask had been removed from my eyes. I was beginning to understand, and immediately I felt a little lighter.

He looked at his watch and grimaced. "Marlene, I hate to end this, but noon is fast approaching and I still have preparations to make before the ceremony. Would you like to come back later this week to continue this discussion?"

"Yes, I would." I stood and gave him an embrace.

"Will you be at the festivities today?"

I shook my head. "I haven't decided about that yet."

He took my hand in his. "Please listen to me, and remember this…our Father does not choose between his children. He has no favorites."

"I know you are mourning your sister's passing, and I want to help you with that. So call my secretary and make an appointment to see me again. Until then, before you go to sleep tonight, read Psalm 46:1. That may help you a bit."

I waved and walked out the door. I hadn't made any big discoveries, but I had learned enough to revive my spirit.

13

Steve was much too comfortable in Amy's car, catnapping with the windows down and the radio playing music that he certainly couldn't hear through his snoring.

"Times up! Gotta gallop, Pokey!"

The man was handsome as ever, even with his hair mussed by a gentle breeze. He sat up, stretching and yawning. "If I'm Pokey, then you must be Gumby," he grumbled.

"Yep. I'm the adventurous one and you're my reluctant cohort." That was a running joke with us, but ordinarily the roles were reversed. Steve was the risk-taker, and I'm the one that always said, "Let's just stay home," when he'd suggest that I try something new. Jumping out of a plane with a parachute or diving to see sharks didn't seem like fun to me. That sounded more like a death wish. I sometimes wondered how we ever ended up together, but more recently I found myself wishing we'd never split up. He had always supported everything I tackled, and I realized that he had never stopped watching over and protecting me and my family. It was like a blindfold had been snapped away from my eyes and I was seeing the truth.

He turned the ignition and asked, "Where next? The country club?"

"That's the plan. Onward!"

The route from Sabal Palm to Amelia Island is beautiful. We drove over several low bridges that connect all of the coastal barrier islands together, passing over salt marshes and beneath thick tree tunnels of weather-gnarled scrub oaks that opened up to the beaches on our east side.

We arrived at the country club about thirty minutes after we'd departed the church. The front doorway was thick with a multitude of busy staff. Frantic club employees worked diligently to spruce up the entrance—washing windows, picking up litter, tidying plants, and sweeping the outdoor carpet.

There was still no indication that the media had arrived, but it was quite apparent that security was in high force based upon the men and women dressed in black, each of them wearing an earbud or carrying a walkie-talkie.

The parking lot was full. We drove up and down the main boulevard and searched side streets, but we were out of luck. About that time, a white van wrapped in a bright multi-colored advertisement for *Christine's Fabulous Cake Emporium* passed us going in the opposite direction. "Follow that van!" I urged him. He did a quick U-turn, kicking up gravel on the berm, and caught up just in time to follow the driver behind the hotel to a rear entrance.

A guard tried to stop us, but Steve rolled down his window and announced, "We're with him!" The guy waved us ahead. Obviously the people in black were not the Secret Service and providence was finally on our side.

Three box trucks from *Tantalizing Events* were backed up

to the loading docks. Tony Gilman's mother, Eloise, stood behind one. Steve stopped the car long enough to let me out. "Park over there," I ordered, and pointed to a spot between two golf carts. "I'll catch Eloise before she goes inside."

While her employees wore monogramed uniforms, Eloise was dressed semi-elegant. I say semi because her makeup was flawless, her jewelry sparkling, and her coiffure much more sophisticated than the ponytail I see her wear in the grocery store. I assumed she would change into something more appropriate for the reception, but at that moment she wore a button-down shirt over khaki twill pants, and white lace-up work shoes similar to the stodgy black ones my elderly aunt always wears.

"What are you doing here?" she asked. "Shouldn't you be getting ready for the wedding? It starts in—" She checked her cell phone. "You'd better leave now if you want to have time to drive back to the island and change clothes. I'm sure sorry I won't be there, but I've got too much to handle at this end."

As Steve walked up he asked, "Can we help?"

The look on her face was unforgettable—a mix of surprise and excitement with a tinge of foreboding to finish it off. "Well, hello, sailor!" She threw her arms around his neck, gave him a giant smooch on his cheek, and used her thumb to wipe off her lipstick when she was finished. "Good to see you!" She glanced from him to me and back. "Great to see you two back together! Uh...um...you are together, right?"

"Yes," Steve said with a sheepish grin.

"And no," I added, not wanting her to read too much into the situation. "We came together as friends. We both needed a date."

She chuckled. "Yeah, we'll see about that. Check back

with me in six months and let me know how friendly you are."

I could tell Steve was enjoying the wordplay, but he was on good behavior, at least for that moment. When one of her workers returned with a hand truck stacked with empty boxes, my buddy jumped right in and helped him reload them for storage until after the event. He flashed a mischievous grin and waved as he nonchalantly followed the sweaty worker back into the building.

"I apologize for walking away from you the other day," she said when we were alone. I'm just so sorry about Lenore. Oh, what was I thinking? You're not going to the wedding, are you?"

"I don't think so."

"Well, I don't blame you, but what are you doing here again? You're not planning to blow this place up with Jon in it are you?" We both giggled. "Oops. I shouldn't tease about such awful things with so many spooks around. This whole thing makes me nervous. You have seen them, haven't you? Gosh, I hope they haven't bugged my truck. If they did, we'll both be spending some time behind bars tonight, and whatever will they do with all my fancy costume jewelry when they book me?"

"You are just what I needed today." I gave her a playful punch. "I'm here because I'm nosy. That's all."

"Tony said you've been snooping around. Something about Lenore." Her smile faded. "Oh, darn! I don't know when to shut up! I'm so sorry. I didn't mean to bring all this up. I know this day is awful for you to begin with, and here I am—"

"Where is Tony, by the way?"

"I haven't a clue," Eloise said, shaking her head in dismay. "I have been so busy planning this wedding reception that everything else, including my son, has been ignored for a few weeks."

I gave her a sympathetic hug. "Don't worry—no offense taken. Today, I've called a truce between me and Jonathan Lucas. This is his day and I'm not going to be the one to ruin it. Lenore wouldn't want me to do that, and it's not on my agenda for this afternoon. I've sworn an oath of polite restraint today."

I watched her demeanor deflate. I'd never been in a situation where so many people were uncomfortable around me. Maybe that's why I was on edge and so suspicious.

It wasn't just the secrets and untruths that bothered me. It was the whispers, changes in conversation, and even people walking to the opposite side of the street to avoid me. Of course I had plenty of people offering their condolences and making sympathetic gestures, but there was an undercurrent of prickly unpleasantness that made my skin crawl. It wasn't my imagination. I knew that as much as I knew that there were people watching me at that very moment.

Eyes were everywhere—eyes that I couldn't see, and ears that could hear a mouse scratch his nose from a mile away. I felt a sudden wave of nausea sweep over me.

"You don't look so good! Let's get you inside!" Tony's mother has always watched over me like I was part of her family. She's known me since I was in first grade. I think she was our room mother because I remember the wonderful parties she would cater for our classroom, and I also remember all the times she came to my rescue on the playground.

She placed her hand on my back and guided me through the back entry and down the hall into the women's room where we found a couch. "Just lie down and rest a bit." Eloise wet a few paper towels and placed them over my eyes. "I'll tell Steve where you are, and I'll check on you in a few minutes."

It didn't take long for the queasiness to subside. True to her word, Eloise came back in to check on me about five minutes later. I assured her I'd be fine and that she could return to her work without coddling me. Although it wasn't the ideal way to gain access to the building, I was pleased to be inside. I splashed my face and dabbed it with one of the lush hand towels that were folded and stacked in a neat pile at the corner of the marble countertop. I left a dollar in the tip jar and retreated to the hallway for a quick look around the banquet wing.

I swear I wasn't out there more than a few seconds when Jon Lucas stepped out of a room a few feet away from me. He looked very debonair. Lenore would have approved, and I was torn about how to react. Would she be pleased for him or would she be sad? Reverend Williams insisted she had moved on with her life, so I imagined she would want me to say something to him. But what?

He turned to me with a look of astonishment. "You're here!"

"Well, yes. I am. And may I offer my sincere congratulations on your pending nuptials."

He was surrounded by a herd of groomsmen, and it became very apparent that some of them were tuxedoed security agents as they hastily stepped between me and the groom. I thought I was going to be patted down on the spot.

"Excuse me, gents," Jon said as he pushed his way through the protective barrier of arms four of the men had created as a line of defense. "She's an honored guest."

The men cautiously stepped behind him, remaining watchful as he walked me away from them.

"I am?"

"Of course you are. Although I didn't expect to see you here since you didn't reply to the invitation. Lenore had assured me you would want to come to my wedding. But now she's gone, and here we are. I am so, so sorry, Marlene."

"You sent me an invitation?"

"I take it you didn't receive it?"

"Nope. I haven't seen one yet."

Right then, Steve walked up, his jaw set and his eyes stern. The throng of agents was about to sweep down upon him like locusts when Jon announced, "They're together. He's a guest as well."

Steve sent me a curious glance and looked at Jon. "I am?"

"I assumed you would be attending with Marlene. Matt insisted you wouldn't be able to make it, but I'm glad you both rearranged your schedule. It's so good to see you two as a couple again."

"If that happens—" Steve reached out and shook his hand respectfully, avoiding my eyes. "Well, we'll make sure to send you and your new bride an invitation."

The best man stepped into the hallway and looked at the three of us with wide eyes. "Marlene?"

"Yes, brother, that would be me."

"What are you doing here?" Matt looked at me, then at Steve, over at Jon, then back to me again. "I thought—"

"Great reunion here," Jon interrupted, "but we need to leave." He looked at me. "We're heading out to the church. Do you want to come with us?"

"No, thanks," I said, trying to smile pleasantly. "We'll be right behind you."

"Then I'll see you at the church. And if not then, we'll catch up with each other at the reception later in the afternoon."

He rejoined his group and they walked away together, disappearing around a corner.

Steve headed for the men's room.

I looked up and was a bit alarmed to see Jon jogging back toward me with one of his watchers following behind him. He turned around, and yelled, "Just wait!" to the man who was trying to catch up with him. He obediently jerked to a stop, backed up, and leaned against the wall to wait for the fugitive groom. "These guys never give me a break," he complained as he approached me.

"Marlene, I meant to thank you. I know Lenore never finished the project, but I've been told everything has been delivered. I imagine you're responsible for that...so, please know how much I appreciate everything you've done on my behalf in the absence of my dear friend."

I stood rigid and speechless.

He gave me a hasty hug and briskly marched out of sight with his shadow tagging along so close that I was sure they would trip over each other.

"Glad I didn't wear the tux over here," Steve said as he re-entered the hallway. "I broke a sweat helping those guys load everything up."

I instinctively smoothed his hair. "You didn't have to do

that much. Once you got in, you were safe to wander around."

"See that deputy by the fake palm tree?" He dipped his head and smiled at the uniformed officer standing outside the reception area, acknowledging his existence. "He's been watching me like a hawk since I came in with the catering guy."

"Well, now that he's seen us with Jon, I'm sure he'll leave you alone." I pasted one of Sylvia's flashy smiles on my face and winked at the man. "And a little flirting never hurts."

"Or does it?" Steve said, groaning. The man didn't smile back, but he immediately left his post and headed our way. "Why did you do that, Marlene? You're going to get us thrown out."

My courage wavered. "We could dash out of here through the back door."

"Uh, didn't you see the walkie-talkies? He's not alone. And besides, you're planning to come back here later, right?"

I laughed nervously. "That was the plan, but I've been thinking about skipping the wedding and just staying here. We've already seen Jon and he said we were invited, but I don't need to watch him marry that woman. Attending the reception should be sufficient for my purposes. What about you?"

"Hey, we got married in that little church. Why would I want to taint that memory?"

I leaned in, gave him a friendly peck on the cheek, and whispered in his ear. "That was sweet. Is he still coming?"

"Affirmative. Think fast because the dude's almost here."

"Dude can hear," the officer said, chuckling. "I've got super powers."

Steve said, plunging his hands into his pockets, "Sorry, guy. You're making me nervous."

"Then I've done my job," the man responded. "This place is closed for a private function today. If you're not an invited guest, then we need to rectify that situation and get you out of here. You both need to show me some identification right now, and then you need to show me your invitations."

I crossed my arms over my chest and took a defensive stance. "You did see us talking to Mr. Lucas, right?"

"I did."

"So you're just harassing us?"

"No, ma'am. I'm just doing my job. Mr. Lucas may know you, but I don't."

Steve pulled out his wallet and handed the man his driver's license and military identification card. The deputy studied them both and handed them back as he turned to me. I already had my license ready.

"Married couple, I see."

"Yes," we both replied together.

He addressed Steve. "Thanks for your service to this country, man. I'm a retired Navy man myself."

I relaxed, imagining we were beyond the scary stuff.

"Now, where is your invitation?"

"Invitation." Steve looked at me. "Invitation, Darling?"

I riffled through my purse, as if trying to find the invitation I'd never received. "I thought I brought it with me." I tried to sound disheartened so that he would pity me and leave us alone. I grabbed a stack of receipts and papers from my purse and sorted through them hectically. "I must have left it at home, sir. I just don't see it in here."

"What's this?" he said, pointing to the piece of junk mail

Steve had scribbled on earlier that day.

I showed it to him, pointing at Steve's sloppy handwriting. "This is the time of the ceremony and where it will be held. We were planning to drive over there, after we helped our friend with some last minute preparations here, but I guess we'll just have to wait here now because it's getting too late for us to arrive at the church on time. I wouldn't want Steve to get a speeding ticket just because you made us late."

The officer took the envelope from my hand and turned it over. "You've never opened this, young lady, but I'm thinking this just might be your invitation and passport into this place."

I grabbed it back. "What?"

I glanced over at Steve and he shrugged. He reached into his pocket to take out the pocket knife he normally carries, but he'd left it home since he expected extra security measures at the wedding and after party.

"Here, let me help you." The deputy took out his tactical knife, slit the envelope open and handed it back to me. "You'll notice it has your name on it, Mrs. Lucas, and you can bring a guest." He turned to Steve. "That would be you, Sport."

Steve winced.

I slipped the contents out and stared at a very formal invitation, not so much amazed that it had gone unnoticed and got lost in my spam mail—after all, I hadn't been expecting it, and I had been focusing on other things recently—but I was astounded that Jon had invited me at all.

"Looks like everything's in order, Mr. and Mrs. Wagner. Whatever you decide, I hope you enjoy today's festivities, and I hope you understand that this was all part of my job. I didn't intend to ruin your day."

"Thank you, sir." Steve gave him a polite salute. "And let me thank you for continuing to serve our country in your capacity as an officer of the law." The man saluted back as he went back to his post behind the palm.

"You didn't have to go that far," I told him when the man was out of hearing range.

"Yes, I did," Steve replied. "You'd better keep that invitation handy in case we need it later. Are we going to the wedding or not?"

"How do you vote?"

"I say we stay here and relax."

I took his hand and began walking toward the lobby. "We don't have time to relax, Pokey. Let's go see what other kind of trouble we can get into before the rest of the guests arrive."

⁂

Before we found our way to the entry, I was intercepted by Christine. She looked much more composed than Eloise and she was dressed in a cream-colored jacket and matching skirt with a white blouse, business attire that looked very appropriate for the occasion yet still perfect for setting up the dessert and cake tables. She wore no jewelry except for her wedding ring, and flat shoes since she would be on her feet a good bit of the afternoon. Her long black hair was pulled back in a soft chignon.

"I'm a little startled to see you this early," she said, holding out her hand to greet me. "I'm also very pleased you're here. If you'll follow me to the main cake table, you can have the honor of setting the cake topper your sister made."

I felt a catch in my throat, and I had no idea what to say. "Thank you."

I had assumed she realized I had created the piece when I delivered it to her store. I gave Steve a censorious look to warn him not to correct her. He put his hands behind his back, as if standing at ease, and followed us into the room.

The banquet hall was so splendidly decorated that it took my breath away. Even though I had visited it just two days before, the finished product was nothing less than magnificent. It looked like the kind of room you see in fairytale weddings, and I was prepared to see the prince and princess arrive at any moment. In the corner of the room, wedding planner Mavis Clarke looked like a very self-satisfied fairy godmother.

Hundreds of delicate pink and lavender glass butterflies shimmered above me despite soft lighting from the chandeliers. That's when I noticed the pink and purple spotlights around the room, each pointing at a strand of butterflies or creating a circle of colored light on the floor between each table. Every round dining table was surrounded by 10 chairs, each one draped with lavender linens that matched the tablecloths, tied at the back with a lovely lace bow.

I did a quick count of the room. There were 50 tables, including the head table, so they were expecting to fill the room to capacity. Sylvia's employees were still working like busy bees, setting the last row of tables at the opposite side of the room with fine china, delicate crystal, and lustrous silverware.

Closer to me, the table settings were complete and I was spellbound by their beauty.

At each place, there was a large dark purple dinner dish topped with a matching salad plate, and sitting in the middle of each one was a beautiful hand blown glass figurine. Tall fluted champagne glasses with long amethyst stems were stuffed with napkins that were a mosaic of purple colors. They were precisely folded so they fanned out like beautiful peacock feathers.

Ten white pillar candles in various heights surrounded a four foot tall centerpiece. I had never seen anything so grand. I wondered if Matthew had created the mammoth vases because they were obviously a custom design.

Every vase was about three feet tall and towered above the seating area so that guests could still converse. The dark purple vessel began with a tall pedestal bottom that blew out into a six inch diameter sphere, about half-way up. The massive vase continued upward another foot in an elongated shape that tapered to a four inch mouth. At the top was an enormous arrangement of white chrysanthemums. The centerpieces would have overwhelmed a smaller room, but in the banquet hall they were spectacular.

The three of us continued to weave our way through the room, over the dance floor, and by the long tables that were stacked with hundreds of wrapped miniature cakes.

In the middle of the far wall, the main cake table was covered from left to right with the assorted wedding cakes we had seen at the bakery. Steve studied each one again, and when he looked up, I swear his eyes were glistening. In the center of the table, with three cakes on each side, was the 5-tiered butter sponge cake with white fondant and lavender lace icing.

Christine stooped over and reached beneath the tablecloth, pulling out a familiar cardboard box. She gingerly removed the bubble wrap and handed the topper to me in three pieces.

"Please do this for Lenore," she said.

I cautiously placed the knitted glass base on the top layer, and stepped back. On top of the base, solid glass tubing formed a big heart joined at the middle by a glass bow. From it, I hung two glass cherubs, facing each other. They flew suspended mid-air, with a horn at their lips, blowing a song to announce the marriage.

"Your sister would be so proud of the work you did on her behalf," Steve said. I barely noticed he had put his arm around my waist because I was so flabbergasted that he had given away my secret.

Christine clasped her hands together. "Did you make these beautiful angels?"

"Yes. I didn't have a design to follow, so I'm not sure the topper is exactly the way Lenore imagined it. I decided to add a second angel—one for the bride and one for the groom."

"It is stunning," Steve said.

With tears in her eyes, Christine stepped up to me and gave me an enormous hug. I was hugged more that day than I think I have ever been hugged in my lifetime. "I am sure Mr. and Mrs. Lucas will treasure your gift."

"You haven't told them about this?"

"I promised you I wouldn't."

I had to wonder what project Jon had been referring to in our earlier conversation. If he wasn't talking about the wedding topper, what was he thanking me for? I hadn't given him the boxes full of colored glass. I was taken aback by the realization that Jonathan was as much in the dark as I was.

I turned to Christine. "Please don't ever tell him."

Her eyes were brimming with tears. "Don't worry, Marlene. I believe a promise is a forever pledge."

14

Saturday, April 1, 2000
2:25 p.m.

Our wedding hadn't been extravagant like Jon and Sylvia's event. A select group of guests joined us—I think 23 showed up. As instructed, they all dressed in beach casual.

I had worn a sundress, my favorite thing to wear on any beach, whether in Florida or on a tropical island.

The unceremonious service was just fifteen minutes long.

After our nuptials, we hosted a laidback celebratory party at the shore. Steve was dressed in beige shorts with a black island-formal shirt covered with brown palms and white plumeria flowers. His sun bleached hair and tanned skin were proof that most of his daylight hours were devoted to the beach or surfing before he enlisted in the Navy. Both of us wore flip-flops, which were perfect for our sedate low-country boil dinner.

I was recently graduated from college and our funds were meager, so we didn't buy rings, with the idea that we would buy them later when we had more money. I tucked a fragrant plumeria blossom behind my right ear and Steve gently repositioned the flower behind my left ear when Pastor Williams pronounced us man and wife. The memory still makes me happy.

✖

I couldn't take my eyes off Steve. He looked dapper, so fetching in the formal suit he had changed into for the reception.

For this extraordinary wedding and reception, fancier clothes were a prerequisite.

A few days before, I had slipped into a little boutique near Mama's gallery when I decided to crash Jon's wedding. I saw the dress I wanted the moment I walked inside the store. It was a captivating little number, made of fuchsia jersey material that hugged every contour of my size 12, wide-hipped figure. Was it appropriate for a wedding? I think so. It had three-quarter inch sleeves, a trapeze neckline, and flattering ruching throughout the body and skirt. With it, I wore a chunky gold bead and braid necklace and strappy gold pumps.

Evidently everything came together perfectly because my appearance made Steve's eyes light up when I joined him. Yes, I admit I was delighted that I could still turn his head by just walking in a room.

"Where did you get that suit?" I asked as I moved around him in a clockwise direction, inspecting him from head to toe. He wore a brown herringbone jacket and pants with an off-white shirt and a burgundy tie, and he was extremely handsome.

"The stores were open late last night, so I took a chance and stopped in one of the men's clothing warehouses. I couldn't believe they could fit me from the rack, and they even gave me a good deal." He tugged at his cuffs and posed proudly as I admired him.

We spent a bit of time outside the lobby, watching the people dressed in black scurry around like squirrels after acorns.

So far, there wasn't much media on site, though I imagined they were still at the church. There were two vans outside, each with a single news videographer representing two local Jacksonville television stations. There were also a couple of photographers setting up tripods, but they were kept well away from the lobby entrance. I wondered if they were paparazzi from *The American Interrogator*.

We walked outside again, checking to see if anyone else had arrived from the mass media. I was still appalled that no national newspaper or television crews were covering what I thought was a newsworthy event. I was sure the marriage ceremony was almost over, and I expected guests to start arriving within the hour. We walked back into the lobby and just stood there speechless, looking at each other.

"What gives?" I asked Steve.

"Looks like Jon's security team did their job. Maybe they've pulled it off and the wedding and reception will go unnoticed."

"How can that be? Everyone in Sea Turtle Beach knows about this. You saw the local news is covering it."

"Two stations—the other two didn't show."

"Are you saying this man is potentially a future senator of this state but people don't care that he is getting married?"

"If he was a senator, the press corps might be here. I stress 'might'. If he had done something newsworthy, or had skeletons in his closet, they'd definitely be here. But, Marlene, we're talking about Jonathan Lucas. We grew up with this guy. He can crack a joke, but the man's somewhat staid. He has nothing to hide or show off."

According to Sherry and her mole at that tattletale magazine, he was wrong on that point. I searched around the lot, looking for Sherry or anybody else that I might recognize from local or national news services.

"And look at the bride he picked," Steve continued. "Amy told me she's an RN. So right now they are just a businessman and a nurse getting married. Jon is big news in his hometown, but not ready for primetime."

I felt a little disappointed. I wasn't really disheartened that the press wasn't going to smear this guy, because no matter what I thought of the man, nobody deserves being roasted by a gossipy supermarket tabloid. But I still wondered why Lenore had been sneaking around with Jon, and I was bothered that all of my family assumed I wouldn't attend the wedding since everybody—including my dead sister—had been invited to this not-so-little soiree.

I kept thinking people were hiding secrets from me, and although I'd been questioning myself, Jon's insinuation that I was involved in a secret project fanned the fire within me. I wanted something to happen, and I wasn't sure what that would be, but I was convinced that it was going to transpire on the day of his wedding. Nothing out of the ordinary was going to take place if his sentinels had anything to say. They had even shut down the media.

"Let's go stakeout a table." I grabbed Steve's hand. "If we go now, before the rest of the guests arrive, we can sit close to the wedding party. I want to be up front, near the action, where I can hear and see everything."

He hooked my arm with his and guided me back inside, through the lobby, and down the long hallway that led to the double doors marked *Stellar Room*. Outside of the room, a large changeable message sign announced, 'Welcome Lucas Party—Congratulations Mr. and Mrs. Jonathan Lucas!'

Inside, we were greeted by a woman in a black suit who asked us to present our invitation. After we got by her, another woman dressed in a catering uniform pointed out the open bar and asked if we would like to order drinks. "Thank you, Jillian," Steve replied, having read her name tag. "We won't be ordering alcoholic beverages today, but can we take our seats?"

She pointed to a podium which was staffed by another member of the *Tantalizing* staff. "Ask Mr. Scott. He has the seating chart."

I whispered, "That may be a problem, Steve."

"Why?"

"I never responded to the invitation." How could I if I didn't know it existed?

He placed his hand on my back and guided me toward the podium. "Excuse me, Mr. Scott. I wonder if you can help us."

The older gentleman had been wiping his eyeglasses with his tie and appeared to be embarrassed when my partner in crime spoke up. He put on his glasses. "My word...is that you Wagner?"

Steve smiled and shook the man's hand. "I haven't seen you since I graduated from high school, Mr. Scott. I see life is treating you well."

The man adjusted his tie and ran his fingers over his gray hair to smooth it. "I retired from the school system several years ago, young man. As you can see, I've given up teaching, but I'm really enjoying my retirement. From time to time, I work for this catering company to earn a few extra bucks. I meet a lot of nice people, and I kind of enjoy getting out and about and seeing how the rest of the world lives. Like this high-society dinner today. This is the first time I've ever been in this country club. Imagine having enough money to pay for a membership."

"Anybody can come to this dining room," Steve told him.

"Oh, no, that wouldn't do at all. I'd feel out of place. This is enough for me." Mr. Scott surveyed the elaborately decorated room with admiration. "I'm an old guy on a fixed income. I'd rather get paid to work here. I can buy a lot of early bird specials with the money I earn today, especially if I get tipped. Now, young fella, how can I help you today?"

"My wife and I are here as guests, but we're surprising the groom who is a childhood friend. We didn't respond to the invitation because we wanted it to be a secret that we would be here. You won't find our names on your chart. Can you help us find a table —something close to the bride and groom?"

Mr. Scott looked around the room. "I can't do that without permission, as much as I'd like to help you out. But if I can find somebody in charge, I will see if they can assist you."

Before Steve could respond, the man walked out of the room.

Everywhere we went, somebody knew Steve. I looked at him in wonderment. "Who is he?"

"He was my homeroom teacher for three years, and he taught me U.S. History. I'm glad he's here today. I'm sure Elmore Scott will love telling his grandkids about seeing a real live senatorial candidate in person."

We waited by the podium, Steve more patient than me, until the man returned.

"Hang in there. I found somebody who will help you when she finds a moment to come in here, but I have to warn you that the two of you will be lucky to get a seat by the rear exit. I was told every table is full. And that thing you said about getting close to the front, well, that's not going to happen. The front tables are for the families of the bride and groom, and there are a lot of dignitaries and influential people coming to this affair. They'll get the good seats, and ordinary people will get shoved to the back."

I fingered the invitation in my hand, still amazed that I had one, and hoped for the best. Steve gave me a reassuring smile and stood in his normal at ease stance. Neither of us talked and the elderly gentleman fidgeted, furtively glancing up to check on us now and then.

Eventually, Mavis Clarke showed up in an elegant designer dress and with an over-inflated ego. It was obvious that she had been working since the early morning hours because she already looked a little weary, and she didn't even try to smile. I was sure she didn't have the time or inclination to fuss over us, so I started to think about what Plan B would be if we got tossed from the room.

She greeted both of us with a halfhearted handshake. "I understand you didn't take the time to RSVP," she said dully. "I may not be able to help you, but you can wait back here while the place fills up, and if somebody doesn't show, you can take their seat. Unfortunately, you may not be able to sit together. I apologize for the awkwardness of that situation."

She held out her hand to me. "May I see your invitation, please?" I handed it to her and she boorishly turned the envelope over to read my address. She studied my name intently, looked up at me, and then back to the envelope. When she looked up again, I marveled as her expression changed and her demeanor softened, miraculously transforming the tactless woman into a radiant and obliging hostess who effusively welcomed both of us with arms that enveloped Steve and me with more uninvited hugs.

"Marlene! I am so very happy to meet you! I have heard so much about you from your sister!" Then, just as quickly, her countenance sobered, her voice cracked, and she tried to console me about my family's recent tragedy. "I know you must be devastated," she said sympathetically.

I wondered how well this chaotic woman really knew Lenore.

Steve thanked Mr. Scott for his assistance and tucked a $20 bill in the palm of his hand.

Mavis marched us to the front of the room. "This is your table," she announced, "and these are your seats." She pulled out two chairs and I stared at the name cards that sat behind our plates. Sure enough, both our names were hand-inked in ornate calligraphic writing.

"How did this happen?" We were to sit at the table located to the left of the bridal party.

"Your sister promised you would be here. I assumed that hadn't changed, even when you didn't respond to the invitation." She smiled at us and walked back to the podium to oversee the seating of guests who were now trickling in.

Steve walked around the table, reading each name card out loud. We were to sit with my parents, Matt and Monica, and the pastor and his wife, Gail.

"Matt is the best man, so why is he sitting with us?" I

wondered out loud.

Steve said, "In the absence of your sister, I'm sure he wanted to sit with his wife and your parents, to diminish any uneasiness they might feel."

Steve walked behind me and pointed at a place card to my right that was inscribed *Josh Fleming*.

I looked up at him and asked, "Who is that?"

He shrugged, then reached over, picked up the card beside it, and dutifully handed it to me. A shiver crept up my spine and tears spilt down my cheeks as I read the graceful inscription: *Lenore Terhune*.

I went to the women's room to freshen my face after crying. On that day, a teenaged attendant was on duty to tend to the guests' needs, such as toiletries and fresh guest towels at the sink. She had even provided a variety of perfumes that were set out on a mirrored tray.

My cell phone rang. Sherry's voice was muffled. I had to move to a more open place to hear her voice. "Hold on!" I tossed a dollar bill into the tip jar and walked through the lobby and outside to a spot where I got better reception.

"Where are you?" she asked. "I kept waiting for you, but you're a no-show."

"I skipped the wedding and went directly to the reception. Can you believe I received an invitation? I didn't find it until this morning. So, I'm on the inside now."

"That's great, Marlene! You didn't miss much here. I'm told the wedding was perfect, but the paparazzi didn't show up so there wasn't much excitement outside where I was stationed. But now, something is definitely up and I thought I should warn you."

I felt a little uneasy, but there still wasn't anything

happening in the parking lot, under the portico, or inside the lobby.

The two videographers were packing up their gear, and the few photographers that had come were milling around, talking to each other. Then I saw both men from the television stations walk over to a police officer, and the photographers ran over to join them. When they were finished conversing, one cameraman returned to his van and stood watching the lobby. The other started raising the satellite dish on his truck.

"Only a few photographers and two television crews showed up here, Sherry. They looked like they were packing up, but now they seem to be staying. What's new on your end?"

"When the wedding party left, people here started packing up to leave. Then I got a phone call from Donna. She told me to rush over to the country club because something big is going to happen. I'm heading to my car now, but I may not get there on time. I'll be on the outside and you'll be on the inside. I'm sure somehow, somewhere we'll see something."

"But what are we looking for?"

"No idea. Just keep an eye out. If you see something, call me."

As much as I wanted to wait outside to watch for trouble brewing, I knew I was expected inside. "I can't. I should return to my family. Call me when you get here. If I don't pick up, just wait and I'll call you back."

"Affirmative," she said. "I'll catch you later."

Automobiles were now arriving in a steady stream and a long line of traffic was growing steadily. Guests pulled their cars up to the front entrance, and security personnel examined their invitations and credentials with meticulous concentration. After the guests were vetted by the sentries in black garb, a uniformed valet presented them with a receipt and delivered their vehicles to a designated car park.

When I reentered the banquet room, the orchestra—yes, an orchestra, not just a cover band—was playing a selection of soft background music that was intended to create an intimate dining atmosphere. The entire ensemble, including the two women in the violin section, wore black, save for the vocalist, a 40'ish gentleman dressed in a white three-quarter length coat. He performed a sweet rendition of *Fly Me To The Moon* as I strolled back to our table, stopping along the way to acknowledge some friends and social acquaintances. I even stopped by the parents' table, which was situated to the right of the bridal party's long table.

The room was already more than half full. By the time I returned to our table, the remaining guests were arriving en masse and my parents were seated to the left of Steve chatting with him amicably. I still wondered how we found ourselves sitting so close to the bride and groom, but my mother explained it was because Matt would be giving the traditional wedding toast. That made sense to me.

Soon after, my brother and sister-in-law appeared at our table followed by Reverend and Mrs. Williams a few minutes later. They both smiled at me, and Pastor Williams gave me a favorable nod to indicate he approved of my decision to attend the dinner. Although Lenore's chair and the one next to it were still unoccupied, nothing was said by any of us.

The conductor tapped on his lectern and the orchestra played a song to welcome the bridal party.

As each bridesmaid or groomsman entered the room, they were introduced by the male vocalist and welcomed with a smattering of applause.

When the bridal party was seated, the orchestra played *Could I Have This Dance* and all of the guests stood and applauded. The newlyweds waltzed into the room and onto the dance floor.

I turned to my mother. "Look how they're dressed!"

Mama glanced at me with inquisitive eyes. "Whatever do you mean, Marlene? This is what they wore for the ceremony. Weren't you there?"

Steve answered before I could open my mouth and stick my foot where it didn't belong. "We had a little mishap. I lost the invitation and it took us so long to find it that we had to skip the wedding and just head over here."

"Oh, I see." Mama looked at Daddy and winked, and he just smiled, saying nothing.

Jon and Sylvia and their wedding party formed a line and graciously greeted every guest with a smile and handshake.

While they held court, my father took my mother's hand and they went from table to table, talking to a multitude of friends.

Twenty minutes later, Pastor Williams stood, clinked his water glass with a silver spoon, and the room hushed as he offered a blessing before the meal.

I've attended many weddings parties in the past, but this feast didn't require invitees to stand in long buffet lines. In fact, every table had an appointed server that tended to that particular table's guests. I couldn't even imagine the amount of money expended on behalf of the bride and groom, all of it just to create a memorable extravaganza.

The food was delightful. I had been fed by Eloise Gilman many times as I grew up, but this meal was extraordinary.

All of the wait staff was attired in formal black attire, but they wore name tags instead of the company insignia.

During cocktail hour, they strolled through the aisles, offering up a diverse selection of eye-catching hors d'oeuvres displayed on shiny silver trays—crispy little phyllo dough triangles called Spanakopitas, stuffed with spinach and feta cheese; Florida sushi rolls; Thai chicken skewers with peanut sauce; cocktail shrimp in horseradish sauce, served in a shot glass with a celery stick; and warm crab cake bites served with a tangy dipping sauce. There were more to sample, but I fought hard to control myself so I'd still have an appetite for dinner.

Jillian came back to the table several times. "Can I get you a beverage, sir?" She overtly flirted with Steve.

"Schweppes for two, please."

I looked at her and smiled. "We'll let you know when we need another." Then I turned to Steve. "When did you stop drinking?"

"When you quit smoking. I meant what I said, Marlene."

"You did that for me?" I was taken aback by his act of friendship and he won immediate brownie points.

"It's obvious I have a problem with liquor. I apologize for drinking beer in front of you, and for demeaning you about your alcohol dependence. That was really very inconsiderate of me, but I thought I was trying to help you. Now I realize I was wrong. We both have our demons to fight. I never drank as much as I have since we split up. Not your fault, Marlene. I did it to myself. But I'm getting older, and I hope a bit wiser. The truth is, I'm working hard to change my life."

"I think I'm doing the same thing," I admitted. "I haven't missed the cigarettes, and that's a surprise. They were always a crutch, like the booze. Something I turned to when I was nervous, unhappy or bored."

We toasted each other with tumblers of club soda on ice. It was another small step in healing ourselves and our relationship. We were becoming friends again.

It was a bizarre turn of events for me. Not just the shift in our relationship, but also how my day had progressed as well.

I'd been on edge for weeks, and when I'd left the house that morning, I'd never imagined me sitting at a table at Jon's wedding, enjoying Pistachio Crusted White Fish ladled with a Sun-dried Tomato Cream. It was scrumptious. At Steve's behest, I also sampled his Mayport Shrimp Creole served over rice. When I took a look around the table, I realized almost every plate had something different on it—steak, grilled chicken, fish, prime rib—and every offering looked delicious.

Matthew proposed his wedding toast, the bride and groomed shared a traditional dance with her father and his mother, and when the band leader invited the guests to join them on the dance floor, I was swept out of my chair, complaining all the way, by my former husband.

The music was gentle and I eventually relaxed enough to enjoy a slow dance, in Steve's arms again. Beside us, the new twosome danced and stared lovingly into each other's eyes. Their vintage attire wasn't to my taste, but I knew I was being hypercritical.

The groom wore a long jacket over matching trousers made of shiny pin-striped material. It was reminiscent of a 1930's zoot suit. Sylvia wore a sleeveless peach-colored cocktail dress with a high collar that wrapped around her neck. The fitted skirt-style bottom ended just above her knees with a large flouncy fishtail running around the hem. It was the perfect dress for the music that followed. What caught my eye was her hat. It wasn't the traditional tiara or wedding veil. Instead, the bride had chosen an ivory headpiece which featured a large feather flower that had an oval rhinestone at its center. Around her head swooped circles of long white goose feathers.

The orchestra was brilliant. They specialized in swing music, but they also played polkas, waltzes, and almost anything by special request.

The dance floor was jam-packed and we moved out of the crowd to join my family and friends back at our table. From there, we watched both young and old people dance to a variety of nostalgic big band arrangements that evoked memories of Benny Goodman, Glenn Miller, Tommy Dorsey and Duke Ellington. The walls resonated with the sounds of three trombones, four saxophones, a clarinet, and an upright bass that played repeated riffs to propel the faster songs. I especially enjoyed the country club's reverberating grand piano with its keyboard under the skilled fingers of a gifted pianist.

Tears bit my eyes and I felt guilt-ridden for enjoying myself. Lenore had dreamed of a wedding like this, but Sylvia danced around the room with Jon, and my sister was just a mere memory as he moved forward in his life without her.

I reminded myself that I was there to snoop around, to uncover new clues, and to ask more questions, but I doubted a room full of fully-fed, appreciative wedding guests would give me any pointers.

My heart fluttered as my father stood and offered his hand to my mother when a female vocalist joined the band and they struck up the first chords of Cole Porter's *Begin the Beguine*. Mama responded with a loving smile, and gracefully strolled with him to the dance floor. They remained there when the singer segued into *Night and Day*, and my mother dreamily positioned her cheek against my father's chest.

Steve led me back to the dance floor. "This is nice," he said, nuzzling his chin on top of my head. "I remember this."

I recalled the feeling as well.

"We need to talk," I said.

"What about?'

"About us."

He took my chin and raised my face so that we stood eye-to eye, still dancing together. "Us? Are we a couple now?"

I smiled coyly. "We've been a couple for a long time. I just needed to be reminded."

He leaned down and placed a tender kiss on my forehead. "I agree."

"I need to apologize—"

He walked me to the edge of the dance floor.

"No apologies necessary, Babe. We both made mistakes. It's not an easy life, being married to a sailor. I know that. I always hated leaving you behind when I went out to sea, especially when you were dealing with one of the biggest losses of your life. The death of our baby was a tragedy for both of us, and it changed us. In fact, it destroyed our marriage because we didn't know how to help each other and we gave up. Now we have been given an opportunity to unravel our problems. We'll talk, and we'll see how we can work together as a team and fix things. But we won't rush ahead this time, okay?"

I gazed into his indulgent eyes. "No rush. We'll do it right this time. Slow and easy."

That's when Jon appeared by my side and asked me to be his partner. I felt a little apprehensive, but I honestly didn't know how to refuse politely.

We danced to an upbeat tune, and he thanked me again for attending the wedding. "You're welcome," I said, deciding not to tell him I had missed the ceremony. "Everything is lovely."

"I really appreciate that you brought the cake topper. Christine had promised us she had a special topper for the cake, but she just told me today that Lenore made it."

I was shocked. "You didn't know about it?"

"I did not. I had ordered the glass ornaments for our wedding guests, but I never imagined Lenore made every one of them herself."

"How do you know that?"

"Your brother told me."

"How about the garland overhead?"

"Tony says he helped her with the butterflies. Speaking of Tony, I wonder where he is today. He was an invited guest."

I wondered too. "Perhaps he lost his invitation like I did."

"Perhaps."

We continued to dance, and I noticed Sylvia was watching us.

"When are you going to introduce me to your lovely bride?"

Jon looked incredulous. "You've never met Sylvia?"

"No, I haven't, so this is your opportunity to acquaint us with each other."

Did I really want to meet her? Not so much. But meeting the effervescent bride gave me an easy way to move away from that uncomfortable conversation and get back to Steve.

We found Sylvia talking with her parents, so I was introduced to them as well. The four of us chatted cordially for about ten minutes, and I will admit that Jon's new wife effused warmth and hospitality. She was welcoming, alluring, friendly, and even funny. Her eyes actually twinkled, and her broad smile didn't bother me anymore. Whether her charm was real or feigned I didn't know.

I was also introduced to several members of Jon's campaign staff. They smiled courteously but said absolutely nothing. Not one of them even said hello. As I continued talking to Sylvia and her mother, I felt Roger Cane scrutinizing me. Why was Jon's campaign manager so interested in me? I felt naked, and my neck actually tingled.

Matt eventually called the couple to the dance floor and announced that it was time for Sylvia to throw the bouquet.

I returned to our table and my mother insisted that I join the throng of younger women in the center of the room. Monica pulled me with her to stand in front of the bride. Then she scurried back to the table.

The room hushed.

Sylvia kissed the bouquet, let out a whoop, and threw it over her shoulder, where it landed at my feet. I was tackled from all sides by squealing women, but I came up intact with the bouquet in my hands.

The room erupted with whistles and enthusiastic applause. "Take the hint!" one of my high school friends yelled from the back of the room, and the onlookers cheered.

I was appalled. How could I lose control and act so

carefree at Jon's wedding? Mortified, I returned to my seat and hoped people would stop staring at me. I felt Lenore's presence in every corner of the room.

My brother laughed as he walked by me, and he gave me a brotherly pat on the shoulder. He winked at Steve, but Steve just studied my face.

Matt pulled a chair into the center of the room and told Sylvia to sit down. Even the sober men in the room left their dignity and decorum at the door as they began to whistle, clap and chant.

Only Jonathan displayed a hint of self-respect as he kneeled at his new bride's feet. His cheeks reddened and his eyes remained cast down as he stared at Sylvia's expensive high-heeled shoes. She mussed his hair. When he looked up, she winked and smiled seductively as she pulled up the hem of her dress to reveal her right knee. They both snickered as he removed the ruffled garter.

Steve joined the swarm of potential grooms who were waiting for the toss. But when the garter was released into the air, every man stepped back and watched as the elastic band sailed into my ex-husband's waiting hands. The men applauded, the women shouted, and my mother mouthed the words "I'm so happy!" when I turned to face her.

My insides twisted into knots.

The male vocalist then announced the cutting of the cake and the impending ritual made my heart race. It was all too much. I'd tried so hard to remain calm and blend in with the rest of the guests, but I needed respite. I left the room and headed for the lobby, deciding it wasn't necessary to be on hand when Sylvia saw the glistening angels on the top of the main cake; and I didn't need to be there when they smooshed the expensive butter cake into each other's mouths.

I just needed to be alone to recover from a grueling afternoon of pasted-on smiles and fighting back tears when acquaintances commiserated about our family's awful experience.

15

I sat on a plush curved divan and settled back on its comfy flowered pillows. Anxiety threatened to overtake me. I sifted through my purse, fretfully searching to see if I'd left just one cigarette inside and found none.

Above me, a large sky dome dimly lit the room with the last rays of Florida sunlight as evening was upon us. The rest of the room's light came from table lamps interspersed throughout the lobby. In the rush of the past couple of days, I hadn't taken the time to appreciate the entrance to the country club. Rich woods, marble flooring, palm trees, and custom-crafted tropical furniture created a casual atmosphere. A translucent glass wall was covered with a gentle waterfall. The fountain acted as a partition between the front foyer and the reception atrium.

To my right was a dark teak concierge desk, where a thirtyish woman in a crimson red jacket congenially answered questions and helped visitors navigate around the expansive multi-winged, multi-tiered building. Between me and the cushioned chairs across from me sat a long, low, woven wicker table with a row of fat pillar candles down its middle.

It was as inviting and luxurious as any five-star resort I've had the pleasure to stay in, and I began to relax. Then I saw Matt and my shoulders tensed as he approached me.

"Do you want a piece of cake, Sis? They all look delicious."

I was relieved he didn't berate me for leaving the room, and he took the high road by not mentioning the cake topper at all. I wondered if he knew I had made it, but I didn't ask.

"I came out here for a smoke, but I didn't bring any cigarettes." He reached for his breast pocket and I said, "Thanks, but I'm okay. I've been trying to quit."

He reached inside his pocket, and presented me with a stick of chewing gum. "This might help. It helped me when I quit smoking last year."

I didn't know he'd quit, but it gave me hope. We've always been competitive, and the knowledge that he'd overcome a vice he'd had since he was a teen made me more determined and strong-willed. If he could quit, I could quit too.

He sat beside me on the sofa. "I miss Lenore."

My emotions expended, I didn't cry. I looked at my brother and realized his eyes were filled with unspilled tears. I leaned to him and whispered, "There's no recovering from grief, I'm afraid, but I'm told there is recuperation."

"Who promised you that?"

"Our pastor." I studied my hands and recalled my earlier conversation with Reverend Williams. "I'm sure I'll be talking to him a lot in the coming months."

Matt agreed. "Sometimes I can't find my own answers, but he always seems to have the right words, or he can tell me where to find them." He looked around the room, then back at me. "Our sister taught me about many things. She's the one that talked me into returning to church. She's the one that explained to me that the only way to recover from pain is to release it."

I looked at him, still holding back his tears. "I see you're still working on that one."

"Yes, I am," he said. He choked back a sob and wiped away the few tears that had escaped in a stream down his cheeks.

I scooted closer to him. "You're a good brother, Matt. I don't tell you enough, but I hope you know I love you." I walked over to a box of tissues on a wall-side table and brought a few back to him, waiting patiently as he cleared his nose. "I apologize for being so stubborn."

He managed a feeble laugh. "We're more alike than you think."

"How is that?"

"Lenore also taught me about forgiveness. I had an awful time forgiving Jonathan, but she insisted that I should do it. She said, 'If I can do it, you certainly can.' And after a time, I realized she was right. It has taken me a few years to trust him again. You know I can be pig-headed, but our sister kept scolding me and reminding me that I had been friends with Jon way before they became a couple."

"Did you know she was making all of those glass pieces for his wedding reception?"

"I did."

"Did you help her?"

"With some of it, but she wanted to tackle most of it. Jon had asked her to do it as a favor, and she felt it was her last step in mending their friendship. She was determined to reclaim her life. She told me she had spent a long time pretending to be happy, but that she had finally found the man she loved and she needed to tie up loose ends before she could start a new life."

"Sounds like something I've said recently."

"I want you to understand that I haven't wanted to butt heads with you, Marlene. It's just my need to protect you, because I obviously didn't protect Lenore enough."

I looked around the room, and realized most of the security people had disappeared from the area, except for one that was standing fairly close to us. I wondered if he'd been listening, and thought we should change the subject until we were alone.

Matt leaned in to me. "You need to stop playing private eye, Sis. I now realize there's more going on than either of us knows about. I've been told to let the investigation go where it needs to go, which means we both need to stand down."

"Who told you that?"

"I can't tell you who I've been talking to—not just yet."

"Are you saying Lenore died from an overdose of drugs?"

"That's what I've been told, but I also know that the M.E. is waiting for results from some laboratory down South."

"Were you there when the body was discovered?"

"Let's not talk about that here, Marlene. Just be patient. I'm sure we'll know more in a few days, and then we'll get together and discuss everything privately."

My phone vibrated and I checked to see who was calling. As expected, it was Sherry Hill. "Anything new?" I asked her as Steve joined my brother and they both pretended not to listen.

"Yes! I'm outside. Are they getting ready to leave?"

"I don't think so. Why do you ask?"

"A slew of police cars just pulled up in front of us, and they were followed by a couple of black SUV's. We were all deliberating about what might be happening inside."

"Who is 'we'?"

"Me, a couple of dozen photographers, and several television crews. Even CNN is here now."

"Oh, really?"

"Do you think they're heading out?"

"No sign yet."

Sherry let out a disappointed huff. "Call me when you have news."

My brother looked at me with squinting, prying eyes. "I'll do that. We'll chat later."

Steve looked at me suspiciously. "Who was that?"

"It was Anita, the young lady that works in Mama's shop." I lied without flinching even a tiny bit.

"Is there something wrong?"

"No, no...she has a big crush on Jon, and she's a little jealous that she didn't get to come to the wedding. She wants me to drop by the shop later this week to tell her all about details."

Just as I stood up to make my way back into the reception hall, I glanced across the room and saw an attractive man with dark wavy hair enter the room. He was wearing dress whites—a naval uniform intended for formal occasions. He stepped up to the front desk and presented the clerk with his invitation. I nudged Steve and when he looked over at the man, he smiled broadly.

"I know him!"

Of course, he did. Steve knows everybody.

"That's Dutchy!"

He scrambled out of his seat and sailed across the room, slapping the sailor on the back. They high-fived each other, a manly custom that isn't exactly suitable in a formal setting, but as I scanned the room, I realized nobody else seemed to care.

Matt looked at me quizzically and I shrugged.

As they approached us, Steve announced, "This is Dutchy. We've served together on Big John, but he's now stationed out of Norfolk." The man removed his cap, greeted me enthusiastically and said, "Nice to meet you finally, Marlene."

I suddenly felt panicked.

He shook my brother's hand heartily, and Matt began a conversation that was just un-deciphered code in my head.

"How well do you know him?" I whispered to Steve.

"I'm acquainted with him, but I wouldn't call him a friend."

"Why is that?"

He looked at me and indulged me with a crooked smile. "The JFK is an aircraft carrier. You know how big it is. With more than 10,000 souls on board, how many of them do you think I know by their full name? We were tasked to different parts of the ship, so we ran into each other a couple of times, and I can't even remember what we were doing."

"You called him Dutchy."

"I did. That's his nickname."

"He acts like he knows me."

"You do now."

I shot Steve a cutting look, and scrutinized the sailor's name tag.

FLEMING.

Suddenly, I recalled the imprinted place card at our table.

Josh Fleming.

How did this man earn a seat by my sister? And then it clicked. *Josh something.* Joshua Fleming, my sister's computer pen pal, and possible suitor, had finally made an appearance.

"Do you see his name tag?" I spoke under my breath.

"I do."

"He has short dark hair, but did you notice it's also wavy?"

He looked at the man and checked out his hair. "Well, yes. Now that you've pointed it out, I guess it is. And if you will also notice, I am a guy. I might give a dude props when he's been working hard, and I might even compliment him on a new tattoo, but as a rule, I don't notice too much about a man's hair unless it's spiked up or colored purple and pink."

"Men." I shook my head. "You can name any car, explain every aircraft, shoot any firearm, and you can even dive deep in the sea, but you don't pay attention to the little details."

"I beg your pardon," he said, losing his smile. "I know plenty of details. It's just that sometimes what a man thinks is important, a woman doesn't, and vice versa. It's what makes the world go round. You're a girl, I'm a guy, and we think differently at times. But that's okay, as long as we have the same values."

I had to smile at that because he was right. We both love God, our families, and our country. We believe in honor and integrity, and we stand up for what we believe. This applies to him more than me because I never had the guts to join the

Navy, even though we had discussed joining together when we graduated from high school. I went on to college and my high school sweetheart joined the military and made a career out of what originally was intended to be a four-year tour. I have proudly watched him move up through the ranks.

We both continued our covert conversation as we followed the two men down the hall toward the bar. Steve leaned toward me and whispered, "Another way men are different than women is that we don't take hints well. We like you to spell things out. So what were you trying to get through to me a few minutes ago? I'm sensing that I've been missing one of your not-so-subtle suggestions again."

I wanted to laugh because he was right on target, but I had to make my point before we joined them for a drink. "What was the name on the place card beside my seat?"

"Josh Fleming."

"Josh *Something*," I said, emphasizing the last word.

Steve closed in on the two men, pushed his way between them, and asked, "How do you know Marlene?"

The sailor stopped, turned around, and asked me, "You are Marlene Wagner? Am I right?"

"I am."

"I'm Josh—your sister's boyfriend, and I'm sure she's wondering where I am since I arrived late. By the way, where is she?"

Matt's jaw dropped.

Josh followed my amazing ex-husband into the cocktail lounge where Steve ordered Ginger Ale for everyone. He forced a smile and asked, "Did you fly back to Norfolk when we came into port?"

"Yes, sir, I did," Josh said with enthusiasm. "I went up

there to check on my folks. Virginia Beach is my hometown, so when I had a chance to transfer, I did. When I got back, I shipped all of my stuff to Virginia. Norfolk is the home port for the USS Harry Truman. We'll be deploying in November."

Josh leaned closer in, whispering to all of us. "I imagine you all have guessed that I'm planning to ask Lenore to marry me. I'm just waiting for the right time." When he looked at me, I hoped he didn't notice the tears forming in my eyes.

Matt stood up. "Sorry, but I've gotta get back to the reception." My brother rigidly shook Josh's hand, and abruptly left the room.

"I want to ask your father for Lenore's hand in marriage," Josh announced. "I want to do this the old-fashioned way. Your sister has said she is willing to follow me to Virginia. I'd like to take her there as my wife."

Steve glanced at me, then back at Josh. "Have you spoken to her recently?"

Josh sat back in his chair. "We haven't been in touch for almost a month, and I'm anxious to see her. She said she would be very busy with a special project—something to do with this wedding."

The bartender served our drinks, positioning them in front of each of us, with the extra one placed in the middle of the table.

Josh asked the man, "Have you seen Lenore Terhune?"

"No, sir, I've never met her."

The bartender walked away and Josh scrutinized the room. "I wonder where she is."

Anxiety overtook me, and I pondered what else I could

say to delay that awful moment of truth. I felt sorry for him, but at the same time, I wondered if his demeanor was a farce. Could he be responsible for her death? Was he lying?

He turned around to face me. "I think it's remarkable that Lenore can stay friends with her former fiancé. She is strong, independent, and very forgiving of others. She knows what she wants from life, and she understands that everyone makes mistakes. That is why I want to marry her—your sister is a special woman."

I took a sip of my Ginger Ale and said nothing.

"Lenore had hoped I would be able to attend this event, but she wasn't sure I could get back here from Virginia in time. So I laid low and decided to sneak in on her. That way this whole weekend will be special, because I'll propose to her before I head up North."

I felt nauseous and wanted to run from the room, like my brother. Josh Fleming had a lot of questions. Whether he was guilty or innocent, we needed to give him answers in order to determine what happened next.

But a wedding celebration wasn't the ideal place to tell him about something I still hadn't come to terms with—the reality that Lenore was forever gone. I couldn't imagine how he was going to handle such heart-wrenching news.

I looked at him and wondered what I should say. The whole situation was unpleasant. Would he be overwhelmed with grief, or would he feign surprise?

Steve stood up and put his arm around the man's shoulders. "Have you had dinner?"

Josh looked at Steve with questioning eyes. "I was planning to meet Lenore…"

"Lenore isn't here right now," Steve said as he removed

the truck keys from his pocket. "But if you'll come with me, I'll find you a bite to eat since they've already served dinner here."

Josh looked at me, as if asking for permission to leave the premises.

"Go ahead," I encouraged him. "I'll catch up with you guys later."

Then, before he could protest, I walked away, silently blessing Steve for taking the burden from my shoulders.

16

As I approached the ballroom, Sylvia approached me at a quick clip, with Monica trailing behind her. "Have you seen Jon?" Her poster girl smile was missing, and I recognized a hint of angst.

"The last time I saw him, he was with you," I answered, wondering why she looked so distraught.

Without another word, she traipsed off in the opposite direction, her skirt swishing wildly.

Monica stayed. "He left the room a while ago with two members of his security staff. Now she can't find him and she's getting worried."

I followed my sister-in-law into the banquet hall and returned to my table.

Monica scrutinized the crowded room. In a far corner, Matt was speaking with Roger Cane.

When she joined them, they conferred in clandestine whispers for a few moments. I observed both men's demeanor. Matt looked concerned, but Cane was visibly agitated. He practically flew out of the room, with Monica and Matt swooping out of sight with him.

The rest of the guests were oblivious to the shifting atmosphere.

The orchestra continued to play, couples continued to dance, kids went back for second servings of wedding cake, and Reverend Williams' conversation with my parents was uninterrupted.

I walked out of the room calmly and mostly unnoticed, but as soon as I was out of sight, I began snooping again. I wished my cohort was by my side, but by that time, I imagined Steve was immersed in a difficult dialogue with my sister's distraught fiancé.

Matt and Monica were standing at the far end of the hallway, conversing with several members of Jon's staff. Cane was nowhere in sight. I thought to disrupt their conference, but my brother shot me a glance that said 'stay away', so I did.

Back in the lobby, I walked around the waterfall, and stared out the glass entry doors. A few spectators had already gathered curbside near the photographers, claiming spots where they could watch the couple depart for their European honeymoon.

Two slack-jawed men disembarked from one of the SUV's and marched through the lobby, turning at the hallway on the left. They were dressed in non-descript clothes.

I walked to the middle of the lobby and watched as they stepped into a conference room, where they stayed for about thirty minutes.

I paced around the room a few times, speculated about the change in events, and then walked outside to call Sherry. I hung up before she answered when I saw movement inside the lobby.

Mr. and Mrs. Jonathan Lucas walked across the room, arm in arm, contrived smiles on their faces. Behind them, the two men, several deputies, and a multitude of people in black kept close proximity. They walked out the door and several paparazzi broke through police lines, dashing under the portico. The security agents cut them off and blocked their way.

Photographers furiously snapped pictures. One shouted, "I'm from *The American Interrogator*! Is it true you were having an affair?"

Sylvia stared down at the ground.

"Of course not!" Jon responded.

A reporter bellowed, "Are you with the FBI?"

And Sherry's squeaky-little voice screeched, "Are you arresting Jonathan Lucas for the murder of Lenore Terhune?"

One agent pushed Jon and Sylvia into the back of the first SUV. The other said, "No comment!" and got into the driver's side of the same vehicle.

Three more men and a female agent had been standing near the second vehicle. They climbed into their seats and hurriedly followed the lead car off the property.

Sherry appeared at my side. "Looks like the FBI to me."

The photographers across from the parking lot scrambled for photos, then ran for their vehicles. Journalists talked on their cell phones, videographers stood in front of the security staff asking unanswered questions, and news anchors reported the story by a live feed via satellite dishes and camera phones.

Roger Cane stepped outside, followed by an entourage of

campaign aides, where he was met by a throng of information-starved journalists.

"Can you tell us what just happened?"

"Do you have a statement?"

"Where did they take Mr. Lucas?"

"Will this end his run for the senate?"

The media were like hungry vultures anxiously picking at a freshly killed carcass.

As I walked back inside, I heard Cane raise his voice above the din. "We need you to leave the premises quickly, ladies and gentlemen of the press, so that our wedding guests can leave this venue. Please respect their privacy. Most of our guests aren't aware of what just occurred. Let's not ruin their evening."

Another, unfamiliar voice added, "We'll be issuing a press release from our office within the hour. Right now we don't know any more details. As soon as we do, we'll announce a press conference, and at that time, we'll certainly entertain your questions."

Emotionally and physically exhausted, I turned and saw my brother sitting on a couch in the center of the lobby. Matt was hunched over, his arms pressed against his knees, and his shoulders trembled as he cried convulsively. Monica stood stoically beside him, staring at his back.

I was devastated. I had come to the wedding reception looking for answers, and I still had none.

Steve had just stepped out of his car to purchase fuel at a gas station when I reached him by phone.

My nerves frayed, I remember hearing my voice warble as I tried to talk. "Honey, something has happened here that you won't believe."

"Is everything okay?" he asked.

"Two intimidating men just took Jon out of here. I'm pretty certain they're from some law enforcement agency, and I think he may be under arrest."

"I'm sorry I'm not there with you, Marlene."

"Can you come back to give me a ride home?"

He hesitated as he considered our options. "Josh deserves answers," he said. "I don't want to leave him hanging, and wondering whether Lenore dumped him. Can you get a ride home with your brother? We're almost at Amy's house."

"Don't worry about me," I answered, feeling just a tad let down. "This is going to be a long, hard night. I'll call you later so we can fill each other in on the events of the day."

On my way to the lobby, I dialed Sherry. "Don't leave yet. I need a ride!"

17

Saturday, April 1, 2000
8:06 p.m.

"It's been a long day for me. I'm heading to bed," Monica said when she called.

"And where is my brother?"

"He's gone out for a while. We'll see you in the morning, when we're all fresh. I've never seen such a wedding...and that ending! I don't know what to think, but the television is buzzing with theories. CNN threw together a full hour of special coverage, including a short bio of Jon, a timeline of his career and foray into politics, vague background on the bride, and footage shot outside the country club today. They had a close-up of Sylvia's face. She looked thunderstruck!"

I said nothing.

"You might want to tune in, Marlene. It's a call-in show and the telephones are hot with viewers debating whether Jon is guilty or not."

"Guilty of what?"

"They say he's being questioned about his relationship with your sister, and that the FBI is involved because he is in the middle of a political campaign. Matt left when they presented a short piece about Lenore. He walked out of here without saying a word about where he was going."

"So, they're insinuating that my sister and Jon were having an affair?"

"I guess so. You know how people get a kick out of intrigue, especially salacious gossip about celebrities and dignitaries."

I was annoyed. "Jonathan Lucas is neither a celebrity, nor a man of any actual notoriety."

Unless he was elected as our state senator or arraigned for my sister's murder.

Bereaved, insulted, angry—I was overcome by all of those emotions. I also felt betrayed by my sister-in-law. As far as I was concerned, she was no better than the rumormongers. Yet, I imagined watching the news was her way of processing the devastating calamity surrounding our family. Despite my inclination to protest, I edited my lecture.

"I won't watch that rubbish."

Why would I? Why would Monica? We had both witnessed the fiasco in person, and the media had seen the same event. If I didn't know what had happened, there was no reason to suppose they would know more.

"Sleep well," I said, trying to end the conversation. "We'll chat tomorrow."

"Are you angry with me?" Monica asked.

"No, I'm just tired. Go to bed."

I was fatigued, but when I went into my bedroom, I pulled Lenore's belongings from my closet one more time. The invitation had been right under my nose, but I hadn't seen it. What else had I missed?

I sorted through the stack of greeting cards again, but they were all leftovers from her adolescent years. The address book wasn't remarkable. I opened the hardback book and wondered about its title again: *Getting Rid of That Man You Don't Really Need.* Could there be a clue inside?

What man did she want to get rid of so much that she needed an instruction manual? Could it be Josh or Steve?

I read through the Table of Contents. It wasn't the kind of book I would buy. I closed the book and put it on my bed. If she had a stalker, why didn't she tell me? Who would she tell?

I picked up the book again and turned to the title page, a page I always skip. Between the book title and the author's name, the following words were written:

My Dearest,

I wish I could be there to help you, but maybe this will help you figure things out.

Just know that you are dearly loved, and I can't wait to come back to you. I pray that you'll never want to be rid of me, because I will love and adore you for the rest of my days.

Yours,
Josh

I held the open book to my chest and tears filled my eyes. Josh was so in love with my sister, and I was sure she had cherished him as much.

How would he handle the news Steve was going to tell

him? His life would be changed forever, as was mine. I knew then that the book's title didn't refer to her sailor, and I knew in my heart that it also didn't refer to mine—my Steve. He had always been mine. Steve knew it, Lenore knew it, and the whole town seemed to know it.

I threw myself against the mattress and wept, sobbing hysterically.

My self-absorption had hurt too many people. No wonder my parents interrogated me, my brother rebuked me, and my sister found new friends to confide in.

Only Steve had the fortitude to stand up to everything I had dished out to him. He didn't run away. Instead, he waited in the wings, offering my sister the friendship and support she needed when I was completely absorbed in self-loathing. He didn't indulge my defeatism. Apologies to everyone I knew were well past due because I had been wallowing in a pit of depression too many years, so long that my sister had never seen me reach this day of awakening.

Tears depleted, I changed into more comfortable clothing and poured myself a glass of cold water. I went back into my bedroom and pulled Lenore's jewelry box from its hiding place.

I opened the lid, withdrew the necklace, and held it high in the air where I could see the sparkling diamond ring hanging from it. It had once been repugnant to me, but now it shimmered and reminded me of Lenore's adoring eyes. She had once been proud of the ring Jon had presented her upon their engagement. Why wouldn't she cherish it? I squinted to make out the engraving inside:

Heart & Soul-Friends Joined Forever-Jonathan

His words confirmed what I already knew—that Jonathan Lucas would never intentionally harm my sister.

"Are you okay?" Sherry was standing in my doorway.

I wiped away my tears, put everything back in the box, and returned it to my drawer. "I'm as okay as I'm going to get, considering the circumstances of my sister's death, and today's events. I was just going through a box of memories. I feel like I'm storing my sister up on a shelf. Isn't that awful?"

She coaxed me into the living room.

I sat on the couch. "My family won't be here. I hoped to put our heads together and figure some things out tonight, but apparently the plan has changed and we'll be doing that tomorrow."

"Is Steve coming back?"

I shook my head. "I doubt it. He took Lenore's fiancé home. The poor man doesn't know about her death, but he will before he goes to bed tonight."

"Fiancé? I didn't know she was engaged!"

"I didn't either, until this afternoon. Everyone in my family keeps secrets, especially from me."

She plopped on the couch. "I'll stay with you tonight, if that's agreeable with you."

"Please do. Did you talk to your friend?"

"Yes. She said she'd call me if she finds out anything new. I promised to do the same. What a day! I could use a stiff drink."

"No alcohol in this house, Sherry. I've quit smoking and Steve has quit drinking. How about a tall glass of pineapple juice?"

She smiled. "That would be perfect!"

We finished the rest of the evening filling each other in

on what we had seen that day. We both wondered why Sylvia was also taken away. Was she being questioned?

"What about Lenore's boyfriend?" Sherry asked. "Had you met him before?"

"No."

"Then he stays on our list of suspects."

"Suspects?"

Sherry plopped her feet up on a foot stool and made herself comfortable. "What else would you call him? Something is going on because now this whole fiasco has become a national matter."

She stared at me, but remained mute as she considered her next question. "Do you still think Steve is involved?"

I looked at the kitchen clock. It was just before 9:30, but I was tired. "I'm exhausted, and I don't want to think about this anymore." I pointed to the pillow and blanket at the bottom of the bed. "Steve has been sleeping here on the couch. Let me get you a change of linens."

She waved her hand in the air. "No need. I'll just sleep with what's out here."

I climbed into bed with my clothes on and let out a big sigh. Steve was right. Things were more complicated then I could handle. It was time for me to get my nose out of a situation I didn't belong in. I hoped the law enforcement agencies would find the answers for me.

I grabbed Lenore's Bible from my bedside and turned to the passage the pastor had mentioned earlier that day. So I wouldn't forget it, I'd been reciting the passage number to myself all day, Psalm 46. "*God is our refuge and strength, an ever-present help in trouble.*"

I rolled over and closed my eyes. "You're right, God," I said out loud. "This is out of my hands. I give every bit of this to you."

❧

It wasn't even two hours later when the phone rang. I picked it up, expecting to hear Steve's voice. I wondered how Josh had handled the awful news.

"Hey, Steve! How'd it go?"

"This isn't Steve." I recognized the baritone voice, one I'd been waiting to hear from for weeks.

"Tony! Where have you been?"

"No time to explain. Get out of the house now!"

"Excuse me?"

"I saw the news just now, and I know what happened at the wedding. If you value your life, you need to leave your house immediately. Go someplace safe, where you won't be found."

My heart hammered. "Do I have time to pack a few things?"

"No. Leave right now. Take your cell phone with you, and answer only if you see that it's me. Do you understand me? If you don't, I'm telling you that somebody may be coming to your house right now to kill you! Now run!"

The connection went dead and I ran into the living room.

"Get up, Sherry! We've got to hurry! Grab your keys, we've got to leave!"

Sherry looked at me through sleepy eyes. "Huh?"

I reached beside her and grabbed the keys to her car. "Follow me and don't ask questions until we get down the road a bit!"

She wrapped the blanket around her, and both of us ran out to the car with no shoes on our feet.

We'd been driving about five minutes when I saw car lights speeding toward us in the rearview mirror. I pressed down on the accelerator and tried to stay ahead of it, but no matter how fast I went, the car matched my speed. For every turn I made, it copied my action.

"What's going on?" Sherry asked. Her voice was an octave higher than usual, and that's saying something for a woman who is already a soprano.

"Marlene, answer me!"

"We're being followed."

She turned in her seat and looked at the sedan that was on our tail. "Why is that car following us?"

"I don't know, but let's not find out. A friend called and warned me to get out of the house and run. That's what we're doing."

"I'm scared," she said, slinking down in her seat. After all, she's a reporter for a small newspaper, not *The Washington Post*.

"Don't worry. I know where I'm going. Just keep your head down."

I drove onto a gravel road that became my shortcut to the main road into town. Dirt and stones were tossed behind me into the air, but the driver didn't swerve, slow or stop.

The car followed me through the tree tunnel to Sea Turtle Beach, and into the old part of town where I turned off my lights. I parked in the dark alley behind Mama's shop to hide. Mere moments later, Sherry screamed when he found us and flashed his headlights.

My wheels spun as I peeled out. Picking up speed, I raced by familiar storefronts, through parking lots, behind the frozen custard stand and in front of our church. The persistent car still chased us.

Finally, I sped into a parking place beside a police cruiser at the STB police station. I felt marginally relieved but my heart still pounded. Surely the driver would drive off and leave me alone, but the dark blue Chevy Caprice pulled up beside me and a man jumped out.

We stayed inside, the doors locked, but Sherry bellowed so loud my ears hurt.

The threatening stranger leaned down and talked to me through the closed window.

"Good move, coming here."

He reached into his pocket and I flinched, expecting him to shoot me right in front of the police department.

Instead, he withdrew his wallet and flashed a photo I.D. "I'm Ed Walker, a private detective. I've been keeping an eye on you for several weeks. Your father hired my agency to watch out for you and your mother."

I rolled the window halfway down and shouted, "Why were you chasing me?"

"I was following you. Why were you running?"

"My friend called and warned me to leave my house right away. He said I won't be safe there."

"Does this friend happen to be Tony Gilman?"

I drew in a deep breath. "Yes."

"I've interviewed him recently, Mrs. Wagner. I know who he believes is responsible for your sister's death and why he is worried, but you can go back home now. Your house is secure."

Sherry blubbered noisily from the passenger's seat.

My heart was still pounding and my temples throbbed with a tremendous headache. Remaining cautious, I looked around the perimeter of the building but no one was in sight, not even a single police officer. I checked the rearview mirror, expecting anything to happen, but the streets were quiet.

"I'm not so sure," I said with a great deal of trepidation.

"I am," he assured me. "My associates have been in contact with the police all night. Anybody who is under suspicion right now is inside that building."

He returned his P.I. license to his wallet and slipped that into his hip pocket. "I'll follow you back to your house. You really don't have to worry. I'll be watching your residence until six. After that, somebody else from our agency will replace me. Your father pays us big bucks to protect you 24/7."

Normally, I'd be annoyed with my father for micro-managing my life behind my back. That dark morning, I felt only relief, and the need to be tucked safely inside my cozy beachside cottage.

18

National headlines blurted: *FBI SEIZES JON LUCAS AS NEW BRIDE CRIES OUT IN HORROR!*

Jonathan was released from police custody 24 hours after being whisked away from his wedding reception. Television crews and reporters camped outside the police station, waiting for him to appear for another bout of questioning—the first and second rounds behind him, led by the FBI and local police detectives.

That evening, all newscasts began with Jon's story, and from that point on he was a tasty morsel for the media to feast on daily.

Lenore's death was now in the limelight, and that was a double-edged sword. I was thankful that her death was finally being investigated, but I was consumed with pain when I considered the possibilities.

Daddy had given me permission to return to Crest Glass, hoping to take my mind off of the ruckus surrounding the now very public police inquiry. What had been so well hidden was suddenly the hot topic at every coffee shop and water cooler, even at our factory. People couldn't get enough of the provocative story. They filled endless hours with hearsay, discussing every allegation in minute detail, and speculating about whether Jonathan Lucas, a senatorial candidate, had killed their colleague.

The police were now calling her tragic death a murder investigation.

Even I found myself recording a plethora of news stories and saving newspaper articles to read when I returned home from my job. It was the only way to keep up with the constantly developing story.

According to all reports, Jon was no longer a suspect. Surprisingly, I was actually relieved, but I was also wary. Who else could be responsible for Lenore's death? The investigation was ongoing, according to the press and every police officer that would accept my phone calls. Everything I heard suggested they had no concrete clues.

It was during that pivotal, uncertain time that I finally broke, following many years of fighting desperate depression, stress and anxiety. After spending just one week back at the glass factory, surrounded by careless whispers, I abandoned my work station and walked out the door. I turned my brain off and drove home to my house, determined to live the life of a hermit.

But Steve wouldn't indulge me.

He showed up at my door with bags of groceries, and he began to take care of me, the way he'd taken care of me when we lost our baby. When I tried to climb into bed for a mid-day nap, he'd pull me from beneath the covers and take me for a ride. It went on like this for about a week.

❧

It was Wednesday, May 17th. More than six weeks had elapsed since the wedding fiasco. Steve woke me early and asked me to get dressed for a luncheon engagement.

When we left the driveway a few hours later, I had no idea where we'd end up. I just welcomed the opportunity to escape from the island.

Thirty minutes later, we were sitting in front of Church of the Palms. "What are we doing here?" I asked. I looked over at Steve as he silently parked the car and turned off the ignition.

He turned to me, staring directly into my eyes, and announced, "We'll eat later, Marlene. Right now, we have an appointment."

"With Pastor Williams?"

He grasped my hand in his, explaining, "I know I should have told you about this, but I knew you'd find an excuse...and we need to do this together."

"Do what?"

"Pre-marital counseling."

We'd talked at the wedding about becoming a couple again, but I hadn't thought much about it since that day, even though we'd passed much of the previous two months together. Admittedly, I was still very attracted to him.

No, I actually realized it was more.

I was still in love with him, and I knew it. But we hadn't even kissed, and I certainly hadn't spoken the *love* word to him yet. My life was in such turmoil that I knew it wasn't the right time to jump back into a real relationship with Steve, but apparently he didn't agree.

I touched his hand. "You know I still care about you, Steve, but right now I'm so consumed with grief that I can think of little else."

He leaned forward, kissed me on my cheek, and quietly said, "You've been grieving for too many years. It's time for both of us to face all of this—your miscarriage, our addictions, our divorce, and now, your sister's death—together…as a couple."

Steve leaned in front of me, reaching into the glove compartment of his truck. From it, he withdrew a familiar ring box, and when he snapped it open I recognized my engagement ring. Where he had found that, I wasn't sure. I had lost the ring in a drunken stupor.

Bad memories.

Yet the ring brought a smile to my lips.

"You've been saving this?"

Without replying, he pulled the ring from the box.

My heart pounded.

"I've behaved like a spoiled brat. Do you really want me to be your fiancée?"

He smiled broadly as he slipped the glistening diamond on my left ring finger. "Absolutely. I'll be honored if you will wear my ring again."

At first, I watched in mute amazement; but after a few moments, I began to giggle. "You do know there was a better way to do this, right?"

His eyes crinkled at their corners and he said with a contented smile, "I admit I'm not very good at this, but I'm trying."

He wrapped his arm around my neck and gave me a tender kiss. "Let's go inside so Pastor Williams can help us."

✻

I looked at the address and compared it to the large numbers on the outside of the non-descript white block building. "This is it," I announced.

JEREMY BROWN – TRANSITIONAL THERAPY was engraved on the plaque over the entrance.

We sat silently for what seemed like endless minutes. Over the past several weeks, our pastor had taught us to rely on God more, through prayer, Bible study, attending Sunday worship services, and to praise God for guiding us through life. He'd also suggested that we should visit a licensed, Christian-based, marital counselor to mend our relationship.

Fear of what I would discover about myself inside that building paralyzed me. I had become desperate for answers that would explain to me why I had walked out of our marriage. After much consideration, and gentle prodding from Steve and Pastor Williams, I was approaching the end of a long dark journey.

Steve looked at me pensively, waiting for me.

I twisted the diamond ring on my left finger and remembered why I had always loved him so much. He was kind, considerate, caring, sympathetic and more patient than I deserved. He was also forgiving in ways beyond my realm of understanding.

I rested my head on his shoulder. "I don't want to lose you again, Babe," I said. "I know this will be hard, but I'm ready. Let's go inside and start figuring out why I'm so broken."

Steve placed his hand over mine, and we bowed our heads, praying together before we took the biggest step in reconciling ourselves. "God be with us, protect us, and heal us...in the name of your Son, Jesus, we pray. Amen."

19

I discovered the whole truth about Lenore's last minutes on a cold winter day, in a trial that took place many months after Jon and Sylvia were whisked away from their reception by the Federal Bureau of Investigation.

I sat in the front row of a crowded courtroom, familiar faces all around me. I was nervous and my hands trembled slightly as I listened to hour upon hour of testimony from prosecution and defense witnesses—including Tony, Jon, and Matt—and a lineup of officials and investigators from various state agencies. I could only shake my head in disbelief, sometimes crying softly, because I was dumbfounded by the magnitude of heartless and cruel exploitation that people commit in order to serve their purpose.

❧

Tony Gilman had talked to my sister the evening she died. He had told me most of his story during the time preceding the trial. Still, I was worried as he approached the bench, took an oath to tell the truth, and climbed up on the platform.

The prosecuting attorney looked daunting. He asked, "What was your relationship with Lenore Terhune?" I coughed, realizing he intended to tear a hole in my friend's heart.

"I was her colleague."

"Just business associates?"

"Yes."

"Were you in love with her?"

My heart skipped a beat. Tony answered, "Yes, but Lenore was in love with another man."

"Were you hurt?"

"Yes, sir, but I've known her for years and I valued our friendship. I just wanted her to be happy."

I realized then that Lenore had finally mustered the courage to tell Tony the truth, and I wondered for a moment if she'd been helped by the book I had found in her apartment. How did I not notice that my good friend was infatuated by my sister?

"Happy in the arms of another man?" The attorney cocked his head. "How did that make you feel?"

Tony looked at the prosecutor, over to me, and back at the ominous man standing before him.

"Well, sir, I never held Lenore in my arms, so I truly don't know how it would feel."

The whole room erupted in a fury of laughter and the judge stifled an imminent chuckle. "Order in this court is required. The next time this happens, I'll clear the room."

With his witness off kilter, the prosecutor—a 40'ish man with a sly smile—changed his strategy. "Strike that question, your honor. I can proceed in another direction." He turned to Tony and asked in an intense manner, "Why were you at

Crest Glass the night of her death?"

Tony, unaffected by the man's demeanor, leisurely leaned back in his seat and crossed his arms over his chest. "Lenore called my house and asked me to meet her at work. She wanted me to help her finish the custom glass order for Jonathan's wedding."

He had already told me in a private conversation that my sister had also phoned me for assistance that night. I'll always regret missing that call.

When I asked him why he didn't disclose that information to me when we met at the studio, he said, "You were upset and I just wanted to get you out of there quickly." I never imagined he had come there to snoop around on his own. I just recall feeling very embarrassed, and somewhat relieved, when he showed up that afternoon.

The lawyer walked over to the defense table and turned around, addressing Tony again. "So you drove to the warehouse to help her?"

"Yes, sir."

"What happened when you arrived at the warehouse?"

Tony responded, "When I got to the warehouse, there was an unfamiliar car parked outside. I called Lenore from my cell phone. She told me to come back in an hour."

"What happened when you returned?" the lawyer asked.

"I cruised around the island for about 30 minutes, stopped by the quick mart to grab two soft drinks, and returned to the main building. When I got back, there were numerous vehicles outside, including a police cruiser and a rescue squad."

"What did you do?"

"I rushed inside." Tony choked up and wiped his eyes on

his arm. "That's when I saw Lenore's body slumped against her work station. Matt was already there. He told me to leave."

"So that evening, you never saw Miss Terhune alive?"

"No, sir."

"Who else was there?"

"Bremmer was there," he replied. "Floyd walked me outside and that's when the rescue squad pulled into the lot. Also, more cops were arriving on the scene. He suggested that I should get out of their way while they did their jobs."

The lawyer asked, "What did you do when he told you to get out of the way?"

"I went home."

"You went home?"

"Yes, I went home."

"Don't you think that's an unusual thing to do, considering the circumstances...after all, your friend had died."

"My mother taught me a long time ago to respect authority. I know Floyd and I figured he wanted me out of the way. He knew where to find me."

"What did you do when you returned home?"

"I woke up my mother and told her about what had happened. Then we stayed up all night, watching the news to see if we could find out more, but we didn't see anything on any of the local stations...and in the following days, we didn't even see anything in the newspaper, except for her obituary."

Tony told me later that when he returned to work the following Monday, Matt advised him to take a vacation. He also said Matt contacted him after our houses were burglarized and asked him to move Lenore's furniture to his garage; but when he got there, the apartment was empty.

All of this made Tony suspicious. He contacted the regional office of the FBI about his suspicions of foul play and went into self-enforced hiding.

❧

Jon testified for the prosecution. His testimony consumed hours of the afternoon, and despite my weariness, I mentally digested his every word—especially when he talked about his campaign manager.

"Roger Cane was a dedicated supporter and staff manager, but he tended to be over zealous with our volunteers at times."

"Power hungry?" the prosecutor asked

"Perhaps," Jon answered. Then he mulled over his answer. "Yes. Definitely. The goal of my campaign team was always to get me elected, so I often acquiesced to their judgment. That was definitely a mistake, because it is now evident that Roger did things and made statements on my behalf that I would never condone."

Images of that man alone in the warehouse with Lenore crept into my brain and I felt instantly ill, but I resisted my compulsion to leave the room.

When the prosecutor said he was finished, Jon asked him if he could add one more thing to his testimony, and with the man's permission, he added, "I would never allow anything bad to happen to Lenore." Jon went on to say that he was never made aware of what Cane did covertly, in the darkness of that particular night; not until the FBI whisked him away for questioning.

※

The court recessed, and the next morning Cane testified in his own defense, but first the prosecution had their way with him.

I had slept well and felt invigorated and prepared to face another long day. Jon's testimony finished, he was in the courtroom that day with his wife and mother-in-law beside him.

The prosecutor stood midway between the witness stand and the jury as Roger Cane swore an oath of honesty. When the man took his seat, the attorney attacked.

"Mr. Cane, why did you go to Crest Glass on the evening of Sunday, March 12, 2000?"

I slid forward, sitting on the edge of my seat, waiting.

Roger Cane sat stiffly erect and answered in a precise, well-rehearsed manner. "I went to the Crest warehouse to ask the woman to discontinue her clandestine meetings with my candidate. I warned her that their liaisons would cause a scandal and cost him the senatorial race."

"What woman were you referring to, Mr. Cane?"

He replied. "Lenore Terhune."

"How did she respond?"

"She showed me some of the glass pieces she was working on for Jon and Sylvia. At the time, she was creating a glass angel. She said she was just helping out an old friend."

"How did you respond to that, sir?

"I told her that she could deliver the product to me, but

that she could no longer have contact with the candidate."

"Then what happened?"

"The lady said she would need to speak to him. That's when she told me about her daughter. She said Jon was the father of her child and that she would eventually tell him about her existence. She said she would wait until after the wedding, but she had decided it was time to tell him the truth."

I glanced over at Jon's wife and saw the shocked expression on her ashen face. Her familiar smile was gone. She leaned over to whisper to Jon and gracefully exited the courtroom.

The attorney paced the floor in front of Cane. "How did you react to that news?"

"I was surprised."

"Did you become angry?"

"Yes, I did. Why would she wait until Jonathan became involved in a senatorial race to tell him the truth about something she had kept a secret since the baby was conceived?"

My hands went from hot to cold and clammy and I wiped them on my slacks.

"Would you say you were agitated?" the lawyer prompted.

"Yes. I was."

"What did you do next?"

"I told her to leave him alone and that keeping the secret for a few more years—at least until Jon was established in the Senate—would be okay."

"What did Miss Terhune say?"

"She told me to get out of there right away…to stay out of

her business and her life, and that she would call the police if I didn't leave immediately."

"Did you leave?"

"No, I didn't."

"Please repeat what you just said."

The defense attorney jumped up. "Your honor, I object! That was just addressed!"

The round faced, black robed judge responded robustly. "I'll allow." He turned to Cane. "You may answer again."

Cane looked mystified and a little restless. This time, his answer was more abrupt. He leaned forward with his hands clasped in his lap, and spoke into the microphone loudly. "I did not leave."

"Why did you elect to stay, despite Miss Terhune's admonitions?"

"I wanted to talk to her a little more...to convince her that anything she did could affect Jon's life and career, and that if she really cared about him, she would heed my advice."

"What happened next?"

"I walked toward her—I meant no offense, sir, I just wanted to get a little closer—and she became extremely defensive. She walked backwards fast. I assume she was going to call the police. But she didn't watch where she was going, tripped on a floor mat at one of the work tables, and flipped backwards. She fell so fast I couldn't catch the poor woman. She hit her head on the floor and lost consciousness right away."

I wanted to throw up.

"So the death was accidental?"

"Yes, sir. It was unfortunate. Such a tragedy."

Steve took my hand in his and squeezed it tightly.

The prosecutor stepped up to the stand, facing the accused eye-to-eye. "Sir, if it was, as you say, an unfortunate accident, why didn't you phone for help?"

"I did. I called 911."

"Did you do that right away?"

Cane nodded. "Pretty much...after I determined that I couldn't help her."

"How did you try to help her?"

"Well, I tried mouth-to-mouth resuscitation on her but it didn't work."

I could taste the bile in my mouth.

The prosecutor walked closer to the jury, turned around, and asked, "Are you a doctor?"

"Of course not, you know that—"

The judge interrupted. "Just answer the question. He'll ask you to clarify as necessary."

The prosecutor turned to the judge. "Thank you, your honor."

He turned back to Cane. "Are you a licensed paramedic?"

"No." He turned pleading eyes to his own attorney.

"Did you move the body?"

Cane shifted in his seat. "Yes, I did."

"And why did you do that?"

Cane leaned into the mike. "I thought if I sat her up, maybe she would breathe better."

"That must have been a struggle," the prosecutor remarked.

The defense attorney rose up, but the judge lifted his hand. "No need to object." He turned to the prosecutor. "You know better. Ask your questions. If that happens again, we'll have a meeting at the bar."

Unfazed, the prosecutor asked the witness, "Was that difficult?"

"Somewhat."

"Did it help her?"

"Obviously not…she's dead, isn't she?"

That's when I left the room.

❧

What was obvious was that the prosecution had done their homework. That became more and more apparent as their case against Roger Cane unfolded over the next two days.

The defense had little to stand on, but they tried their best to show Cane was a devoted, church-going, family man who made a few mistakes in judgment. They had a multitude of character witnesses, and it was apparent that he was dedicated to his candidate, but in the end the prosecution won their case.

My family had seen the coroner's report. They had ruled that Lenore died immediately, the result of hitting her head on the concrete floor when she tripped and fell. Because of that determination, the fanatical campaign manager was not implicated in her death.

The M.E. also ran innumerable tests to determine if drugs were present in her blood or tissues, but they only found prescription drugs and Acetaminophen in her body.

Even so, I emotionally needed to be in the room every day, watching the attorneys present both sides of the case. My parents stayed home. Matt sat in the back of the courtroom. We all needed the fiasco to be over so we could, as my father said earlier, get back to our lives.

Although Roger Cane never actually stood trial for my sister's death, he was prosecuted for many other crimes associated with that night, including tampering with evidence. The police, the FBI, a private eye, my brother, the prosecutor, and the jury determined that Cane had staged Lenore's body and lampworking equipment to indicate she had succumbed to noxious fumes…or committed suicide.

The prosecutor said in his closing statement, "Mr. Cane did call an ambulance, but only after he had moved the body. Remember, he was still trying to save the campaign. And after he finally called for help, he left the scene. Roger Cane left Lenore Terhune alone in her death. That is the tragedy of this case…that he thought of his candidate, he thought of the campaign, and he thought of himself first. I'm not sure he ever thought anything more of Lenore Terhune, except that she was an unfortunate mistake in his candidate's life."

He paced the room and his voice became loud. "Ladies and gentlemen of the jury, when Roger Cane went to see her, it was with malice. He did not go to that warehouse expecting her to acquiesce to his pleas, but he was determined that he would make her go away."

He turned to look at the accused, Roger Cane. "When she died, it was a fortuitous turn of events for this man."

He turned back to the jury. "And when he walked out of that building, leaving her alone, that was not an accident. Roger Cane knew exactly what he was doing when he disappeared into the night, when he told his staff what to do to cover up his mess, and when he lied to his candidate and the people of the State of Florida."

He turned to the judge and announced, "I rest my case, your honor."

❧

Four members of Cane's staff were also involved, prosecuted, and found guilty of the many things they did to conceal anything they perceived as a threat to Jon's campaign. The list of charges against Cane and his cronies was extensive and included three house burglaries. They stole Lenore's laptop computer, the key to her lockbox, and the furnishings from her townhouse. Although they didn't find anything at my parents' house, they went there searching for the pieces of glass she had made for the wedding—the custom glass the groom had purchased as a special gift for their wedding guests.

Along the way, the saboteurs made mistakes.

In Cane's panic to get out of the warehouse undiscovered, he didn't pick up the broken angel or the list of pieces my sister was creating. One of his flunkies snuck into our office, printed the purchase request, and deleted the entire order number from the computer system, just in case they didn't find the missing items. They did everything they could to sidetrack the custom order—the one thing that would tie Jon to Lenore—but they failed because Tony and I had found the initial hand-written order and decided to fulfill it ourselves.

Daddy had discovered more boxes of Lenore's glass in Mama's Lincoln Navigator. With his approval, Tony had completed the remaining glasswork at a workbench in his garage. I recreated the glass angels in my mom's gallery studio. We never discussed our plans with each other.

We both snuck our creations into the banquet hall at different times, but everything was in place before an astute campaign aid—the one that had grabbed the rest of the custom glass from Lenore's Miata—delivered the remaining pieces to the country club just in time for the wedding. I wish I had seen his face when the miscreant saw the glass butterflies floating in the air above his head.

I also didn't get to see the expression on Cane's face when he saw all the sparkling baubles on every plate, and I should have been in the room when the bride and groom stepped up to cut the cake. I'm told my brother took a microphone and announced, "This magnificent glass angel topper was made by my sister, Lenore Terhune!" Steve says the man probably wanted to faint on the spot.

The problem with a lie is that it always multiplies.

Matt and Floyd suspected something was amiss from the beginning. They were always in contact with the state police and the Medical Examiner.

My brother told lies to everyone—me, my parents, and anybody else that asked—in order to keep us out of the delicate investigation. He was also afraid I would stir up the culprit, who was still unidentified. The newspaper editor, as a favor to Matt, held back on the story until all the details were known.

Although I didn't know it, the scheme to convert the

townhouses into condominiums had been planned for over a year. My sister never mentioned it because she was planning to move to Virginia with Josh. Cane's minions purchased the unit when they emptied it, just in case they had missed any item that would point their way.

The sales manager said she neglected to tell me Lenore's unit had already been sold because it was proprietary information. I tend to think it also had something to do with the classy roadster we saw her driving.

I was right. Certain people were lying to me, and I now have my answers.

❦

I had always suspected Lenore's secret admirer had been responsible for her demise, but Josh was only a man in love. He was mortified when Steve and Amy told him the truth about her death. The attachment my sister had referred to was Josh's devotion to his elderly parents in Virginia.

And Steve? He was always my faithful husband—my sister's friend—who patiently waited for me to listen to my heart.

Epilogue

Sometimes we take detours in life, but we end up where we need to be. In my opinion, this is absolute proof that God has bigger plans for us than we can ever imagine. We may not always see our path, and we often experience pain along the route, but when we follow our hearts instead of our heads, he will show us to our destination.

It took me a long time to come to terms with my sister's death, and I eventually realized that all of those weeks of questioning and searching were never really about how Lenore had died. I was questioning God about why he had taken her from me.

I felt guilty for not being there to accept her call, because I imagined that I could have stopped what happened to her; guilt for not realizing she was having problems and for not keeping up with everything that was occurring in her life; and guilt for always being envious of her.

My pastor helped me immensely. He reminded me that we are all human and not perfect. Only God is perfect, and that is why we need to rely on him in good times as well as during bad times.

The therapist was also amazingly insightful. I learned that I wasn't just mourning my sister's death. I was still grieving the loss of my child and our marriage, and I'd been placating myself with alcohol, cigarettes and sometimes food. When I was overwhelmed, I went into hiding. I was tired of hiding, and I was tired of being alone.

We spoke about life in general and specifically, covering all the things I had experienced since childhood, how I had handled problems by acting out, and how I could deal with anything looming in my future as long as I kept an open connection to God.

The changes in me didn't happen overnight, but I can remember singular moments of clarity when I realized I had made bad decisions, said the wrong things, and took actions that affected not only my life but the lives of the people around me.

I remembered things I had worried about and pondered on my own, and understood that I could have handled them differently with a little help from friends, family and my pastor. We are not intended to be alone in this world. God gave us friends and family for a purpose.

I began to examine my relationship with Lenore. As much as I loved my sister, I finally realized how consumed I was by jealousy, and that I had always measured myself against her achievements. That set me up for failure in so many ways and placed a lot of unnecessary burden on my shoulders.

As a result, I focused the turmoil inside me on those around me. My parents, my brother, and Steve were the victims of my angst. They were co-dependents and had at first enabled me to mistreat them by forgiving me time after time, without making me suffer consequences for abusing them.

I always imagined they expected more of me, but the truth was that they, along with Lenore, were my steadfast supporters. My problem was that I couldn't accept their help without questioning their motives or my abilities.

When they finally tried to help me by setting boundaries, I left Steve, and turned away from my family, without confronting my issues.

I took the easy way out. Instead of addressing my chaotic emotions, I pushed them deeper into my inner self, and allowed the confusion and pain to swallow my spirit.

The only person I'd given access to the real me was my sister. And when she died, I was consumed with sorrow.

I now realize that if my father had allowed me to return to my job, I would have worked myself to exhaustion so that I didn't have to confront her death. Instead, he gave me time off and I was forced to channel my energies elsewhere. I searched for the reason for her death, but along the way I found myself again.

The biggest lesson I learned was about forgiveness. I know now that you cannot live a fulfilling life without forgiving people or yourself. That was a major lesson.

Pastor Williams suggested that I had blamed God for every bad experience that had happened to me, especially my baby's death.

He was right.

That's when I realized that God is so forgiving that he loves me despite my shortcomings, and that he had always been with me, even when I ignored his presence in my life. He waited for me to ask him for help, instead of trying to deal with my problems by myself. God already knew my pain, but my fervent prayers finally showed him that I acknowledged him, and that I really wanted to change my life.

And I did.

I'm sure Lenore would be amazed that I now go to Bible study on Wednesday nights. Through daily prayer, Steve and I became closer to God, and in turn, closer to each other. Returning to church, and the parishioners who had always prayed for me, helped me immensely. I rediscovered fellowship with devoted friends, as well as a better understanding of what God expects and requires of me. He gives us family and friends for a reason—to love and support each other.

I had married Steve, promising to honor and cherish him forever, but when our unborn child died—when we needed each other the most—I failed him.

As I marched down the aisle toward the love of my life, I marveled at how handsome he still was, and thanked God for blessing me with his unfaltering love, devotion, faithfulness and understanding.

I walked by so many familiar faces—Tony, Christine, Eloise—too many friends to list. In the front row, Mama and Daddy sat with Monica and Matthew and the rest of our family.

Jon and Sylvia were in the pew behind them. He had withdrawn from the senatorial race and resigned from politics. He returned to the private sector where he is now the CEO of a transportation and warehousing conglomerate based in Northeast Florida.

It has taken me a long time to adjust to his presence in my life. I now call him my friend. Sylvia and Steve have helped us cultivate our relationship. It came from a seed Jon and Lenore planted eighteen years before, when they created a child together.

Their daughter, Angela, now lives with her adoptive family in southern Georgia, where she has a good life. Even though my sister had not told him about their child before she died, I realized that I could no longer keep the truth from him. Why would I? Lenore intended to tell him, and that truth was slammed upon him in a courtroom.

When I discussed everything with Jonathan and Sylvia, they immediately wanted to meet Angela, but they honored my sister's wishes and waited for his daughter to contact him.

That happened just before her 16th birthday, and they have spent almost two years getting to know each other. The four of us—Steve, Jon, Sylvia and me—are her second family, and from that our friendship has bloomed. Jon and Sylvia are now expecting another child in their lives, a little boy they are adopting.

Steve reenlisted in 2001, following the attacks on the World Trade Center. Both Josh and Steve served with the Navy in Operation Desert Storm. They are retired now, and operate a scrap diving business together at Sea Turtle Beach.

Amy and Josh became best friends while he was at sea. She corresponded with him, sent him care boxes, and offered a sympathetic ear during the hard months after Lenore's death. Two years later, they got married.

Tony still works at the glass factory, and he's still my good friend.

❧

At the altar, my husband waited with our best friends, Amy and Joshua Fleming, who were standing up with us as we exchanged our vows for a third time, this time in a vow renewal ceremony to commemorate the 10th anniversary of our second wedding. Amy had been my matron of honor, and Josh was Steve's best man a decade before.

There were also two beautiful little girls standing to the left of Pastor Williams. One was our 8-year-old daughter, Mary Lee, and the other young lady was 6-year-old Eleanor Fleming, Josh and Amy's oldest daughter. Our 5-year-old, Timmy, held his daddy's hand.

Pastor Williams asked, "Are you ready?"

I grasped Mary's tiny fingers, and Steve picked up Timmy.

"Absolutely!"

Pastor smiled and said to us, "We are gathered together today because you have chosen to reconfirm your pledge to each other. Life has brought you both wonderful blessings and difficult challenges over the years. May this ceremony remind you that despite the stresses life has put in your path, God has always been with you. As you continue in this marriage, you already know that it will require a lot of love, commitment, and work to keep your relationship an ongoing success."

"Do you now wish to reaffirm your promise to each other?"

We both said, "I do."

And then he read from the Bible:

Love is patient, love is kind. It does not envy, it does not boast, it is not proud. It does not dishonor others, it is not self-seeking, it is not easily angered, it keeps no record of wrongs.

Love does not delight in evil but rejoices with the truth. It always protects, always trusts, always hopes, always perseveres.

Love never fails.

FOR COUPLES SEEKING HELP

Statistics on the divorce rate in America vary, but the general consensus is that about 50% of first time marriages end in divorce. I find that statistic to be surprising and sad, and I wonder how many people dissolve their marriage before they fight for it. How many marriages could be saved if the couple made a pact to work it out and seek counseling for their problems and addictions, discussing and mutually tackling their problems, and above all seeking God to guide their path?

If you need help in your marriage, here are some resources:

1. *Psychology Today* – Find a Therapist: http://therapists.psychologytoday.com
2. *American Association of Christian Counselors:* http://www.aacc.net/

May God be with you always, blessing you and yours with an abundance of love and forgiveness.

In Memory of
Freddie Weber

ACKNOWLEDGMENTS

I know this page is most often found in front of the book, but I had oodles of people to thank, and I didn't want to take away from the atmosphere I wanted to create in the first chapter.

It takes a lot to write a book, and in my experience, it took a decade to write BROKEN ANGEL, my second, novel. I am blessed with many people who continue to support me in all areas of my life.

Thanks to my husband, Lorenza, who helps me with research and brainstorming. You are my partner in all things, just as you promised me more than 20 years ago.

To my son, Christopher, I cannot tell you how proud I am of you. Thank you for the cover design. It is perfect.

Much appreciation to my friends who helped proofread the manuscript, especially Renz, Patty, Cyvette and Dana, who had very constructive input and remarks.

In the course of writing this book, I had to pause several times to deal with medical problems, including two open heart surgeries.

My sincere appreciation to heart surgeon, Dr. Richard Agnew; Dr. John Butcher; Dr. Thomas Hilton and all of the cardiologists and staff at Baptist Heart Center/Beaches; Dr. Thomas Gaddis and his staff at Hematology-Oncology Associates; Dr. R. David Heekin and Dr. Timothy Sternberg at Heekin Orthoepedic Specialists; Dr. Omar Kawwaff; and to the following hospitals in Jacksonville, Florida: Mayo, St. Vincent's, Memorial, and Baptist Beaches.

Finally, to Dr. Jason Hosch, PHD, thank you sincerely for

helping 'us' find 'our' way after all the heartache.

Thank you all for taking care of me in so many ways!

And to God, I give all the glory for saving me too many times to count. You ARE the reason.

ABOUT THE AUTHOR

Claudia McCants has been married to her beloved husband, Lorenza, since 1992. They live in north Florida, where they raised their son. Christopher McCants, who is now in college, designed and created the cover for this book.

After a decade of fighting serious illnesses and a life crisis, with God's help, Claudia has returned to the church feeling renewed and invigorated.

She has also returned to writing, but under God's guidance, she has changed her approach to this novel to reflect her Christian faith. She hopes her testimony and her future stories will encourage you to let God direct your life path. She says, "Trust God."

Claudia is a travel enthusiast, enjoys making jewelry, and loves art glass.

You can learn more about this inspirational author on the Internet at www.claudiamccants.net.